SCREEN Kiss

ANN ROBERTS

T0124563

BELLA BOOKS

2019

Bella Books, Inc.
P.O. Box 10543
Tallahassee, FL 32302

First Bella Books Edition 2019

Editor: Katherine V. Forrest
Cover Designer: Judith Fellows

ISBN: 978-1-64247-033-8

Other Bella Books by Ann Roberts

Romances
Brilliant
Beach Town
Root of Passion
Beacon of Love
Petra's Canvas
Hidden Hearts
The Complete Package
Pleasure of the Chase
Vagabond Heart

General Fiction
Furthest From the Gate
Keeping Up Appearances

The Ari Adams Mystery Series
Paid in Full
White Offerings
Deadly Intersections
Point of Betrayal
A Grand Plan
A Secret to Tell
Justice Calls

Acknowledgments

My parents watched three or four movies every week. It wasn't uncommon for my mother to break into song on a Sunday afternoon, grab one of us kids and foxtrot across the living room, while singing a show tune from a Broadway hit that had been made into a movie. I love film because of them. As an architect, my father instilled in me an appreciation of old and repurposed buildings, maintaining they were the best constructed since most of the new stuff was "crap." He loved the old theaters, buildings truly worthy of something magnificent like a wonderful cinematic experience. This book blends those two loves.

I'm indebted to Becky Bailey, a transportation supervisor with Lane County, for sharing her stories, experiences, and insights about the world of public transportation and those who ride. She helped shape Addy's character significantly.

Julie Blonshteyn, the owner of the real Bijou Theater in Eugene, Oregon, is a shining example of tenacity, as she risked everything to achieve her dream of owning a movie theater. She explained all the ins and outs, the technical aspects, and the challenges she faces to survive as a small independent. My first visit to the Bijou, a magnificent refurbished and repurposed building, planted the initial seeds for this story. Thanks, Julie.

Linda and Jessica Hill and the crew at Bella Books down in Tallahassee work tirelessly to publish our stories, even in the face of natural disasters like Hurricane Michael. I so appreciate their support.

My wife Amy continues to be my greatest cheerleader. She's the protector of my writing time, the kitten and puppy wrangler, and the most honest critic I have. I love you, honey.

A huge thanks to my editor and mentor, Katherine V. Forrest. Each time an edited manuscript from Katherine arrives on my doorstep, I take a deep breath, hoping she's happy with the story—and she was! I'm incredibly fortunate to have a pioneer of lesbian fiction guiding and pushing me toward the best story I can tell.

Finally, to all of my readers, I'm honored and forever grateful that you continue to spend your money and time on my writing. I'll keep writing if you keep reading.

About the Author

Ann Roberts is the award-winning author of nineteen mystery, romance, and general fiction novels. Ann's most recent romance, *Vagabond Heart*, was a Lambda finalist, and *Conference Call*, the collection of stories she edited in 2017, was a Goldie finalist. She lives in Eugene, Oregon, with her wife and a growing collection of fur kids. When Ann isn't writing her own stuff, editing someone else's, coaching a newer author, or remodeling her home, she can be found exploring Oregon's wineries or strolling along a beach, preferably near a lighthouse. To learn more about Ann, please visit her website, annroberts.net.

Dedication

For those who preserve our old theaters and the independent filmmakers who tell our stories.

CHAPTER ONE

A murmur of excitement buzzes through Lane Eight—Addy Tornado's checkout line. When she scans the customer faces, most of whom are Value Shop regulars, her gaze lands on the famous Princess Meritain of Merutious. She has just joined Addy's line, right behind Mr. Flanders, who is skimming the latest edition of Guns Around the World. He clearly doesn't realize he is rubbing elbows with royalty, mainly because he never faces forward, too busy looking at the impulse purchase items available on his left and right.

Princess Meritain takes a step back from Mr. Flanders and his elbow thrashings. Her regal chin turns upward. While she is a diminutive woman, her erect posture and proper carriage creates the impression she towers over all. Perhaps it is her royal training that gives her command of Lane Eight, that or the four-inch, red, don't-fuck-with-me heels that complement her black, tight-fitting A-line skirt. Addy permits herself one long graze of the princess. She drinks in the shapely calves, curvaceous bottom, thin waist, stellar bosom, red lips, long eyelashes, and eyes so blue she can see them from three customers away.

Her grazing complete, she returns her attention to the MOST IMPORTANT CUSTOMER, the one standing in front of her. Value Shop policy reminds its employees that the customer currently being served is the MOST IMPORTANT CUSTOMER in the store. Mrs. Kaminsky is one of Addy's favorites, a delightful retiree who has just returned from summer vacation with her son's family. Mrs. Kaminsky frequents Addy's line at least four times a week, and she has confided she is lonely and enjoys Addy's company, if only for a few fleeting minutes while Addy rings up her purchases.

As she regales Addy with yet another story about granddaughter Chloe's antics in the hotel swimming pool, and a game of Marco Polo gone awry because of some deflated floaties, Addy sneaks a second glance at the princess, who offers a cold, hard stare. Addy immediately looks down, flustered.

"Hey, Addy," Mrs. Kaminsky says. "You just charged me four ninety-eight for a bunch of radishes."

Addy gasps and apologizes. She voids the item and focuses on her work. Mrs. Kaminsky leaves with appropriately charged radishes and as Addy's line moves forward, the princess draws closer and unloads the contents of her little shopping basket onto the conveyor belt with the disdain befitting a task beneath her. She flings a package of overpriced plastic cutlery with such force, it somersaults over the dividing bar and lands in Mr. Flanders's stack of purchases. He discreetly nudges the cutlery back to the other side, his gaze never straying from the article he's reading.

Addy frowns at the behavior of the princess. She has a reputation for being callous and insensitive, and her treatment of the cutlery affirms the stories. Addy allows herself another quick glance while Mr. Flanders debates whether or not to purchase the magazine and finish an article on German rifles from WWII.

He finally placed the magazine in his shopping bag, exchanges a smile with Addy, who rings it up and hands him his change.

Princess Meritain steps to the pay station and stares at Addy as if she's nuts.

Of course, Addy greets her with the required Value Shop smile— while she groups each item by prominent color before scanning it and placing it in one of the Value Shop paper bags.

Addy can't help herself. When she looks at any object, its prominent color pushes forward, whether that is the color of the packaging, the letters on the label, or the color of the item. It's like a spotlight turns on and all Addy sees is one color. Thus, bananas are always grouped with yellow squash, banana popsicles and various cheeses, while lettuces, cucumbers and margarita mix journey out of the store together. Her regular customers have learned her system, but of course Princess Meritain of Merutious has not. But how could she? Addy again forgives the princess this understandable faux pas.

As the princess's luscious lips curl into displeasure, Addy offers, "I'm all about order," as an explanation for her behavior.

"I'd rather you not touch my things any more than necessary," *Princess Meritain replies, in a breathy voice Addy finds very sexy.* "It's not sanitary."

"I promise you, I sanitize my hands after I touch the register or handle money or credit cards."

Princess Meritain raises an already high-pitched eyebrow. "Every time?"

"Every time." *And then Addy leans forward, resting her elbow on the check-writing desk, and whispers,* "My hands are so clean right now that I could feed you a strawberry." *It's a risky flirt, and Addy watches the princess's response carefully.*

The eyebrow descends and joins a face of the creamiest skin Addy has ever seen. She gazes into the extraordinary blue eyes for another second before completing the princess's transaction.

Princess Meritain gazes into the bag and screams, "What the hell? Why is the Drano in the bag with my tomatoes? That's disgusting!"

"Well, tomatoes and the bottle of Drano are the only red purchases you have. If you'd bought something else that was red, I could've started another bag."

The blue eyes turn a darker shade. "I demand to see your manager."

Addy crosses her arms. "No."

The high-pitched eyebrow returns. "Excuse me?"

"You may not see the manager. I won't allow it. That will be twenty-seven dollars. Even."

The princess turns up her regal chin. "I won't pay it."

"Then you can't have your Drano."

With a swoop, Addy pushes the bags into a corner of the bagging area and welcomes the next MOST IMPORTANT CUSTOMER, Mrs. Delano. While she offers her sweetest smile to Mrs. D., she remains cognizant of the princess's stare.

So she gives her a show. She quickly lines up Mrs. D's reusable bags and scans her items, correctly grouped by dominant color. She swipes and taps keys at lightning speed, stealing a glance at the princess, who seems entranced by her grocery ballet, an homage to efficiency.

As Mrs. Delano departs, Princess Meritain steps back to the pay station, licking her lips.

Addy knows that look.

"I'd like to pay now."

Addy completes the transaction, her gaze locked on the princess's gorgeous eyes. When she hands her the receipt, she says, "Value Shop encourages you to follow this link and complete a survey regarding my service and your level of satisfaction. Are you satisfied?"

"Not yet," the princess whispers.

Addy glances at the next customer in line, a young woman engaged in a battle of wills with a preschool-age boy. He wishes to add a candy bar to their otherwise healthy purchases that fill the conveyor belt— and are not grouped by color. Addy sighs.

Suddenly the princess is behind her, pressing into her back. "Meet me in frozen dinners," she says, in a voice almost as smoky as her blue eyes.

Addy nods and drops the CLOSED sign at the end of the conveyor belt. She completes the young woman's transaction, including the candy bar, in record time, given the plethora of colors involved.

She scampers toward the frozen food section as the princess makes a quick turn from an adjoining aisle and pulls in front of her. Addy is afforded the luxurious view of Princess Meritain's ass, her butt cheeks rising and falling with each step.

She stops suddenly, but Addy is so entranced with her backside that she almost plows her over. She grabs a door handle just in time and rights herself. Princess Meritain's amused look is striking and sexy. Addy is smoldering, but she doubts stuffing a Lean Cuisine down her shirt will help.

The princess faces a refrigerated case and slaps the glass with both hands. She grinds her center against it, right in the Green Giant's line of sight.

She glances over her shoulder and says to Addy, "Can you satisfy me now?"

Addy presses against her. She matches her rhythm, kissing the side of her neck while her hands and lips explore the princess's sultry curves, enjoying the continuous undulation of their pelvises. The silk buttons of Princess Meritain's shirt come undone, as does the clasp of her bra, neither a match for Addy's nimble fingers. When the princess's bare nipples meet the cold glass, she gasps and lolls her head to the side. Addy pulls that regal chin up and connects their mouths for a deep kiss. Then she steps away.

"No, please," the princess whines.

Addy, still fully clothed, adjusts her Value Shop polo shirt and nametag, which hangs askew from her gyrations. The glass is fogged and she wonders if it's possible to spoil the food from the outside of the case. Princess Meritain's tiny skirt suddenly drops to her ankles, revealing a sheer, pink thong that matches the bra Addy has already woman-handled. When the princess sloughs off the silk shirt and bra, Addy almost grabs them, protecting the fine garments from the dirty, scarred linoleum floor.

But the princess doesn't notice. She spins around, stepping away from her discarded clothes toward a fresh case, one that hasn't been a victim of their heat. She presses her back against the frosty glass, her eyes grow wide and her lips form an O.

"Feeling a chill. Come warm me up, Addy."

The princess is a sight. Her face is flush, her nipples firm, and the blue eyes have turned a cooler shade of crystal. And she still gyrates, only now her back and buttocks are assaulted by the cold. She spreads her legs wider, beckoning Addy. When Addy doesn't respond immediately, she caresses her own breasts, splays her fingers across her belly and moves the manicured digits closer to the thong, the only strip of clothing she still wears.

"Let me," Addy instructs, sliding in front of the princess, disregarding the inevitable dirt stains on the knees of her white pants.

She yanks down the scrap of material and brings the juicy center to her mouth.

"Addy? Hello, Addy?"

Addy blinked. Her gaze shot left and right. She was at work, sitting in the driver's seat of Bus 29, the crown jewel of the Wilshire Hills Transportation Department. It was Thursday in late August. Her bus idled in front of Rhinehart's Mini-Mart, stop number six on her route. The bus's front door was still open. Thankfully, the brake was still engaged, but the hot summer wind blew inside and devoured the A/C.

She looked up into the full-view mirror above her driver's seat to acknowledge the passenger who had called to her. Mrs. Gelpin waved from the second row, a gentle smile on her face. At eighty-four, she was a long-time resident of Wilshire Hills, and one of Addy's regulars. She understood that periodically Addy took a mental vacation, and it wasn't always at the most convenient time.

"We're all on board, Addy. Ready to go," Mrs. Gelpin called. Then she gave a little cough and her index finger touched her chin.

Addy's hand immediately went to her own chin. It was wet and sticky. She glanced at her left hand, resting on the bus's steering wheel. It held a half-eaten peach.

CHAPTER TWO

Dr. Ivy Bertrand, dean of the School of Music at Cammon University, stared at Mazie Midnight with a look that could wilt flowers. Mazie imagined Dr. Bertrand practiced the look at home while she stood in front of the mirror and tied—and retied—her trademark bow tie until it was a perfectly symmetrical work of fashion art. Today's bow tie was a conservative blue and green striped number that popped against her crisp, white Oxford button-down shirt. She'd perfected her stony stare and undoubtedly intimidated thousands of graduate students, because if practice made perfect anywhere, it would be at the School of Music.

"I'm serious, Ms. Fenster," she reiterated, peering over the top of her reading glasses. The whites of her eyes contrasted with her dark chocolate skin, which only intensified her flinty gaze. "If you don't complete the *performance* element of your required program of study for your master's degree in music *performance* by the end of the fall semester, I will be forced to enter a failing grade in your *performance* workshop because you will not *perform*. Are we clear?"

"Quite," Mazie said, although in her mind it came out as *quit*. Something she'd done far too often. She hoped Dr. Bertrand didn't comment.

She bit her bottom lip. She wanted to share her new name with Dr. Bertrand. She very much wanted to tell her that she'd left May Fenster at the Oregon-Idaho state line. She'd changed her name to Mazie Midnight, honoring Grandma Mazie, the person who encouraged her to sing, and Midnight—the exact moment in time that her new life in Oregon began. She felt an explanation trip across her tongue, attempting to push out from her lips.

"Is there something you'd like to say, Ms. Fenster?"

Dr. Bertrand was intuitive. That was why she was one of the best. Mazie opened her mouth, her tongue moved and her lips parted. Yet no sound escaped. A far too familiar condition. Dr. Bertrand sighed audibly and signed Mazie's program of study. She closed her fountain pen, set it lovingly in a special mahogany holder, and clasped her hands.

"In the event you have further contact with my old friend, Maestro Larkin Lamond, you can tell her that by admitting you to this program, I consider our past debt paid in full. Can you remember that?"

"Yes, Dr. Bertrand."

She put an index finger at opposite corners of the Program of Study form and deliberately pushed it toward Mazie, who signed in the box above Dr. Bertrand's commanding signature. She didn't look at Dr. Bertrand, remembering Larkin's advice. She'd said, "Be deferential. She's really a big pussycat but you'll never see it unless she drinks an entire bottle of vodka with you."

Mazie doubted that would happen, but she imagined vodka had something to do with the debt Ivy Bertrand owed their mutual friend Larkin. Perhaps they had been lovers.

Dr. Bertrand reached for a beautiful wooden sphere and rolled it between her fingers. Mazie guessed her hands never stilled for long, as she was an accomplished violinist, a world-renowned conductor, and a brilliant composer, having written some of the greatest composed music of the twenty-first century.

"Is there anything else, Ms. Fenster?"

"No, Dr. Bertrand. May I be excused?"

"Yes."

She snatched her messenger bag and headed for the door. It squeaked open just far enough for her to disappear into the corridor when Dr. Bertrand said, "May I ask…"

Mazie took a breath and turned around. Dr. Bertrand's face had softened.

"Maestro Lamond sent me a recording. I've heard you sing. You have the chops. When did your stage fright consume you?"

"I don't know."

Dr. Bertrand's lips turned up slightly in a conspiratorial smile. They both knew Mazie was lying.

As Mazie traipsed across the Cammon University campus, she felt like an imposter. At forty-one she didn't belong here. Nearly every backpack-carrying student was half her age, and judging from the topics she overheard them discussing, most were oblivious to the obstacles, pain, and outright cruelty that awaited them in the world outside the university. Their chatter about economic summits, new scientific discoveries, and the age-old question, "But does he *really* like me?" illustrated the bubble in which they lived, one that Mazie envied and missed.

She'd loved college, bouncing from her bachelor's program in finance and urban planning to a master's degree in music. While she'd spent the first four years of college earning a respectable degree that would draw an income, singing was her heart and soul; student loans be damned. And then…

She shook her head. It wasn't worth rehashing again. "This is my time," she whispered. "This is my chance. This is my *second* chance. I will. Yes, I can do it."

She reached the eastern edge of campus, which hugged the old downtown area of Wilshire Hills, Oregon. Across the street sat the majestic Gallagher Hall, a former theater from the twenties. During its heyday it had been the Orpheum, housing vaudeville, plays, movies, even burlesque, until it closed in the late eighties. Attempts to bulldoze the iconic treasure had been

met with such stiff resistance from the local historic society that it
had sat vacant for another decade. Then, as the new millennium
began, Dr. Ivy Bertrand joined Cammon's School of Music and
the Orpheum regained the spotlight. For years Wilshire Hills
politicians and city socialites had quietly suggested Cammon
acquire the Orpheum, but the funds weren't available and no
one with enough clout or vision had taken the lead—until
Dr. Bertrand arrived. It took another decade and millions of
fundraised dollars, but the theater was fully restored and now
housed the performing arm of Cammon University. As the
Orpheum it lacked a clear identity, so it was renamed Gallagher
Hall, in honor of the first female music professor ever to join
Cammon University, Katherine Gallagher. Mrs. Gallagher was
now a professor emeritus and regularly attended performances,
sitting in her reserved seat—third row center.

Mazie gulped. It would be inside Gallagher Hall that she
would sing—or fail. The day her friend Professor Larkin
Lamond suggested Mazie finish her degree at Cammon, Mazie
had laughed at the farfetched notion of acceptance into one
of the finest schools of music in the world. Then that night
she'd dreamt she was singing on the Gallagher's stage with
her deceased grandmother sitting in the audience listening.
The next day she'd talked with Larkin and told her she'd go to
Oregon.

Mazie crossed the street to Gallagher's massive front doors.
Of course, they were locked. She peered inside at the expansive
lobby. Unique and tasteful glass chandeliers floated over the red
and blue carpet. She pressed the side of her face to the glass,
gazing at the oak portal doors that led to the auditorium.

"You know, they give tours," a voice called.

Mazie turned to the speaker, a woman in her mid-twenties
wearing an army jacket and a beret, leaning against a bus stop
sign. "Oh, really?"

She nodded and pointed at a notice taped to the glass.

Mazie scanned the details as a bus pulled up. "Thank you."

The woman offered a mock salute and boarded. Mazie's
attention returned to the notice and she took a picture of it

with her phone. Perhaps touring the facility, sitting in the seats, maybe even standing on the stage, would help her prepare for her performance. "It couldn't hurt," she told herself.

She turned away and noticed the bus was still in front of the stop, its door open. She looked left and right, expecting to see someone charging toward it before the doors closed. She glanced inside at the female driver, a young woman wearing a light blue, long-sleeve button-down shirt, navy walking shorts and an eight-point hat, similar to the ones police officers wore fifty years ago. It looked rather ridiculous on her, especially since it sat askew on her head. She was incredibly skinny and her pasty white legs looked like toothpicks. It was odd to wear a long-sleeve shirt with shorts in August, but perhaps the dress code didn't allow for short sleeves. The driver stared out the front window as still as a statue.

"Excuse me?" No response. "Excuse me?" Mazie asked louder.

The driver jumped and her hat fell onto the enormous steering wheel. She had an oval face with dimples on her cheeks, which were now flaming red. Her dark brown hair stuck out at all angles, and she quickly returned the hat to her head.

"I'm sorry," Mazie said. "I didn't mean to scare you. I thought you might've been waiting on me, and I'm not getting on the bus. I was just admiring the Gallagher."

The driver seemed to look through her, or rather, her gaze focused on something below Mazie's face. She wondered if the driver was staring at her breasts, but when she adjusted her messenger bag on her shoulder, the driver's gaze followed the movement.

Mazie pulled the bag around to her front, studying it, wondering if a snake was crawling out from under the flap. Seeing nothing except the colorful tie-dyed fabric, she locked eyes with the driver. "Are you all right?" The driver ignored her question, quickly closed the door and drove away while Mazie shook her head, muttering, "Definitely an odd duck."

CHAPTER THREE

As she pulled into the bus depot, Addy checked the time on her phone, six-fourteen. "Crap."

She was nineteen minutes late, which meant she wouldn't clock out on time—again. It was the third time in two weeks. Once or twice more and she'd wind up on the district manager's shit list. Clocking out on time was the most important expectation of bus drivers. Not only did it prevent overtime wages, it signified a driver was staying on schedule. A late arrival home meant the schedule was off.

And her schedule was off, but only slightly, as she never took a lunch and her regulars were sympathetic people who didn't report her. The infrequent riders assumed the tardiness was a glitch. She knew she was pushing the system, taking advantage of the kind and sympathetic community culture that defined Wilshire Hills. Eventually she'd have to deal with it.

As she turned in to her parking space, she wasn't surprised to see Jackie Correa, her supervisor, waiting for her. Jackie was ready to leave, her jacket draped over one arm and her lunchbox dangling from her shoulder. She was the only woman Addy knew who looked good in the city-issued polyester pants, which outlined the shapely curves of her buttocks.

Addy had firsthand knowledge of those buttocks, having caressed them once, when she and Jackie had attempted to expand their relationship, an experiment that failed miserably, at least from Addy's perspective. Still, Jackie was fine about it and Addy had no problem ogling her, an act Jackie appreciated. She'd freed her dark black hair from its traditional bun and taken a moment to freshen her lipstick. Addy imagined she was headed to Lolly's, Wilshire Hills's only lesbian bar.

Addy slowly completed her post-shift inspection and collected her things. Perhaps Jackie would get impatient or be summoned to an urgent matter before she debarked.

"Come on, Addy," Jackie said sternly. "I know you're stalling. I'm not going anywhere."

She groaned and hopped off the bus. "Sorry I'm late." She stared into Jackie light brown eyes, asking for forgiveness.

Jackie blinked and sighed. "I already clocked out for you," she whispered.

"Thanks."

"Addy, it's getting worse. Do you see that?"

She looked away. She knew it was true, but there was nothing she could do about it. Clicking heels approached, echoing in the enormous bus bay. Another driver, Pratul, sauntered by. He was stout with jet black hair and a mustache that reminded Addy of a caterpillar. He offered a wave and a glance but didn't stop on his way to the locker room.

"Goodnight, Pratul," Jackie called in a sickeningly sweet voice.

"Goodnight, boss."

"I don't trust that guy," Addy whispered.

"You shouldn't. He wants my job and you fired. In that order. You need to stop giving him ammunition. Damn homophobic asshole." She took a breath and added, "See you at home," before she walked away.

"See you later," Addy said. "And thanks again."

Jackie didn't acknowledge her, making Addy feel worse. She headed to the locker room to change. She heard a locker door slam and one of the new hires came around the corner. She was an older woman with short curly hair and a great smile that would make her popular with passengers.

"Hi, Addy," she said cheerfully.

"Hi. Hey, I'm sorry. I forgot your name."

"Oh, that's okay. I'm Quinoa. Like the food. I had hippie parents." She waved. "Have a nice night."

"You too."

Addy headed to the last row of lockers, aware that she was alone. The locker area creeped her out, and many slasher movies included a creepy scene in a locker room. She grabbed her street clothes and ducked into a changing room. Since the locker room was co-ed, private changing rooms were provided. Even if it were just a women's locker room, Addy would've used the changing room. She didn't want anybody seeing her skinny-ass, as her mama called it. That was part of the reason she'd never connected with Jackie. *Well, that's one part.*

She quickly changed and as she headed out, she heard a sneeze. *Pratul.* He was still in the locker room, possibly watching her. She'd caught him once, and he'd insisted he was looking in her direction but not at her.

She hustled outside and retrieved her bike. Passengers and other drivers often found it ironic that a bus driver didn't own a car. Addy saw the simple logic. She spent all day driving and had no desire to do so after the workday. And the ride home from the bus depot was therapeutic.

The wise city council had determined the bus depot, like so many other unsightly buildings, would sit on the outskirts of town where the big box stores and large industrial companies had been banished. For decades the various mayors and city council members—regardless of political party—shared the common belief that Wilshire Hills should maintain its quaint and charming status. Consequently, strict urban growth laws prohibited rich entrepreneurs from dotting the downtown with tall buildings. Small business owners were favored over large chains attempting to bully their way into a prestigious college town, and the varying ecosystems were preserved.

One such example was the Willowick Creek Wilderness Area. The "Willy" as locals called this thin artery of the Columbia River, spawned marshlands between the heart of Wilshire Hills and the bus depot. Miles of bike path paralleled the creek that ran to the town of Sweet Home. The six-mile ride to her house provided the solitude she craved after eight hours of smiling, chatting, and sometimes confronting the bus passengers. She'd often veer off the direct route to her neighborhood and go exploring. Sandwiched between the tall grass on her left and the creek on her right, Addy often got lost in her thoughts, and more than once, she'd just gotten physically lost.

In the winter months when the sun set before she finished her route, she had to pay particular attention to avoid crashing into squirrels, possums, and nutrias crossing the path. More than once she'd swerved to miss a creature who froze in place, blinded by the light on her bike. Once she'd actually crashed and broken her wrist. It had forced her to a desk job for six weeks since she couldn't turn the bus's enormous steering wheel with one hand.

She felt guilty that Jackie was covering for her tardiness and even guiltier because of the reason Jackie continued to do it: she had a crush on Addy. While Addy had been clear and honest that she didn't feel the same way, not even after viewing Jackie's glorious derriere, she knew Jackie wasn't over her—and had told her as much.

It didn't help that they lived together, or rather, Addy lived on Jackie's property in a tiny house Addy had built with the help of three bus route regulars. Since her one-night make out session with Jackie, she had contemplated moving the tiny house, especially after she realized Jackie still had feelings for her. But Addy didn't know where she'd go.

As she rode toward downtown, she contemplated Jackie's comment. *It's getting worse. Do you see that?*

Yes, she saw it. She'd read lots of articles about daydreaming, fugue states, and hypnosis. What happened to her was all three rolled into one. Different things sent her down the rabbit hole, the name she'd given to the place her mind went. Most often she remembered the scenarios, like today's tryst with the princess in the frozen food aisle. It was her own movie that she created, but how many movies had pickup scenes in grocery stores?

But what if she lost control of the bus? What if Pratul, who deserved the moniker homophobic asshole, found out about her daydreaming and reported her? What if she didn't stop at a red light, too busy fantasizing about her dream woman? Sweat dripped into her eyes and she wiped her hand across her face.

Instead of the frozen food aisle, maybe she and the woman of her dreams would be doing it in a steamier place—like a sauna.

Skin slick with heat. That's how women exit the Whispering Pines sauna, their bodies glistening with sweat. Some wear a terrycloth robe back to the showers, while others wrap themselves in a plush cotton towel from breast to thigh. Still others…just nude, a trail of steam following them.

These are the women she admires the most. They have risen above body shaming. Yes, some have toned and lean figures and know it, but many are chunkier, displaying stretch marks from their pregnancies and scars from their surgeries. They are proud to be women. Two such women, Mrs. Sattlewhite and Mrs. Elder, pass Addy and offer a nod. Both sit on the cusp of senior citizenhood with sagging breasts and a roadmap of varicose veins. Yet their naked strut across the lobby convey their complete lack of care.

As the steam room concierge, Addy sees it all. It's normal for her to have a conversation with a naked grandmother about grandchildren or be flattered by the flirtations of a married woman, her enormous diamond ring the only jewelry she wears into the sauna. Often Addy is asked if she's single. Sometimes she lies. Sometimes she tells the truth.

Usually a woman catches her gaze at least once a week. Their eyes hold for a beat too long, and she knows. Sometimes the woman provides an added hint, such as dropping her towel.

"Could you put some lotion on my back?" a brunette now asks.

She is completely naked, her full breasts lifted cosmetically and her tummy tucked. Her Botox-laced lips curl into a smile. Addy guesses she's in her late fifties, but she has a great surgeon.

"Of course."

"Make sure you warm it up." She says warm with a trace of a Southern drawl.

"I will," Addy assures her.

As she massages the lotion between her hands, she realizes they are completely alone. Not only is the dressing room empty, no one is in the steam room. Such excellent timing. She rubs the lotion into the tanned, smooth back, over rippling muscles that are regularly exercised, probably rowing. As her thumbs cross more real estate, the woman hums. It isn't a tune, just a purr of pleasure.

"Lower," she whispers.

Her fingers work another dollop of lotion into the skin, careful not to take liberties and cross her obvious tan line from the tiny bikini briefs she must wear to the tanning bed or the pool.

The woman laughs. "C'mon, Addy. Lower." She giggles and stands on her tiptoes for a second, encouraging Addy's palms to her creamy white derriere. Addy circles her cheeks, longing to plant a kiss on each one. "You're being far too gentle," the woman snaps in a throaty voice. "If I wanted gentle, I'd just ask my wuss of a husband."

Addy squeezes her buttocks and she moans. Then she leans forward, thrusting her rear end into the air. "Spank me. Leave a mark."

Addy complies, growing more lustful with each swat. When both cheeks are red as a young girl's blush, she drops to her knees and kisses them tenderly. And since she's already down there… She dips her head between the woman's legs, parting the soft folds with her tongue. The woman tastes divine, and with each tongue lashing, she sighs. She buries her fingers in Addy's hair and pushes her tongue deeper inside, riding Addy until she cries out.

Her legs quiver and Addy helps her to the cedar deck. After a few deep breaths and a quick glance into the mirror, she paws Addy's polo shirt and unzips her walking shorts. She twists the stretchy fabric in a fist.

"In thirty seconds I'm ripping off your uniform, so you better run out to the waiting area and flip over the closed sign. Today the sauna is reserved for a private party of two." She parts her legs, giving Addy a clear view of her throbbing clit. "I'll keep myself in the mood until you

*get back." She licks a middle finger and pleasures herself while Addy
stands rooted in place, watching. She laughs and says, "Go!"*

*Addy races out to the tiny lobby, pulling up her zipper, in case a
client has wandered inside. Perhaps another beautiful woman could be
enticed to join a threesome?*

"Well, well, what is going on?"

*Pratul sits on the love seat in the reception area, his arms
outstretched along the back of the cushions, wearing a shit-eating grin
and sunglasses. "Addy, you know you're in trouble, right?"*

Addy nods.

*"I'll make you a deal. Let me watch your unnatural act with that
woman and I won't report you. Okay?"*

Out of the corner of her eye, Addy saw movement. She
jerked the handlebars, nearly knocking herself over, but ensuring
the surprised squirrel made it across the bike path. Once she'd
regained her balance, she let out a heavy sigh. These "mental
vacations," or whatever they were, really could be the death of
her. Last night she'd watched *Steam* with Jackie and their friend
Nadine, so apparently it was still trolling her psyche.

She exited the Willy, crossed into downtown, and rode past
the rows of closed shops. It was just past six p.m. and the bars
and restaurants hummed now that the fall semester at Cammon
University would begin soon. Couples enjoyed candlelit
dinners on the outdoor patios, soaking up the pleasant late
summer weather Oregon provided. Lolly's, one bar that catered
to lesbian clientele (although almost all bars were LGBTQi
friendly) was quiet, waiting for the bar crowd.

She turned right and grinned. The entire street was bathed
in neon glory from the Bijou's enormous marquee, which
advertised a lesbian double feature, *The Small of her Back* and
Days Without End. A converted church with only two theaters,
the Bijou played the indie and artsy movies that came to
Wilshire Hills, mainly for the academic citizenry at Cammon
who wanted more than just chase scenes with exploding cars.

Addy came to a stop in front of the movie posters. She
checked the time and realized the next showing of *Days Without
End* was in forty minutes. She parked her bike and bought

her ticket from a young girl sitting in the box office outside the theater. Her nameplate said Tango, and Addy guessed she must be new, a college student hired for the school year by the manager and owner, Almondine, a flamboyant woman who spoke English with a terrible French accent just for fun. She said it was her ongoing tribute to French filmmakers, the true masters of the craft.

"Enjoy the show," Tango said, handing Addy her ticket stub.

"Tango. That's a cool name."

"Thanks," she replied politely with a nod.

"I'll bet a lot of people comment on it, right?"

She smiled and nodded again.

"Well, I can relate. My name's Addy Tornado. I'm a regular here, and people ask me about my name all the time."

The girl furrowed her brow. "Addy? What's weird about that?"

Addy blinked. "No, not that part. Tornado. My last name. People ask where it came from, and a lot of government types don't think it's real. When a police officer pulled over my bike one time, we got into an argument because he thought my driver's license was a fake."

"A cop pulled over your bicycle? Really?"

"Yeah, sometimes I go pretty fast."

"Oh."

Addy waved. "Well, nice to meet you, Tango."

"You too, Addy Tornado."

Addy laughed and ventured inside, her stomach rumbling for a popcorn and soda dinner. And maybe some licorice too. As she stepped up to the concessions counter, she gasped. She couldn't believe what she was seeing! Billie, the concessions clerk, had previously accommodated Addy's one request: group the candies by predominant wrapper color. But now the reds mixed with the blues. The yellows and greens were interspersed with purple and orange. How had this happened?

It was almost as bad as the moment earlier in the day when the woman outside Gallagher Hall had spoken to her—a tie-dyed bag draped over her shoulder. Addy thought her head might explode. Tie-dye was the ultimate disrespect to color, and in fact was created in the sixties as a statement of disrespect to the establishment. At least, that was her theory.

Fortunately, the tie-dyed bag lady hadn't boarded the bus and Addy had quickly looked away and closed the door, thinking it was kind of her to tell Addy she wasn't boarding. Most people weren't that considerate. They just stood there, usually on their phones, and when Addy went to close the door, they'd run up to it, pounding on the glass, yelling at her for almost driving off without them. "Then get *off* your cell and *on* the damn bus!" she wanted to scream. "What are you standing around for?"

But Addy rarely screamed. It just wasn't her nature, and she believed in true customer service. She was dedicated to helping all the citizens of Wilshire Hills reach their chosen destinations.

There was no one in the lobby or at the concessions counter. Where was Billie? What had happened to the display? She scratched her head and thought it couldn't hurt to be proactive. She flipped up the hinged countertop and went behind the glass case. She knew what she was doing. Often when the line was long and people were impatient, she'd duck under the counter and help a grateful Billie.

Almondine had fired Billie a few times for yelling at rude customers, including one uppity college boy who really deserved the Dr. Pepper shower Billie bestowed upon him. Of course, Almondine rehired Billie before closing. Few employees put up with Almondine. She needed Billie.

"You're my lifesaver, Addy," Billie had said many times.

Addy crouched and opened the lighted cabinet. Her hands deftly swapped out candies, creating a uniform rainbow of color.

"What are you doing?" an angry voice asked.

When she turned around, the first thing Addy saw were a pair of great legs with cute knees. Definitely not Billie. Her gaze slid up the woman's skirt, over a shapely abdomen to a pinstriped, button-down shirt that accentuated a noticeable pair of breasts. She had a round face with rich, brown eyes. Her skin was darker than Addy's, a light shade of cocoa that matched her hair. She wasn't Addy's type, but she definitely had some nice features. Her gaze settled on two red lips formed into a scowl. Then Addy remembered. She was tie-dyed lady.

CHAPTER FOUR

Mazie couldn't believe what she was seeing. A grown woman stealing candy from the concessions stand! And not a bag lady type—no, a woman with a very nice bottom and muscular calves. But that wasn't the point, she reprimanded herself. Now wasn't the time to ogle a hottie.

She stepped up to the woman and demanded to know what was going on. The woman's slow, long gaze convinced Mazie she was being checked out, a fact that pleased her immensely, even while she was angry. She'd spent an hour regrouping all of the candy after suggesting to Almondine that a better way to display products for sale was by price—not by color. Almondine had replied with something unintelligible but approving. That had been their standard communication for the past two days. Mazie attempted to understand Almondine but relied much more on tone and facial expression.

The thief looked stunned, obviously ashamed of herself.

"You've got a lot of nerve coming behind the counter and stealing stuff!"

The woman stood, her green eyes blazing. "I'm not stealing." She looked around, distraught. "Where's Billie?"

Mazie shrugged. "I don't know who that is. I was hired yesterday. Almondine said something about a kayak trip?"

The woman processed that information and scratched her head. For some reason, Mazie thought they'd met before. She crouched and shook her head. "Why are you touching all of this?" she asked as she put the candies back where they belonged. "It's not sanitary."

"Don't!" the muscular woman cried. "You're messing it up." She dropped next to Mazie and put a hand on her arm.

"Don't touch me! Move back to the other side of the counter. Customers aren't allowed back here. Do you even have a ticket?"

"I do!" The woman pulled out a ticket, her gaze riveted to the candies in the display. "Just put them back."

Mazie sighed at her distress. "Why?"

"It's just not right. The yellows all need to go together. And the blues."

The creaky door to the manager's office opened and Almondine appeared. Mazie thought she said, "Addy, what's going on?"

"She changed Billie's system!"

"That was a system?" Mazie asked sarcastically. "Having everything by color doesn't encourage patrons to buy anything. They have no idea what anything costs."

"It's all the same," Addy said.

Mazie cocked her head. "Seriously?" She looked at Almondine. "You really charge the same amount for a little box of gummy worms as you do for a king-size candy bar?" When there was no reply she added, "No wonder the bubble gum expired in 2016. No one is buying it. Why would I pay a dollar for a blob of gum when I can have the peanut butter cups for the same price?"

Almondine closed her eyes and took a deep breath. Then she offered Mazie a hard stare. "I know you're new here, new to Wilshire Hills and new to the Bijou. Here we believe there are more important things than money."

Mazie gave an exasperated sigh and looked at Addy. "Of course there are more important things, but I spent most of my adult life as a CPA." She turned to Almondine and said, "I'm here to tell you that money helps. That's one reason you hired me, right?" She glanced around the lobby before she whispered, "You do want to stay in business, right?"

"Of course," Almondine said, pressing her palm to her forehead.

Once Almondine learned Mazie was a CPA during her initial interview, Almondine stopped asking questions about coming to work on time and counting change and asked instead for feedback about her business plan and an analysis of the Bijou's finances for the last year. She agreed to give Mazie the second apartment above the Bijou—and a paying job as the manager—in exchange for one small thing: Mazie needed to save the Bijou, which was bleeding money and would close within a year if something wasn't done.

Mazie stood and crossed her arms. "Everyone knows that movie theaters make their money from the concessions stands. If you're not turning a profit there, you're not turning a profit. Period." She whipped around and faced Addy. "Which do you like more? Coming here to the Bijou or looking at color-coordinated candy? Because if this place doesn't make money, it won't be a theater for much longer."

Addy's face crumpled. "I love the Bijou," she said sincerely. She looked at Almondine. "Are you closing?"

"No," Almondine said. "Of course not. Mazie will make sure of it." She turned on her heel and retreated to the office as if her pronouncement solved everything.

Mazie tried to look as reassuring as possible, although she wasn't sure of anything. She felt a pang of empathy for Addy, whose eyelashes were almost glamorous. "Do you have OCD?" she asked gently.

Addy's expression turned hostile at the use of the term. "None of your business," she spat. "But if you must know, I'm just peculiar."

Three more moviegoers came into the lobby, and while Mazie sold them snacks, Addy filled a bucket of popcorn and dispensed some lemonade from the fountain. Before she picked up her refreshments, she deposited money in the register, rummaged through a cabinet, and withdrew a new sleeve of napkins. She filled the dispensers and returned the remainder of the napkins to the cabinet.

"You're almost out of sugar packets too," she mumbled as she grabbed her refreshments.

Mazie admired her retreating derriere and returned to the candy reorganization—again. She glanced at the theater door where Addy had disappeared. Maybe there was a way...

Addy tried to concentrate on the movie while she enjoyed her popcorn and lemonade dinner, but she couldn't stop thinking about the candy display. She and Billie had organized it together. There had been major discussions since some of the wrappers had two dominant colors, and while Addy deferred to Billie's superior organization skills, the process reminded her of an economic summit between superpowers.

It wasn't often that people listened to her, especially at work. Most of the bus drivers ignored her if she made a suggestion, except for Jackie, and fortunately, Jackie was the supervisor in charge of her shift. There had been talk of promoting her, and while Addy would love to see Jackie move up the food chain, Addy wasn't sure she could work with any of the other supervisors.

She'd already decided that if someone new took over the day shift, she'd quit. "Bus driver" would just be another entry on her extremely long list of occupations that already included journeyman electrician, driver's ed instructor, sommelier, butcher, termite inspector, and construction worker. At twenty-nine, she'd held more jobs than anyone she knew. Her résumé was nine pages long, filled with a patchwork of jobs, most of which hadn't lasted longer than six months—except the bus driving gig.

She'd been a "Grade Two Transportation Associate" for eighteen months, and she gave all of the credit to Jackie. Addy had quit her previous jobs because of poor management and a failure to provide an understanding environment, namely her need for color organization. Such had been the case at the wine shop. The owner had been none too happy when she reorganized four hundred and twelve bottles of wine—by label color. The chardonnay, pinot gris, and sauvignon blanc mingled with the red blend, Malbec, and cabernet sauvignon. So despite her incredible taste palate, she was pressured to resign.

A moan echoed through the theater and her gaze returned to the screen. After some witty repartee, the two love interests had fallen into bed together. Both had incredible bodies and knew exactly where to touch the other. Of course, the filmmaker left much to the imagination, unlike Addy's own fantasies, which included visuals of every erotic female body part, because she believed the entire female anatomy was sensual and sexy.

Not that she knew from experience.

She was a virgin. But she imagined she would enjoy tracing the fine curve of a woman's calf nearly as much as cupping a large breast or tasting the folds of a woman's labia—if she could get past her intimacy issues. But before that, she'd need to meet a woman who wanted a second date. She'd had a multitude of first dates, but the minute they saw her separating anything by color, they usually inquired politely, and once she shared her peculiarity, they'd offer an understanding look that said, "No big deal." But they never called again. One woman excused herself to use the restaurant's bathroom—and never returned. She was hot and Addy would've enjoyed seeing her labia. *But then she'd probably want to see mine…*

She shifted in her seat, becoming turned on by her own thoughts and the increased grinding and moaning from the actresses on the screen. The scene was reminiscent of the love scenes in *High Art*. Her fingers thudded against the bottom of the popcorn barrel. She'd eaten it all and was still hungry. On any other night, she'd be opening a package of red licorice, but she'd become so flustered by Mazie that she hadn't thought to purchase any. And besides, it hadn't been sitting with the other blue-wrapped candy. It was tainted.

She glanced back at the exit, debating whether to run out to the lobby or not, when she spotted Mazie leaning against one of the columns, watching the movie. Her long, curly hair served as a pillow for her head and the gentle locks draped around her face. She had fine lips—symmetrical and plump. She bit her lip, and Addy's breath caught. It was incredibly sexy. Addy could tell Mazie was enjoying the steamy scene. She wondered if Mazie saw the similarities to *High Art*. Did she even know anything about movies?

Suddenly Mazie's gaze flicked from the screen to Addy. Addy blinked and faced forward. Mazie had caught her staring, but how did Mazie know where she was sitting to stare back? Unless she'd been staring at Addy too.

She focused on the movie as the plot shifted to the next day, but she desperately wanted to look back at the pillar and see if Mazie was still standing there looking like a movie ingénue, but she didn't dare. Besides, she wasn't attracted to Mazie, so she shouldn't give her so much "brain space," as Dr. Pfeiffer called it. Mazie would never be the type of woman she fantasized about—too plump, too plain and way too careless with colors, as evidenced by the candy display fiasco.

She suddenly remembered she had a baggie full of blue M&Ms in her knapsack. She gleefully fished them out and spent the rest of the movie living in the problems of beautiful lesbians while munching on chocolate joy.

By the time the credits rolled, the lesbians were living happily ever after (as if a lesbian romance would end any other way!). She quickly bolted up the side aisle near the wall, hoping to exit the theater before Mazie saw her. She was embarrassed when she thought about the way she'd ogled Mazie. It was very disturbing and inappropriate in the light of the "Me Too" movement.

As she crossed the lobby, her gaze strayed to the concessions stand. And she halted—so quickly that a college guy nearly ran her over.

"Sorry," he mumbled in a not-sorry way as he raced past her.

She couldn't believe what she saw. All of the candies were once again clustered by color—and each candy had an individual price sticker.

"Do you like it?"

Addy turned to find Mazie beside her. She wore a meek smile, as if she was imploring Addy not to be upset. "It's genius," Addy said. "Thank you for going to so much trouble."

Mazie grinned at the compliment and her full lips parted slightly. For a second Addy wondered what it would be like to kiss those lips.

"It didn't take too long to do, and you're clearly a Bijou VIP."

Addy knew it was her turn to say something but being called a VIP momentarily stunned her. "I really liked the movie," she blurted. "It reminded me of *Elena Undone*."

"I agree," Mazie said.

"And the sex scenes were filmed like *High Art*."

Mazie made a face. "Not a fan."

"You didn't like *High Art*?"

"Not really. I like movies that are more straightforward like *Fried Green Tomatoes* or *Bound*. And *Everything Relative*."

"Wow. That's an oldie. So you don't like artsy films?"

"No, I do, but I think sometimes they're trying to be artistic and they fall flat. But others, like *The Gymnast*, are really beautiful. I loved that movie."

"Me too," Addy said.

Mazie offered a slight smile. "So we agree."

Addy shuffled her feet and glanced at Mazie once more. She could talk about movies to someone like Mazie for hours.

Mazie held up the broom and dustpan and said, "Well, I'm off to cleanup duty. See you soon, Addy."

"Bye," Addy called, relieved, as she headed for the front doors with the crowd.

Outside she took a deep breath, pleased with the events of the evening. The movie was good and she'd never again be deprived of her licorice. She knew such joys were not that important in the grand scheme of life, like surviving a hurricane or beating cancer. Still, for her they rated.

She biked five blocks before she realized there was nothing on her back. She'd left her knapsack in the theater. She'd been so busy thinking about Mazie's full lips and the unorganized candies that she'd forgotten to pick up her version of a purse.

She groaned and turned her bike around. Fortunately, the last patrons were just exiting, and she caught the front door before it closed. She knew Almondine's routine. She always locked the front doors midway through the last showing as a security measure. The patrons could leave but drunk creeps couldn't enter.

As Addy crossed the lobby, she admired the wooden beams across the pitched ceilings. The Bijou had once been a church. While the original lobby remained, the sanctuary now served as the larger theater, accommodating one hundred and ten patrons. Outside across the courtyard was Theatre Two, which had once been a meeting hall.

She stiffened as she walked through the courtyard, another place to gather. The little chairs and round tables dotted the thirty by forty space. Hanging planter boxes provided color, and a few trees lined the border. In the summer Almondine would host poetry readings and serve cappuccino. While a lot of people didn't attend, those who did found it most enjoyable.

She grasped the large door handle for Theater Two but hesitated. She imagined she might encounter Mazie again, and goose pimples sprouted on her arms. She hadn't seen those since her teen years when a friend made her go to the haunted house at the county fair.

She cracked the door open—and heard singing. She didn't know the song, but it was bluesy, and she found herself swaying, caught up in the rich, deep sounds. She guessed Mazie had turned on the radio to the jazz station so she could listen while she worked. The song grew softer, and Addy pulled the door open a little wider to catch the next set of lyrics. It was catchy, one of those songs people hummed along with because the melody was easy to follow.

The singer caressed each note the way the lesbians caressed each other in the movie. Addy decided to get the song from iTunes, but since she was terrible at remembering song titles or lyrics, she hit the record button on her phone.

Just as she poked her head through the doorway, holding out her phone, the most powerful crescendo she'd ever heard burst forth. From Mazie. Addy's eyes widened as she gazed at Mazie, standing on the little stage in front of the movie screen. Her back arched, her arms opened wide and her entire body shuddered as she belted out the chorus. Addy imagined colors emerging from her lips, alongside the glorious notes—blues, greens, yellows...and deep purple.

Addy couldn't believe it. Those lips she'd studied uttered the words of the song, like a gift just for her. She closed her eyes and those lips were upon her...

"What are you doing here!"

Addy blinked. Mazie had stopped singing and was staring at Addy, her face red with anger. Addy suddenly realized the music had pulled her through the doorway. She was standing at the head of the aisle. She quickly shoved the phone into her pocket.

"I said, what the hell are you doing here?"

"I, I...left my backpack." She pointed wildly toward her usual seat.

"Get it and get out," Mazie said, turning away.

Addy hurried down the aisle and retrieved it. Mazie had abandoned the stage and was furiously sweeping the opposite corner of the theater as if an entire dumpster had overturned and a pile of garbage littered Row A.

"Your singing...your voice. I've never heard anything like it. You're amazing."

Mazie whirled around and faced her, teeth gritted. "Get out!"

CHAPTER FIVE

Addy's least favorite month of the year was September, when the leaves, flowers—everything—started to die. It was also the month she celebrated her birthday. Her mother had declared her birthday was always the day after Labor Day, the first day of school. Once Addy understood calendars, she realized her birthday was always a different date, and her mother confessed she struggled to remember Addy's actual date of birth, so she just proclaimed it to be the day after Labor Day, saying "labor" was the reminder she needed about the trip to the hospital and Addy's appearance in the world.

Addy had heard the story many times, whenever her mother decided to make her feel guilty for being born. Twenty hours of labor. She'd almost died. Addy had almost died. Her mother vowed never to return to a hospital, claiming the nurse nearly killed her because she hadn't given her the right medications. Addy didn't understand this at all, but she'd always found herself apologizing for existing right before she blew out the single birthday candle her mother stuck in a Ding Dong, Twinkie, chicken pot pie—whatever was convenient.

A few days after her declared birthday, Addy was still thinking about her confrontation with Mazie. How could someone with such a beautiful, melodic instrument turn it, in an instant, into something shrilly, horrible and nightmarish? It was almost as if Mazie had been possessed, like Sissy Spacek in *Carrie*. So which voice belonged to the real Mazie? The singer or the screamer?

Get out!

She exited the changing room and returned her street clothes to her locker. As she passed Jackie's office on her way to the time clock, Jackie called, "Addy, in here, please!"

She pivoted and leaned into the doorway. "Can it wait, Jac? I haven't clocked in."

"Clock in and come back. And what's that tune you're whistling?"

She cocked her head to the side. "What?"

"You were just whistling." Her eyes narrowed. "Weren't you? I'm not losing my mind…am I? I'm not over forty yet." She shook her head. "You really didn't just hear yourself whistling?" Her expression grew troubled. Addy had seen it happen every so often, when Jackie's leadership ability and confidence seemed to evaporate. "Middle age strikes again," she muttered. "Go clock in and come back."

Addy nodded and sighed. She retreated down the hallway toward the Bull Pen, the aptly named lounge, since ninety percent of the Wilshire Hills Transportation Department was male.

As she entered, Pratul said, "And the second guy says, 'I may not have a right hand, but at least I'm not a fag!'"

Four of her colleagues—all white males, obese, homophobic, approaching retirement, and somewhat racist, laughed heartily at his punchline. She ignored them and strolled to the time clock, passing by Jennifer, one of the other few female employees. Jennifer was between shifts and engrossed in a book. She claimed it was her way of blocking out the testosterone. She glanced at Addy as she passed and they exchanged nods.

"Hey Addy!" Pratul called. "You just missed my joke. Want me to tell it again?"

She took a breath and faced him. "No, I don't need to hear it."

"Why not? It's funny."

She cocked her head to the side and tapped her chin. "Funny like, 'how many Muslims does it take to build a bomb?' That kind of funny?"

His expression turned stony. She knew he wished her physical harm, but he enjoyed the cushy salary and benefits provided by Wilshire Hills and wouldn't sacrifice those for a quick backhand to her mouth.

"And for the record," she said, "I don't think jokes about Muslims are funny either." She turned on a heel and headed back to Jackie's office.

"There! See? You're whistling." She slapped her desk. "I am not crazy."

Addy shrugged and slumped into the chair across from Jackie's desk. "Sorry. Didn't realize I was doing it."

She looked at her shrewdly. "You're awfully chipper for just running the gauntlet through the Bull Pen. Did you let Pratul have it?"

She nodded. "Yeah, a little."

Jackie looked at her sharply. "Be careful, Add. I'm telling you, he's looking for a reason to take you down."

"I know," she said, "but I'm not taking his shit."

"And I'm not asking you to." Jackie held up a folder. "Now, the reason I called you in here—"

The radio next to Jackie cackled. "Supervisor, this is Luanne on 19."

Jackie rolled her eyes and picked up the radio. Addy knew Luanne was a new driver and prone to mistakes. Two days before she'd managed to pull her bus into a dead-end alley. Another driver and several passengers had to help her back out.

"This is supervisor, Luanne. What's up?"

"Uh, I know you're probably going to be upset..." Luanne sniffled and sounded as if she were crying.

Jackie leaned forward. "It's okay, Luanne. Is anyone hurt?"

"No, no. It's nothing like that. I'm on I-5, and well…I had my window open, and all of my directions for the route, you know, the left turns, the right turns…all of it blew out the window. Gone. I've got no idea where I'm going."

Jackie bit her lip and tried not to laugh. Getting lost and missing turns was part of the gig. Addy motioned for the radio and Jackie handed it to her. "Hey, Luanne, it's Addy. Tell me the next sign or landmark you see."

"Uh, the outlet stores are coming up."

Addy nodded. "Okay, take that exit. Then go right at the first stop sign, that's Goode Street. You got two stops on Goode, and then turn left on Nashua Boulevard. Three stops there and it's the end of the route. There's a Dollar Mart store at Nashua and Washington. Pull in there and get yourself set up with the bus's GPS."

"Aw, Addy, I hate using all the fancy technology," she whined.

"I know, but you gotta, right?"

"Yeah, okay. Hey, thanks, Addy. You're the best. Over and out."

She grinned and Jackie offered a high-five. Jackie set down the radio and looked at Addy thoughtfully. "How did you know where she needed to go? That's nowhere near your route."

She smoothed the creases of her shorts. "When I came on and didn't have any seniority, I did all the routes."

"And you remember all the turns for each one?"

She shrugged. "I don't know. I guess so." Jackie looked doubtful. "No, really, I remember everything I drive. I don't know why."

"You know, you could be a trainer. Ever thought of that?"

Addy shook her head. "I don't think so."

"Well, I do. I think you'd make a great trainer, but there's a distinct possibility you won't be employed with us after tomorrow."

"What?"

"This is why I called you in here. You haven't filed your insurance papers. If I don't get the form completed by tomorrow morning, you won't have health insurance. And you have to be covered. It's part of the union agreement." Addy nodded but said nothing. "You understand you need to do this, right? Our new carrier, Meritain, demands it. If something bad happened, you'd be fucked."

"I know. I just…" How could she explain that she didn't understand the jargon? She'd had an anxiety attack just trying to make sense of the forms. She didn't like to think about being sick. She'd only been to a doctor twice in her whole life. Her mother never had the money, and fortunately she and her brother weren't sickly. And the times she should have gone… She wasn't going to think about those times.

"Look, would you like me to help you fill out the papers?"

"Would you?"

"Yes. This needs to get done." She paused and looked at her uncomfortably. "Addy, have you checked to see if your doctor is on this plan? You know, the psychiatrist you see every once in a while?"

Addy shrugged. She hated talking about Dr. Pfeiffer. She hated talking to Dr. Pfeiffer. She was ashamed to tell people she actually paid someone to discuss her…issues, especially the colors. She'd tried talking to Jackie, but Jackie didn't feel like she could help her. And then it made their relationship even stranger than it already was.

"Get going and come by my place tonight after you get off work," Jackie said. "We'll go through everything and celebrate your birthday—just a little bit."

She smiled and Addy nodded. "Thanks." Jackie understood she hated big birthday celebrations, but she didn't mind a quick drink or a quiet meal.

"Hey," Jackie said before she ducked out of the office. "That tune you were whistling? I figured it out. Great blues number called 'My Mama Don't Allow Me' from the forties. How do you know that song?"

"I…must've heard it somewhere."

"My grandma used to sing it. Used to make my racist granddad mad because it was 'black' music." She looked away wistfully. "He was such an asshole." She smiled at Addy. "Catchy tune. Have a good day."

"You too."

She headed to the bus bay, scratching her head. She didn't know that song. Where had she heard it? As she filled out her log and performed her pre-check routine before she departed, she suddenly remembered. It was the song Mazie had been singing in the theater the night before.

Addy started her route, which she affectionately termed "the oven mitt," for it was shaped like an oven mitt—or the state of Michigan. She'd added the thumb of the mitt herself by including a slight detour for one of her regulars, a detour that neither Jackie nor the Wilshire Hills Transportation Department knew existed. While she thought it was for a very good reason, she doubted the stuffy executives who ran the city and probably never had ridden a bus would agree—and would insist on punishing her if they found out.

She rarely collected passengers at her first two stops since the nearby sawmill had closed six months ago. When she'd been hired eighteen months before, her route was the one no one wanted. It was known as the "Buzz Kill" for two reasons, the first being the sawmill. She'd almost quit during her first week after facing a sea of men, mostly clad in offensive plaid shirts—Addy's least favorite pattern ever. Plaid was a world where colors practically slammed against each other, separated only by thin black lines. Many of the men asked her out or made sexual comments, all of which she ignored. By the end of her shift each day, she had routinely found the floor and seats covered in sawdust, making her cleanout process long and cumbersome. She was probably the only person in town who'd cheered the sawmill's closure.

"Buzz kill" also referred to Doobie Scoobie, the most popular marijuana dispensary with the Baby Boomers in Wilshire Hills. Jeff, one of her favorite regulars, had explained the inferences from the popular 60's cartoon, *Scooby Doo*, a show about a group of teenagers who solve mysteries with their dog,

Scooby Doo. Jeff maintained a lot of weed got smoked inside their van, the Mystery Machine, when they weren't solving crimes. Addy routinely picked up people going to or coming from the dispensary, and while there were laws about smoking weed in public places, the acrid smell that often filled the bus suggested many people didn't care about the law. Sometimes she felt like she was high just from the proximity. At least the stoners were a mellow group, and she always preferred them to the sawmill guys.

At the fourth stop, her favorite regular, Bianca, boarded and gave Addy a big hug that made her heart race. She secretly crushed over Bianca, and it was for Bianca that Addy had added the thumb of the oven mitt to her route. Bianca was in her early twenties, a half-Asian and half-Hispanic bombshell who oozed an infectious joy. She always wore brightly colored scrubs with cute designs. Today's scrubs were Addy's favorite: sunflower yellow with little dogs wagging their tails.

After giving Addy her usual hug and swiping her bus pass, she waved to everyone and shouted, "Good morning!"

The other regulars replied, "Good morning, Bianca!" and even the few newbies cracked a smile.

She turned to Addy and said, "I know it's early in the morning, but happy birthday, Addy!"

The whole bus cheered and Addy felt her cheeks burning. She held up her hand and nodded.

"Who wants a popsicle?" Bianca shouted, holding up a grocery bag full of treats. She gave Addy a cherry one and proceeded down the aisle, handing out popsicles to all the passengers. She exclaimed, "It's a great day!" several times and everyone agreed.

And it was a good day whenever Bianca was on the bus. She made it better for everyone else, which was part of the reason Addy was willing to break the rules for her. Addy glanced up at the mirror and watched her slide next to Mrs. Jones, another regular who was on her way to the farmers market. Soon Bianca was laughing, and Addy couldn't help but smile.

She wished Bianca would notice her more—beyond her role as nice bus driver. While Bianca wasn't really Addy's type either, her personality was magnetic. Addy had never met anyone more beautiful on the inside. Bianca was cute. Addy just wished she had bigger boobs. Granted, they weren't *that* small. It wasn't like her scrubs top lay flat against her chest. There was a little contour.

But Bianca's chest was nothing like Nurse Segal's.

Addy injures herself on a rusty nail and goes to the emergency room. Her eyes nearly pop out of her head when Nurse Segal sashays through the curtain, her breasts practically entering the room before the rest of her. Her long, brownish-blond hair harkens back to the sixties, the ends curl around her head. She reaches for Addy's chart and asks, "Do you go by something less formal than Addison?"

"Addy," she replies.

"Cool name."

She moves about the small triage room, bending over for gloves, opening drawers, and reaching for the sphygmomanometer. It's during this fluid movement that Addy realizes Nurse Segal isn't wearing a bra. Her chest sways left to right, and when she plops onto the stool beside Addy, her boobs give an enormous jiggle. For a moment Addy pictures Nurse Segal hula-hooping.

"Your blood pressure is high," Nurse Segal observes. "Are you nervous? Stressed about something?"

"No," Addy whispers. I'm just picturing your hips gyrating in one direction while your boobs jiggle in the other.

"Let me listen to your heart," she says, rising from the stool and moving closer.

As she places the stethoscope against Addy's chest, her breasts graze Addy's cheek. She smells of lavender, Addy's favorite. Addy takes a deep breath and rests her face in Nurse Segal's cleavage.

Nurse Segal whimpers. "I'm not getting an accurate reading."

"I am."

She reaches underneath her scrub top and cups her breasts, pushing them up through the V and feasting on her glorious nipples. Nurse Segal abandons the stethoscope and grabs the examining table stirrups for support. Addy's hands rake over her muscular abdomen, headed for the vulnerable drawstring that secures her scrub pants at her waist. One tug and the little bow unravels.

"Yes," Nurse Segal cries, a look of anticipation on her face.

Addy pulls off her top, and the willing nurse hops onto the exam table, lays back and plants her feet in the stirrups. "I'm ready for my exam, Dr. Addy."

She swings her legs wide open, and under the harsh lights of the exam room, every fold of skin is exposed, all leading to her glistening and throbbing center.

"Please, Dr. Addy!" she moans.

"Uh-uh," Addy chides. She lifts Nurse Segal's right hand, licks two of her perfectly manicured fingers, and places them over her clit. "Touch yourself."

Nurse Segal complies and Addy massages her thighs, her strokes matching the rhythm of Nurse Segal's ministrations.

"I'm going to come without you!" Nurse Segal shouts.

"We can't let that happen."

Addy strips off her clothes, steps onto the foothold, and lowers herself on top of Nurse Segal. Her tongue slides into Nurse Segal's mouth, and she places her own throbbing center against Nurse Segal's clit. They merge and rock. Just before they climax, Addy hears laughter.

A voice shouts, "It's about time you lost your virginity!"

Her gaze shoots to the doorway. Standing there is her mother.

"Addy? Addy, what are you doing?"

She blinked and turned to the open bus door. Mazie stood next to her—in front of the Bijou, one of the last stops on Addy's route. She glanced up at the mirror and saw the bus was quite full, certainly fuller than when she picked up Bianca—who was gone. She wiped her face with her hand. She'd stopped seven more times and made her unauthorized detour to drop Bianca off at the memory care center where she worked—and she had no recollection of it.

Mazie swiped her pass and touched Addy's arm. "Are you okay?" she whispered. "When you pulled up and opened the door, I realized I'd left my bus pass in my other purse. I asked you if I could run back upstairs to get it, and when you didn't say no, I ran back inside. I apologized to you just now, but you kept staring out the window. Like you were in a fugue state."

Addy shook her head, hoping to knock her damaged brain parts back into order. "I'm fine," she said, pulling her arm out of Mazie's reach. "Please take your seat."

CHAPTER SIX

Mazie thought about Addy throughout the day. She'd behaved so oddly when Mazie boarded the bus. Sitting ramrod straight, her gaze focused on the front windshield, offering no greeting—even when Mazie apologized for screaming at her the night before. But she'd felt violated, knowing someone else had heard her practicing. She asked Addy for her forgiveness, but Addy didn't reply. Then Mazie realized she had the wrong purse. When she asked Addy if she could wait just a minute, it seemed Addy was ignoring her—and her anger returned. What was it with this woman?

She knew something was wrong, though, when she reappeared two minutes later with her other bag, and neither the bus—nor Addy—had moved. She called her name three times and Addy finally blinked. Her gaze traveled the length of Mazie's body, stirring a swirl of butterflies in Mazie's stomach. There was something about Addy's eyes…When their gazes met, Addy commanded her to take a seat, but she didn't sound like Addy. But I don't really know her, Mazie reminded herself as she wheeled a cart through Costco. She'd lucked out finding a job and a place to stay at the Bijou. She'd always loved movies. Her grandmother lived down the block in her childhood town of Louisville, Kentucky, and twice a month on Sundays, Grandma Mazie took her to the weekly double feature. It was the late eighties, and she remembered the first time she saw *Die Hard* and *Rain Man* at the enormous Cineplex, but more importantly, she'd seen *Heathers* at the Louisville Arthouse, a great indie theater that had been a church. That experience hooked her on indie films and charming theaters. Then in 1991, Grandma Mazie took her to see *Fried Green Tomatoes*—and she saw herself in the Idgy Threadgood character. She came out to her grandma over chocolate shakes after the movie. She was barely fourteen. Her grandmother declared she knew before Mazie even finished uttering the words. Not long after, Grandma crossed over, as her mother liked to say, and in her will she'd left Mazie free admission for a lifetime to the Arthouse for her and a guest.

Finding the Bijou was destiny. Almondine was charging her practically nothing for rent in the hopes Mazie could find the magic formula to save the theater. Independent theaters rarely thrived in the world of multiplexes. After her friend and mentor Larkin suggested she attend Cammon to finish her masters, she put her urban planning skills to work and studied Wilshire Hills. It was an impressive place, a community determined to lock arms against the big box stores, uncontrolled sprawl, and outsiders in general. She concluded the Bijou would've failed several years prior in a less supportive town, and she worried her business acumen wouldn't be sharp enough to prevent it from closing.

Owning a theater and going to the theater were two different things. She was learning about the role of a "booker," the person who actually acquired films, and the politics of working with studios, distributors, and competitors. She was still grappling with Box Office Essentials, the software that kept track of their ticket sales, and the digital and streaming systems that showed the movies. Sadly she'd realized the days of movie reels and canisters were long over, and now most movies arrived on a hard drive or were a virtual upload. Mazie imagined technology had saved the studios millions, and she could only wish they would share more profits with the struggling indie art houses. Almondine's previous business manager, a man she referred to only as Toupee, had taken an enormous and completely wasted monthly fee as her "investment advisor." A B-actress in Hollywood for twenty years, Almondine had been on every long-running television show at least once, which explained why Mazie thought Almondine looked familiar and why the fate of the Bijou was so precarious—Almondine had no business sense. A fact she'd proven that morning when they had met to discuss the Bijou's state of affairs, and Almondine appeared at Mazie's door with three square boxes.

"What's this?"

Almondine made a grand sweeping gesture with her hand. "You…information…here," was all Mazie understood.

"I thought we agreed to give up the French so we avoided miscommunication," Mazie reminded her.

Almondine closed her eyes and inhaled deeply. When Mazie requested Almondine minimize the theatrics, it seemed to cut her in half. She made a fist and stuck it in her mouth, as if she were in agony. Mazie had stopped herself before she rolled her eyes. *Once an actress…*

"Yes, I remember," Almondine whispered. She turned to the boxes. "This is everything I have. Hopefully among the receipts, the memories, the samples, and the real estate papers, you'll find something useful."

Mazie cocked her head. "The samples?"

"Of course! I kept everything, including the samples presented by vendors seeking a contract with the Bijou. Are you aware there are ten different types of restaurant napkins available in the greater Linn County area?"

"Uh, no." She eyed the three boxes and carefully raised the flaps of the first one, afraid of what she would find. Sitting on top was a glossy brochure from a company in California that made theater seats. "Did you use this company?"

Almondine shook her head. "Their seats weren't comfortable."

"Then why do you still have this brochure?"

She pursed her lips and looked away. "I'm a bit of a hoarder. I don't throw things away."

Mazie suddenly had a bad feeling. She removed the brochure and uncovered a stack of various receipts—large, small, stapled, tattered. One had actually been folded into a paper airplane. She showed it to Almondine.

"Toupee was easily distracted," she explained.

Mazie gave the box a cursory inspection, noting important items like the Deed of Sale, tax documents, and employee evaluations stuffed between inconsequential detritus: old movie posters, phone messages and résumés—one of which was smudged with jelly and had affixed itself to the cover page of the 2016 Oregon Tax Code.

She expelled a long breath before she met Almondine's hopeful expression with one of her own. "Okay, it's going to take me a while to look through everything. Could I make some folders? I won't throw anything away without your approval, but I think it would help to group similar information together."

"Yes, that does make sense," Almondine agreed. She touched her temple with her hand. "Please organize this."

So Mazie found herself buying legal-and letter-sized manila folders in bulk at Costco, as well as boxes of candy to replenish what she'd trashed—candy that was likely purchased for the Bijou's opening four years before, but had never sold because Almondine had made everything the same price to accommodate Addy.

She maneuvered her shopping cart toward the candy aisle. She remembered Addy's stricken face when Almondine admitted the Bijou was on the edge of financial ruin. Addy had looked lost and terrified. It was obvious the Bijou was very special to her, and Mazie vowed never to see that look again. She would figure out a way to keep the Bijou afloat—and finish her degree in music performance.

She'd made one request of Almondine. During the off hours when no movies were shown in the smaller second theater, Mazie wanted to practice performing in front of the empty seats. She saw it as the crucial first step. Then she'd imagine people sitting in the chairs. Finally, if Almondine agreed, she'd ask to give a brief performance after a movie ended. She envisioned her first attempt to sing in front of strangers would be a complete disaster. If her rubbery legs managed to walk onto the little stage in front of the movie screen, words would probably fail her. She'd smile and run off. Audience members would shake their respective heads, gather their belongings, and hurry home. Then the next night, she'd try again. And again. She'd try until she could finally sing a song from the first note to the last.

Only one thing could go wrong: if she couldn't sing in front of the easygoing Bijou crowd, she'd never be able to perform at Gallagher Hall and earn her degree. Thus, she had concluded that her Bijou singing experiment would be successful if the audience members weren't cold strangers. She would commit to memory the names of Bijou customers when they paid their admission or bought their concession items with a credit card. She'd hand the card back and say, "Thank you, John, for your patronage."

If she overheard conversations where names were used, she'd call those people by their names. In a few weeks, when she sang on the Bijou stage for the first time, she'd know some people in the audience and focus on their (hopefully) pleasant faces.

She reached the candy aisle and filled the cart with as much as she could manage on the bus. She'd convinced Almondine it was cheaper to purchase candy from Costco than the wholesaler who stocked the big multiplex on the edge of town. The Bijou didn't buy enough to get the best price, and when she showed Almondine the numbers, Almondine admitted she'd spent more time ogling the candy wholesaler, a woman with bulging biceps.

Once she paid for the candy, Mazie headed outside. She transferred the folders and the sweet-smelling boxes into the two-wheel cart she'd brought with her and headed to the bus stop. She replayed the moment when Addy had said, "Genius," in response to her new candy organization. The compliment warmed her, and for a brief second, she imagined wrapping Addy's skinny body in a bear hug. She'd trace the contour of her jaw, turn her chin toward her lips and offer a gentle, but earnest kiss.

"Why am I thinking like this?"

"Excuse me?"

Mazie jumped and turned toward an older woman sitting in the bus shelter. Her hair was streaked with steel gray, and a set of creases, shaped like matching apostrophes, sat at the corners of her mouth. She smiled broadly and her green eyes danced in amusement. An open book rested in her lap and her right hand gripped a cane.

"Oh, my apologies," Mazie said. "I was thinking out loud."

The woman's shoulders rose and fell in laughter. "I do it all the time, dear. Nothing wrong with that. At my age, it's how I know I'm still alive and can speak coherently."

Mazie smiled and joined her on the bench. "I'm…Mazie." She realized she was still getting used to her new name.

The woman nodded. "Pleased to meet you, Mazie. I'm Kit. Forgive me for not shaking your hand, but as an older person, germs seem to take up residence inside my withering carcass. Can't chance it."

"I understand." Mazie surmised Kit was much older than she looked, a benefit from residing in a damp climate. "Have you lived in Wilshire Hills for a long time?"

"Most of my life," she replied. "I left for college but came back as soon as I could." Her gaze swept from left to right, as if she were surveying the entire town.

"What was your occupation?"

"Teacher."

"Oh, that's wonderful!"

"Not really," Kit said. When Mazie shuddered, Kit laughed. "I'm kidding. Best time of my life."

Mazie instantly thought of the Bijou and replied, "Oh, that's a relief. I'd hate to think you spent your entire life doing something you didn't like."

Kit eyed her shrewdly. "That would be a waste, wouldn't it?"

"Absolutely."

She again gazed out into the distance. "Too many people live 'lives of quiet desperation.' Thoreau," she clarified. She paused and asked, "What are you doing in Wilshire Hills?"

"I'm finishing a music degree at Cammon."

"What area?"

"Vocal performance."

Kit's eyes brightened. "You're a singer."

She gulped and felt her cheeks burn. "I hope so."

The rumbling of the approaching bus smothered Kit's next question, and Mazie stood, grateful for the interruption. She had no desire to explain her academic shortcomings to a teacher.

The bus door whooshed open and she was face to face with Addy. *From one embarrassment to another.* "Hi Addy," she said, glancing away as she swiped her bus pass.

Addy nodded coolly but said nothing. Mazie looked toward the back but found the few seats left were near the front. She dropped next to a teenager composing a text, his thumbs popping up and down on his phone. He was so engrossed he didn't notice her slide next to him, nor did he eyeball the stacks of candy she set in the aisle. Kit leaned over and whispered to Addy before a dapper young person in a three-piece suit jumped up and motioned for Kit to take the window seat beside him—or her; Mazie couldn't tell if the well-dressed individual was male or female. The gray suit and shiny black wingtips suggested male, but the slight frame and smooth ivory skin that contrasted with his/her red bow tie suggested female. And when Kit called him/her Shawn, that didn't help either.

Kit and Shawn continued to converse as Addy closed the bus door. Mazie looked up to the mirror that sat above Addy's head just in time to catch Addy staring at her—before she quickly returned her gaze to the road. At the next stop, Addy opened the doors and hurried down the stairs. Curious, Mazie looked out her window. Addy rushed to a middle-aged woman balancing a toddler in her arms while pushing a stroller. Addy took control of the stroller and helped the three board the bus.

The teenager next to Mazie looked up from his phone, jumped up and bounded down the stairs, leaving the seat open for the woman and toddler. She offered a smile as she settled next to Mazie, taking the infant into her arms, leaving the toddler stuck between herself and Mazie, and dabbing at the sweat on her face with a tissue. Addy gave Mazie a sharp look before she returned to her driver's chair.

Mazie studied the toddler's nearly circular face, deep-set eyes and tiny nose. She thought he was a boy, dressed as he was in denim overalls, a T-shirt, and sneakers. His blond hair was long and its uneven lengths suggested his locks were rarely shorn. His grin was as wide as his cheeks and he laughed—at nothing. Mazie couldn't help but return the smile. She and her first partner, Steph, had talked about adopting children, but the idea never moved beyond the talking stage. Raising a child rated up there with their talk of taking a trip to Australia. Neither was ever accomplished. When Mazie caught Steph in bed with one of Mazie's co-workers, their relationship ended. Mazie couldn't forgive Steph, who didn't really seem to be all that sorry she'd cheated.

The toddler reached for Mazie's necklace, and she automatically placed her hand over his fingers. "No, no," she said gently.

"Sorry," the woman said. "He does that to everyone."

"Oh, it's fine," Mazie replied. And it was. She'd long ago decided the simple interactions and exchanges with other people's children would satisfy the puddle of maternal instinct she stepped in from time to time.

"Weather, where are you going?" Addy called to Mazie's seatmate.

"Up to Fifteenth Street. The butcher shop."

Addy nodded.

"I didn't know there were still butcher shops," Mazie said.

"Absolutely. They're expensive but Mr. and Mrs. Brewster only want the best for Huxley and Coda."

"Who?"

Weather offered a patient look, as if she answered that question frequently, and smoothed the baby's head. "This is Hux, and this little firecracker is Coda." She tickled the toddler who laughed maniacally.

Coda's cherubic face undoubtedly melted hard hearts wherever she went. She could've been a model the way her smile puffed out her rosy cheeks and accented her button nose.

Fascinated that someone would name their child after a musical term, Mazie said, "Do you have any idea how they decided those names?"

Weather cocked her head to the side, and at this angle Mazie could see dark circles under her eyes. "Um, Huxley was named for Mrs. Brewster's favorite writer and Coda got her name because she kept repeating the same movements as a baby, or something like that." She shrugged. "I'm just the nanny." She leaned closer and whispered, "Addy does me a solid and stops the bus in front of my destination, or she gets me as close as she can." She blew her bangs off her face and Mazie noticed her labored breathing. "I have the beginning of COPD, and it's hard to walk. But nobody knows that except Addy, so please don't say anything. I think the Brewsters would flip if they knew I was sick."

"I won't say a word."

The bus stopped again and Shawn, as well as a scraggly young guy who seemed to be Shawn's antithesis, debarked together, chatting as they headed in the same direction.

Weather stood and took Coda's hand, interrupting the Peek-A-Boo game Mazie had just initiated as a way to keep Coda from grabbing at her necklace. "Sorry, we're moving. No offense."

"No problem," Mazie said, although she was disappointed.

Weather headed for the empty seat vacated by Shawn, and Coda ran into Kit's open arms. She pulled Coda onto her lap and fussed over Huxley at the same time. The children seemed thrilled to see Kit. They certainly weren't strangers. Mazie watched the scene with interest until the bus stopped again. She looked up. They were sitting in front of a nursing home she didn't recognize. She'd been on this route once in the evening, and she didn't remember ever stopping here. A young Hispanic woman bounced up the steps and greeted Addy.

"Hi everyone!" she said to the passengers.

"Hi, Bianca!" many of the passengers replied.

Since Weather had vacated the seat next to Mazie, Bianca took it. "Hello," she said with a tired smile.

"Hi, I'm Mazie. I'm new to the area."

Bianca's face brightened. "Welcome to Wilshire Hills," she said cheerily.

As they pulled away, Mazie glanced at the driver mirror and once again noticed Addy staring at her. "Forgive me if I'm wrong, but is the stop in front of the nursing home actually on the bus route?"

Bianca blushed and shook her head. "No," she whispered. She touched Mazie's arm. "Please don't say anything to get Addy in trouble." When Mazie didn't reply, Bianca said, "When I changed jobs, I wound up on this new route with this sleazy driver who made passes at me. It made me terribly uncomfortable."

"Did you tell the bus supervisor?"

She shook her head. "If I told Jackie, that's the supervisor, about Pratul, he'd get mad and take it out on Addy because she's a lesbian. I don't want her to lose her job."

"He could really get her fired?"

Bianca nodded. "Besides, it's only a few blocks off the route." She motioned to the other passengers. "None of the regulars care, and nobody else even knows it's not on the route." She took a breath. "I hope that convinces you. I really need this job. It's important. I help the elderly."

Mazie smiled. "I won't say anything."

"Thanks," Bianca said, letting out a sigh. She thrust her chin toward the front. "Addy's a great lady. She helps everybody. Ride on this bus long enough, and she'll save your ass, do something kind for you without being asked, or both."

A teenager with headphones around her neck, sitting in the seat behind them, tapped Bianca on the shoulder and asked about her long weekend. Bianca introduced Keisha to Mazie and then launched into a story about losing her house key. Mazie feigned interest, but really she was soaking up all she had learned—particularly about Addy. She hoped Addy would come back to the theater soon, as Mazie didn't think Addy had heard her apology when she'd boarded the bus, too lost in her daydreams.

It seemed there was a tight community on the bus. Addy supported the passengers and they supported her. Mazie guessed each one of them would go under the bus—literally and figuratively—to save their favorite, quirky driver. A warm, pleasant feeling overtook Mazie. She'd been invited into the inner circle and felt special.

When she looked toward Addy for what must have been the sixth or seventh time, Addy was again staring in her direction. So Mazie stared back, watching Addy's clearly distracted gaze ping-pong between the road and her passengers. And when she stopped at the next bus shelter and the exchange of passengers occurred, Mazie had a sobering revelation: Addy wasn't staring at her. She'd been staring at Bianca.

CHAPTER SEVEN

Addy heard the music as she coasted her bike to the side gate, her private entrance to the tiny house she rented from Jackie. She took a deep breath, inhaling the tangy, sweet smell of barbeque chicken, Jackie's favorite grilling option. During the summer months Jackie turned her patio into her kitchen. Addy calculated she'd spent thousands on her backyard landscaping, including the stone barbeque, pizza oven, and elaborate fire pit. It was beautiful and inviting, and many of Jackie's neighbors appeared unannounced, including Nadine, a local CPA who helped both Addy and Jackie file their respective tax forms each year. Nadine was also known as Squeegee in the roller derby world because she wiped out the competition a few nights each week.

Addy ducked inside the tiny house before either of them could see her. She changed out of her uniform, put away the morning dishes, and sifted through the mail, color coding anything to be kept. She opened a window to allow the heavenly barbeque smell into the house. She was hungry and debated whether or not to join Jackie and Nadine.

When she'd made it clear to Jackie that she only wanted to be friends, they established boundaries and limited time together outside of work. The exception was if other people were included. Addy was always invited to any of the many parties Jackie hosted during the summer and fall, and Jackie would be invited to Addy's, if Addy ever had a party. But they both knew the likelihood of that occurring was slim.

While she knew a lot of people on the bus, they were just professional relationships. She hardly spoke with them during the route, since conversation with the driver was strictly forbidden when the bus was in motion, and she never hung out with anyone after hours.

Her stomach growled, so she ambled over to the fridge for a yogurt. Before she opened the door, she touched the four by six photo held up by small black magnets on each corner. It was a picture of her with her mother. Sitting between them was Addy's birthday cupcake. She couldn't remember if it was her ninth or tenth birthday, but it didn't matter. They were both smiling, as if the cupcake had magical powers and made everything better. This was the one birthday memory Addy kept.

A burst of laughter from the yard drew her to the window. Nadine, who Addy believed was a true iron woman, leaned against a patio post, her shoulders hunched so her head didn't hit a rafter, a beer in hand. She was somewhat girly, with a French manicure, highlighted hair and gold jewelry. Addy was especially fascinated by the manicure and how she managed to keep it from being destroyed when she skated. She was also the tallest woman Addy knew, possibly because she was transgender.

She was much different than her alter ego, Squeegee. Nadine was calm and soft spoken, usually listening rather than talking, while Squeegee barreled through the opposition, sending women tumbling across the polished floor like bowling pins after a strike. Addy had cringed at their cries, but she'd been aroused by Squeegee's power.

Like a woman made of steel...
Dark steel helmet. A breastplate shining under the moonlight. Chainmail armor that disguises every nuance of her femininity. The horse slows to a trot and circles Addy, who is dressed in a peasant blouse and skirt, holding a wooden basket filled with apples. She knows the knight is staring, despite the helmet that masks her eyes. In a single motion she pulls the helmet off, freeing a tumble of long blond hair. She shakes it from side to side, mesmerizing Addy, who wonders how it fits under the tight metal prison—and why she would ever hide her beautiful face.

"Open the door, wench!"

Addy realizes they are standing in front of a barn, and she quickly pulls the handle.

"Follow me," the knight orders, guiding the horse inside.

Addy scowls at her tone but complies with the request. While the knight is definitely Addy's type, her people skills are lacking.

The horse trots to the farthest stall and the knight dismounts. Addy sets her pail of apples in the corner, awaiting her next command.

"Remove my gloves, wench, but be careful."

Addy immediately sees why. The chainmail is sharp and the gloves are weapons themselves. She frees the first hand, exposing a perfect French manicure. "Your nails are lovely."

The knight's harsh expression softens. How could any woman resist such a compliment? She offers a dazzling smile, and Addy feels a familiar stirring between her legs.

"Ouch!" Addy cries. She's so mesmerized by the knight's smile that she cuts herself on the left glove.

She holds up her bleeding middle finger and the knight frowns. "I had such plans for this finger." From somewhere in the folds of the suit of armor she withdraws a bandage and quickly tends to Addy's injury. She holds it up for inspection and sighs in disappointment.

"I have another," Addy says, holding up her right hand and wiggling the digit.

The knight snatches it between her lips and sucks it furiously. Addy gasps and imagines the knight's skillful lips on other parts of her. Lost in her reverie, she falls backward, but the knight scoops her up and gently lays her on the immaculately clean straw. Eager lips find Addy's neck—and bites.

"Ouch again!"

"Pain and pleasure go together," *the knight whispers.*

"Do you always talk in rhymes?"

"Yes, I hail from an adult fairy tale."

"What is your name?"

"Lancelust."

"Oh, that's interesting."

"Fuck the talk," *the knight orders.*

She rips apart the buttons on Addy's blouse, revealing a tight corset. Addy blinks in surprise, realizing her labored breathing is caused by the corset, a ludicrous contraption. Its only positive: offering Lance a heaving bosom, which she kisses while searching for the corset's entry points.

Addy clears her throat. "Your breastplate... It's a little chilly."

Lance sits up. "It is not my desire to quash your internal fire."

She extends her long arms behind her, and after a few motions, flings the breastplate and accompanying chainmail into another stall. Only a cotton undershirt that clings to her large breasts remains between them. Before Addy can remove the flimsy undershirt, Lance gyrates her hips, swings her arms left and right, and the chainmail drops from her bottom half.

"Is this better, now that I'm unfettered?"

"Yes, but please, let's not talk anymore," *Addy whines.* "I'm seeing images from Dr. Seuss." *They lock lips and work in tandem to remove the rest of their clothing. Soon nothing but skin and sweat join them together. Lance's muscles bulge with each exertion and Addy can't help but trail her fingers across the lines of definition. Lance is worthy of a sculpture.*

"I yearn, and it's your turn," *Lance says.*

"I thought we agreed..."

In a single movement of agility, strength, and imagination—something that could only be accomplished in an adult fairytale—Lance lifts Addy against the stall wall and settles between her legs. While her lips devour Addy's cleavage, one—two—three fingers slide inside her. The more she rocks her hips, the deeper Lance penetrates her. The splintery barn wood that grates against her bare bottom is a small price to pay for the climax roiling inside her. "Oh my…"

A loud bark and a thud drew Addy out of the fantasy. Standing at her kitchen window was Hermione, Jackie's giant sheepdog named for the Harry Potter character. Jackie loved all things related to Harry Potter, which explained why she'd named the neighborhood feral cats Harry, Ron, and Drago.

Hermione's nose pressed against the small pane of glass, her signal to Addy that it was time for her snack. "Okay, girl. I'm coming." Addy pulled open the door and offered Hermione a treat shaped like a dog bone.

Nadine's rich, deep laugh floated across the yard. Addy automatically smiled. Nadine was the kindest and nicest person Addy had ever met. Nadine believed roller derby was responsible for her sunny demeanor. She'd once said to Addy, "I go out on that rink three times a week and literally pour out my anger and frustration until there's nothin' left, just like I pour out the remains of my morning coffee. You can't feel it if it ain't there."

Addy thought those were words to live by. While she rarely got angry, she often was frustrated, and her peculiarities peaked whenever she was anxious. The first time she'd gone to the roller derby, she'd hoped she could vicariously pour out her own metaphoric coffee cup by watching Nadine, but instead she found herself anxious *for* Nadine. She'd wrung her hands the entire time, worried the nicest person in the world would get hurt, and the mix of yellows worn by Nadine's team, the Yellow Jackets, and purples worn by the opponents, the Big Bruisers, made Addy almost barf.

When Nadine saw her, she threw open her arms. "Addy!"

"Hey, Nadine."

Addy offered Hermione a scratch behind the ears and followed her to the patio.

Jackie handed Addy a beer and said, "Cooked up some wings and there's plenty to share. I imagine you're hungry since you never get lunch."

"Why don't you get lunch?" Nadine asked. She threw a disapproving glare at Jackie. "Doesn't your boss make sure you have a lunch break?"

"Oh, she has a break," Jackie said. "But instead of using it, she makes an extra stop for one of her regulars."

"How do you know that?" Addy asked.

Jackie leaned closer. "I know everything."

Addy shuffled her feet. Was Jackie watching her throughout the day on the bus cameras? What if she saw Addy during one of her trances? Regardless of how she felt about Addy, she'd have to fire her in the name of public transportation safety.

"Tell me about this woman," Nadine asked pleasantly.

Addy got all warm inside, but she tried to play it cool in front of Jackie. "It's just one of those straight crushes. She's not gay, but she's cute and wonderful."

They loaded up their plates with wings and Addy snuck a look at Jackie. She was attacking her wing viciously like a rabid dog.

"So Addy, this cute and wonderful person must be something, considering you're violating company policy for her," Nadine said.

"She is. She used to ride my bus, but then she changed jobs. Now she's supposed to ride with someone else, but he's sexually harassed her, so she won't ride his bus."

Nadine turned to Jackie. "Did you know about this?"

"Uh-huh," Jackie said as she chewed. She wiped her mouth and added, "I believe her and Addy. But there's no proof. Pratul is sneaky. He's out to get both me and Addy and he's very careful when he knows he's on camera. I figured letting her help Bianca is the way to go for now."

Nadine nodded her agreement. "So what's the long-term plan? How do you get rid of him?"

Jackie shrugged and popped the top of her next beer. "Not sure. Got any ideas?"

"Well, he could get run over by an entire roller derby team, but I imagine that would make the cops very suspicious."

Addy tossed a bone onto her plate. "It just sucks because he's harassed other women—not just passengers, drivers too. But like Jackie says, he's sneaky. He makes sure no one else is around, and on the bus he leans a little to the right just to be out of the camera's view."

"And," Jackie added, "he made life miserable for the one driver who actually took the time to file a grievance. Now she's gone and he's still there."

"The system is fucked," Addy declared.

Nadine caressed the side of her beer bottle like it was a beautiful woman. Addy found the gesture mesmerizing. "I may have an idea."

"Please share," Jackie said.

Nadine's lips curled up mischievously. "Oh, no. If you're ignorant, you have plausible deniability. When we finally nail Pratul's shriveled little penis to the wall, his attorney won't be able to assert conspiracy."

Addy and Jackie exchanged a nod, trusting Nadine's approach. In addition to being a CPA. and roller derby goddess, she was a licensed PI.

CHAPTER EIGHT

Mazie did a little dance before she carried the film hard drive up to the projection booth. The newest arrival, *Dragon Mamas*, was a celebrated indie documentary about Mormon mothers and their gay children. It had already garnered Oscar buzz, and best of all, it was playing exclusively at the Bijou—thanks to Almondine's address book.

During the two months Mazie had worked at the Bijou, she'd witnessed the leverage Almondine possessed with the entertainment industry. One afternoon they'd argued about a certain A-list actor's presence in a ridiculous and embarrassing B-rated film. Almondine pulled the overstuffed address book from her desk and found the number she was looking for. She made the call and Mazie was blown away when the actor answered.

After he sheepishly confirmed his participation in the film and hung up, Mazie grilled Almondine about who else she knew—many people—and how she acquired their personal phone numbers.

"I'm friendly and discreet," was all she said in her fake French accent. "On a set the primary players will often reach out to their subordinates if they believe you have an empathetic ear and a confidential nature. I possess both," she said proudly, handing the book to Mazie.

The nearly disintegrated and thick address book was held together by two large, red rubber bands. The cover was a very old picture of a world map, which included countries that no longer existed—like Persia. She sifted through the first few pages, stunned by the names in the "A" section. "Every agent from Hollywood to New York would kill for some of these numbers."

Almondine only chuckled and waved her hand dismissively. "Part of the reason I have those numbers is because their owners know I would never betray them." She paused and added, "I know many secrets and the tabloids have tried—and failed—to obtain them."

"I see."

They had let it go, but Mazie's wheels began to turn, and she gently coaxed Almondine to use her friendships to keep the Bijou afloat. At first Almondine hesitated, but once Mazie assured her they wouldn't do anything to harm her relationships with any Hollywood bigwigs, she was willing to reach out to her contacts. One such phone call secured the film Mazie now held in her hand.

She decided to watch it after the last showing of the night. Once she'd shooed everyone out, swept the aisles and practiced, she'd fill up the last tub of buttered popcorn and take a seat in the middle of the auditorium. It was a date with herself, the only kind of date she'd had in a long time. Too long. But she couldn't think about that now. She needed to focus on her goal—complete her master's degree by performing at Gallagher Hall in December.

As the evening crowd filed in for the final showing of the latest foreign film, Mazie scanned the crowd for Addy, who hadn't been by in over a week. Mazie had grown accustomed to chatting with her before a feature started, and she was grateful for Addy's help when the concessions line was long. She was patient, building her friendship with Addy brick by brick. She just hoped the bricks weren't building a wall between them.

Mazie had tried to discuss with Almondine closing the tiny ticket booth that sat outside the theater and combining ticket and concession sales—but Almondine wouldn't hear of it. Only a handful of theaters on the west coast had a true ticket booth, and Almondine found it charming, just like the old-fashioned marquee that sat above the theater entrance. It didn't matter that the glorious marquee routinely increased the electric bill by fifty dollars a month or that Mazie easily spent two hours changing it every time a new film arrived. "Charming" cost time and money, but Almondine was willing to pay the price.

As the final patron entered Theater One with his drink and hot dog, Mazie frowned. No Addy. Almondine stuck her head out of her office, and when she saw the empty lobby, she said, "Can you come here, please?"

Mazie knew that voice. Almondine was in distress, and Mazie guessed she was reconciling the month's receipts, and they were in the red—again. Mazie sighed and followed her into her office, where she flopped into her desk chair and dramatically covered her eyes with her hand.

"I don't know what to do," she said, waving at the open ledger on her desk.

Mazie skimmed the monthly entries. Once again the Bijou continued to bleed money despite Mazie's cost-saving ideas. Not enough people were coming to the theater. It was that simple. Mazie scratched her chin. She knew there was an audience out there. She knew that each year Cammon University accepted new students, and a decent percentage of them liked artsy and indie films. She just had to publicize better.

"We need an event," she concluded.

Almondine raised her head. "What kind of event?"

"I don't know but something to attract the recent arrivals to Wilshire Hills, mainly the new students. We should hold a big gala."

"Tried that. About thirty people came."

Mazie bit the inside of her cheek and didn't comment. More than likely Almondine's event had little "gala" or pageantry—because she wouldn't spend the money. Mazie pictured a few bowls of peanuts and some crepe paper streamers, as if the Bijou was hosting a kiddie party. Mazie simply nodded. She had tried to explain to Almondine that to make money you had to spend some money, but what Almondine was willing to spend wasn't enough to garner the buzz they needed. Mazie would have to do an end run around Almondine if they planned an event.

"I'll work on it," she said, turning to go.

A rustling noise filtered into the office and Mazie quickly headed to the concessions stand. Addy was filling up her soda. Mazie automatically smiled.

"Hey," she said.

Addy turned and grinned. "Hey."

"Are you excited to see the new film?"

Addy nodded. "I read some of the reviews. Should be sold out for most of the run."

"I hope so," she replied, although she seriously doubted the theater would be packed for any showing.

Still, Addy's optimism was refreshing. So much about her was refreshing. She grabbed her drink and popcorn and crossed the lobby to Theater One, Mazie at her side.

"How was your day?" Mazie asked.

Addy rolled her eyes. "Not so great. Had another tweaker on the bus. Those guys are the worst."

"Did he become violent?"

"No, fortunately not. But he threatened Mrs. Gelpin. She was pretty shaken up."

"What did you do?"

"I called our security team and they met us at the next stop. They took him off and interviewed Mrs. Gelpin. It made everybody late, and the other passengers I picked up were really cranky. I told everybody why I was late, but still…Even Bianca was angry, and she never gets angry."

Addy opened the door to head in, but Mazie touched her hand. "Can I ask you a question?"

Addy peered inside. "Is it a quick one? I don't want to miss the previews."

Mazie laughed. "You won't. I'm running the projection booth tonight." She checked the time on her phone. "We still have two minutes."

"Okay, what's your question?"

"Do you have something going on with Bianca? Are you two dating?"

At the mention of Bianca, Addy's face and ears grew red. She shook her head but said nothing.

"Is she someone you'd like to date?"

Addy looked down and shuffled her feet. She mumbled, "I'd rather not discuss my love life," before she darted into the theater.

Mazie sighed. She'd only asked the questions as a way to get to know Addy better. At least that was what she told herself for now.

The front doors opened and a group of twentysomethings entered, all wearing Cammon University apparel. Mazie raced back to the concessions stand to serve them before she started the movie.

It wasn't until she was perched in the projection room, looking out at the patrons below in Theater One, that she thought of Addy again, sitting by herself in the fourth row in the north section. Few people were around her, which was how she liked it. Mazie pictured an impenetrable plastic bubble surrounding Addy. No matter how hard anyone tried, that bubble couldn't be pierced. Addy wouldn't allow it.

Two hours later Mazie dropped onto a couch in the lobby. Theater One was about to let out, and although she'd been looking forward to her private screening of *Dragon Moms*, she'd probably fall asleep if she attempted to watch it tonight.

She'd worked nonstop since walking Addy into Theater One. Someone had thrown up in Theater Two. Another customer, whom Mazie suspected was drunk before he got to the Bijou, threw a fit over Milk Duds that he claimed were stale. He'd become abusive, pelting the candy at her before he stormed out. Then a homeless man dropped an empty bottle of whiskey outside the front doors, necessitating a cleanup before the crowds exited the theater.

She sighed. She was tired. It was hard being over forty. It was as if her body sent a memo announcing it was slowing down and certain bodily functions would only be available during a narrow window of time each day. And some parts had gone on strike. Of this she was certain. Still, she didn't *feel* older.

The alarm on her phone went off and she hustled up to the projection room to end the movie in Theater One. While most everyone left once the credits rolled, Addy remained glued to her seat. Mazie smiled. Addy was a diehard fan of cinema too. They both thought it was courteous to stay through the credits as a way to thank the people behind the scenes, like the best boy or the line producer.

She headed down to the lobby until it was time to climb the stairs and repeat her routine. Once everyone had left, she retrieved the cleaning cart and headed to Theater One. She realized she'd missed saying goodbye to Addy, who must have left while she was putting out the fires.

But Mazie found her still sitting in her seat, in the trance-like state Mazie had witnessed that day on the bus. She hesitated to disturb her, but she was exhausted, and she still had the other theater to clean as well. She flipped open the dustpan and started sweeping the back row. Every few minutes she'd glance at Addy, who remained unmoving—until Mazie emptied her full dustpan into the garbage can. The rumble of cascading trash startled Addy and she jumped. Then she whipped around to get her bearings.

Mazie smiled when Addy's gaze landed on her. "Hi there. I thought you'd fallen asleep."

"Yeah, I did," Addy replied, but Mazie knew she was lying. Addy quickly gathered her things and deposited her empty popcorn tub, licorice box, and drink cup into Mazie's can. She headed toward the back exit. "Bye."

"What do you think of this movie?" Mazie blurted. "Is it one of your favorites?"

Addy turned, her eagerness to depart apparently vanquished by her desire to discuss film. "Yeah, I think it's terrific. So rarely do you see lesbian cinema where they get all the parts right, you know? It's either a bad story, poor actors, or poor quality because the filmmaker couldn't get appropriate financing. Usually one or more of those pieces is missing."

Mazie leaned against her broom, nodding. "I know. Remember *Go Fish?*"

Addy laughed and rolled her eyes. "Uh, yeah. Or *Salmonberries.*"

"Oh," Mazie groaned. "So bad. But here's what's ironic. *Desert Hearts* was the first lesbian film, right? And it was great."

Addy grimaced. "Um, *Desert Hearts* might've been the first real mainstream lesbian movie, and I think it's fabulous," she quickly added. "But there were others before it. Like *Therese and Isabelle.* That's a classic. And *Bilitis* from seventy-seven. And *That Tender Touch* from sixty-nine."

"I've not heard of those." Her eyes narrowed. "Those aren't like *The Children's Hour* or *The Killing of Sister George* where it's really a lesbian-bashing movie, or one character isn't really gay? You know, straight housewife takes her libido out for a spin?"

Addy laughed. "There were a lot of those movies in the sixties and seventies, that's for sure. *Tender Touch* was one of those, but the other two weren't." She paused and her gaze dropped to the floor. "I've got them if you ever wanted to see them. And other stuff too."

Mazie's heart fluttered. "I'd love to see them."

"I could bring them to you. I mean, we don't have to watch them together if you don't want. But you'll need a VCR for *Bilitis* and I know a lot of people don't have those anymore." She paused awkwardly and finally said, "Do you have a VCR?"

Mazie shook her head. "I'd be happy to come by your place, and actually, I'd like to see them with you and hear your thoughts. It seems we think alike when it comes to cinema."

Addy glanced up and nodded again. "I've noticed that too. I think it's really cool that you work here." She looked around, clearly admiring the old building.

Mazie took two steps toward her, careful not to get too close, for fear of scaring her away. "Okay, so it's a date? Kinda? Sometime soon?"

Addy didn't respond, but she continued to stare. Mazie wondered if she'd heard the question, or if she'd taken another one of her mind vacations. Then Addy closed the distance between them and kissed her. The broom clattered against the seats and Mazie pulled Addy against her. She felt Addy relax as one kiss turned into two, and she desperately wanted to touch her everywhere, but she wasn't going to push it—and not just because they were standing in Mazie's place of employment.

She slowly broke the kiss, noting that Addy hadn't moved at all. Her eyes were still closed and her lips remained puckered. "Addy, are you with me?"

She blinked. "Of course. Did you hate it?"

"Oh, no. I thought it felt wonderful. I just..." She had no idea how to broach the subject with Addy, who seemed to run away any time she said the wrong thing. And since she wasn't sure what was right or wrong...*But if we're ever going to be more than friends...* "Where do you go?"

Addy looked stricken and Mazie instantly wished she could retract the question. At least Addy hadn't bolted out of the theater, but she hadn't replied, so Mazie rephrased it. "I mean, what do you think about?" She hoped she looked inquisitive but not nosy, interested but not condescending.

Addy shrugged. "Different stuff."

Mazie imagined those two words led to a very long conversation, one they could never have until a bridge of trust had been built. Perhaps if she wanted Addy to share, she had to do so first. "I think I'm going to fail and not get my degree."

"What?"

"To earn my Master's degree in Vocal Performance from Cammon, I must perform at Gallagher Hall. In front of people. A lot of people."

Addy looked puzzled. "But I've heard you sing—"

"Alone. You've heard me sing to an empty auditorium."

"Yeah, I guess a place full of people would be way different, huh? I couldn't do it."

Mazie groaned. "Well, unfortunately, at this point, neither can I."

"How many people will be in the audience?"

"I don't know. At least my whole committee, so at least five."

"That's not very many," Addy said hopefully. "It's not a crowd..."

Mazie dropped into a seat. "Right now, it doesn't matter how many people are there. Right now one is a crowd, and I'm scared shitless." She looked into Addy's understanding face and it fueled her to tell more. "What's worse, they'll be evaluating me. It's not just that I have to sing. I have to sing *well*. It's a test."

Addy shivered. "Oh, I hate tests." She touched Mazie's arm. "But there's some medicine you can take to help your nerves. I've taken it a few times," she added.

"Actually there's several medications for test anxiety, and I've tried most of them because tests have always been rough. None of the drugs have ever helped. During eleventh grade I actually threw up. On my state math test. Then they had to use this powder to clean it up. They got mad because they'd gone to all that trouble with the expensive powder and there wasn't anything written on my test."

"Oh, snap."

Mazie didn't know what else to say. She glanced at Addy, who rested her chin on her upturned palm. She thrummed her fingers against her cheek, seemingly deep in thought. Mazie closed her eyes, savoring the sound of silence.

"If you hate tests and performing in front of crowds," Addy asked, "why are you getting a master's degree in performance? I'm sorry if that sounds mean."

"No, it's a good question."

Addy's hand rested on the seatback that divided them. Mazie squeezed it, surprised by the strong grip that met hers. Addy had slender, well-manicured fingernails. She imagined those fingers tracing the inside of her thigh... It had been so long. Then she remembered the look Addy had given Bianca on the bus. She remembered Addy's curt reply earlier when she'd attempted to ask her about her feelings for Bianca. But then they'd kissed... It was still very confusing. She removed her hand and stood.

"I need to keep working. I still have another theater to do."

Addy jumped up. "Oh, well, I'll get out of your way."

She started toward the back door, and Mazie blurted, "Hey, a really interesting documentary arrived. It won't premiere for another week, but I'm dying to see it. Would you like to join me for a private screening tomorrow night after the last movie?"

Addy grinned. "Sure. Sounds fun."

"Okay. See you then."

They both stared at each other until Mazie felt uncomfortable. She grabbed her broom and swept furiously.

Addy pushed open the back door and whirled around. "You know what?"

"What?"

"You're going to pass your test, Mazie. I'm going to help you. I'm not sure yet what I can do, but I'm going to make sure it happens!"

CHAPTER NINE

Addy couldn't sleep. She'd replayed her final words to Mazie at least ten dozen times, and she couldn't understand why she'd told Mazie she would help her pass her performance test. *I don't know a damn thing about music or singing, not a thing.* Now she'd given Mazie false hope, as if she could magically wave a wand and Mazie wouldn't have stage fright anymore. *Who the hell do I think I am? I'm not a shrink. I'm not Dr. Pfeiffer. I can't get into Mazie's head and turn off her fear. If it were only that easy.*

Then there was the kiss. She'd kissed Mazie! She couldn't explain why she'd done it, but it had felt so good. So she'd done it again. And then she'd gotten scared, but Mazie knew just the right thing to say next so it wasn't awkward. She didn't know what the kiss meant, but it looked like Mazie didn't know either. If she was going to be clueless, at least she wasn't alone.

She stared at the ceiling. It was two thirty a.m. "Not gonna happen tonight," she murmured. She gave up on sleep and descended the ladder from her loft bedroom, which immediately dropped her into her living room. Surrounding her sixty-inch

TV were rows and rows of movies, many of them lesbian films. Buying lesbian films was her one splurge. She didn't spend a lot of money, putting most of it away for the future or a rainy day. And there were plenty of those in Oregon.

She scanned the titles for something to take her mind off Mazie and the ridiculous promise. She wanted something funny but not too romantic. She plucked *But I'm a Cheerleader* from the shelf, powered up the DVD and brewed a cup of tea.

Are you and Bianca dating? Mazie's question clanked around her brain. She liked Bianca a lot, but she knew Bianca only saw her as a friend. She didn't think Bianca was gay. For most of the last year Addy had listened closely to her conversations with other passengers. One time she'd mentioned someone she was dating, but she kept saying "they," and not he or she. Once Bianca had mentioned a name—Terry—but that could be a male or female.

Addy had thought about asking Bianca out but was certain she'd be turned down. Bianca was so…smooth. On the bus she never struggled to engage people in conversation. She never said anything impolite or cruel. Even when someone like Pratul hassled her or hit on her, she was always polite and kind. More often than not, she turned around bad situations, and by the time they reached Bianca's stop or their own, she had them laughing and waving goodbye.

One time a big, awful guy had made Bianca very uncomfortable. Addy almost pulled the bus over, but luckily Carter, a regular who worked security at Cammon, stepped in and had a few words with the creep, who had turned pale and disembarked at the next stop. Addy guessed Carter said something not sanctioned in the Wilshire Hills Public Transportation Policies and Procedures Manual, but Addy didn't care. He'd protected Bianca and that was all that mattered.

Why are you thinking about Bianca when you kissed Mazie? She knew the answer. Bianca was off in the distance, and it was much easier to fantasize about someone she couldn't have— probably never would have—than to step forward and have a real relationship with very real kissing. She'd never had a real relationship. "I've never really had sex," she mumbled. The closest thing she'd had was the necking session with Jackie, who'd stripped off her clothes in the hopes that Addy would do the same. *But I wasn't ready then. Am I now?*

She sullenly sipped her tea and tried to engage in the movie. She loved Natasha Lyonne. She was great and her hair looked like cotton candy. She usually laughed during the intervention scene, but it wasn't working tonight.

She and Bianca wander the midway between the rides and the food booths. Addy cringes at the noxious sweet odor of cotton candy, but Bianca pulls her toward it. She buys a swirl as tall as great-aunt Norine's beehive hairdo.

Bianca's tongue scoops up bits of the pink cloud while Addy watches. Eventually Bianca tips the cotton candy toward Addy, and she takes a big bite that leaves a pink goatee on her chin. "Let me get that for you," Bianca says. She swipes her forefinger across Addy's face, collects the stray candy and deposits the sticky finger between her own lips— painted ruby red. Perfect lips with just the right amount of contour. Addy traces them with her thumb, not caring who notices. Bianca's mouth opens and she sighs. Addy desperately wants to turn that sigh into a moan, but she needs someplace private.

She yanks Bianca between two rides—death machines as great- aunt Norine used to say. Bianca laughs and munches on the cotton candy, allowing Addy to swirl her between the tents, rides, and food trucks. They stop in front of the legendary Dipper, the carnival ride with the most checkered past in all of fair history. If stories were to be believed, hundreds of kids had fallen to their deaths when the little cages turned upside down and the doors flew open.

Bianca doesn't know or doesn't care, for she discards the rest of the cotton candy and pulls Addy up the platform and into a little deathtrap. A heavily tattooed woman missing her two upper front teeth says, "Enjoy the ride," before she slams the cage shut, sends their little car upward, and stops them again as another set of passengers board.

Bianca wastes no time and plants her ruby lips against Addy's neck. She licks Addy's ear as if it were cotton candy, and she gently tugs on Addy's earlobe with her teeth. Pleasure and pain bring forth a moan from Addy as the little car ascends again, putting more distance between them and the earth.

Bianca unbuttons Addy's uniform shirt and claws at her bra, freeing her breasts. She sucks greedily on each one. Pleasure and pain. They move higher and the little car sways. Addy isn't sure if gravity or Bianca is responsible, and it doesn't matter as long as Bianca continues feasting on her chest. Trapped underneath the questionably-safe metal bar, she can only do so much, but it's enough. Bianca parts Addy's legs and slides her hand inside Addy's shorts, her fingers moving toward heaven. Addy gasps when Bianca's recently-covered-in-cotton-candy digit enters her.

Addy rocks her hips—and the car starts to spin. Around and around they go—and the ride hasn't technically started! Her eyes fly open just as the music blares and the motor cranks to life. They flip over and over. The ride operator laughs each time their car passes, clearly enjoying what she can see through the iron mesh. Bianca nips at Addy's breast and plunges inside her, sending a shockwave through her. While the other riders scream, Addy moans, over and over. Dipper is certainly an apropos name for this ride.

Five times around and the motor slows to idle. Addy is spent. She opens her eyes. They sit at the top and the spinning has stopped. Bianca's head rests on Addy's shoulder, while Addy gazes out at the bubbly lights, inhales the colliding sweet and salty smells, and endures the clash of music and sound. Yet she is absolutely certain there isn't a single fairgoer having as much fun as she is. Her heartrate slows as they reach the bottom, only the ride operator has changed. It is no longer the tooth-missing woman. Now the operator is Pratul. He leans into the metal cage and leers at her. She pushes him aside and emerges, looking for Bianca, who has suddenly disappeared. Instead, her gaze lands on the rider waiting to board the Dipper—Mazie.

They smile at each other and Mazie asks, "Would you take a spin with me?"

Addy's thundering alarm clock boomed, and she sat straight up, disoriented. She was on her couch in front of her TV. She saw the But I'm a Cheerleader DVD box balanced on the edge of the TV stand, but the TV was off. She wiped a hand over her face and grabbed her phone. It was nearly five thirty a.m. The carnival sex wasn't one of her usual daydreams. It had been an actual dream, but it was different. Mazie was there. Addy wondered if she would've gone for a spin with Mazie had her alarm clock not sounded.

She smiled at the thought but shivered at the presence of Pratul. Jackie had said he wanted her fired. She'd caught him talking about "faggots" two mornings ago when she crossed the Bull Pen to clock in. He made a big production of apologizing, but he couldn't hide the hint of a smile that lingered at the corners of his thick ugly lips. She'd heard from one of the sympathetic male drivers that Pratul regularly talked about her. He'd said her body was like three toothpicks stuck together with glue. He couldn't believe any woman would ever want her, and she'd probably never had sex in her life.

Despite the story's truth, when Addy first heard it, she'd been so mad she'd almost burst into the breakroom, grabbed the fresh pot of steaming coffee and pitched it onto him. Fortunately, Jackie had strolled into the breakroom to deliver the box of donuts she always brought on Friday. Addy decided it was enough to imagine his gut-wrenching screams as the scalding liquid met his flesh.

"He'll get his, Addy," Jackie had said a few months before. "He'll get his. Karma is truly a bitch, and like a city bus, it'll pull you right under a wheel and turn you into a soupy mess."

Addy could only hope that was true.

CHAPTER TEN

Mazie realized she needed more to do. Her only class at Cammon was her performance seminar, which was a fancy way of giving her credit for her performance preparation. But since she was paying for the course, it all seemed a little backward. She'd been practicing daily, standing on the empty stage after the movie audiences had left, and she'd been collecting names of the regulars. Of course her favorite regular was Addy, who stayed after the movie and listened to her practice. Addy had said she'd help Mazie prepare for the performance, but she already was helping by being an audience of one.

In another week she would begin phase two of her plan: singing for the Bijou regulars. She'd spent two weeks visualizing them sitting in the audience, smiling up at her. She'd even pictured a few people frowning, others loudly crunching popcorn, and still others yawning. One regular, Dr. Jimenez, a snooty assistant professor of mathematics at Cammon, constantly looked morose and crabby whenever he came to the Bijou. Ironically, he looked no better when he left the theater two hours later—even after watching a comedy. She pictured him sticking his tongue out at her throughout the song, but her managing to finish it despite his distractions.

Still, practicing the three songs she'd chosen long ago didn't take much time, nor did talking with Almondine about strategies to save the Bijou. They held short, daily conversations, and Mazie quizzed Almondine about the address book.

Mazie had spent a week slowly reading and deciphering each page. The book contained so much more than just names and addresses. She imagined that while Almondine talked on the phone, her hand held a pen in motion, capturing key points— and secrets. She probably didn't recognize she was journaling the thoughts and ideas of the rich and famous, but they were written on the blank address spots, the margins and the inside cover. Extra sheets of paper were stuffed in between and sticky notes drooped over the sides.

Mazie realized the book not only revealed celebrity secrets, but a few of Almondine's secrets as well, including an affair with the well-known lesbian actress/director and African-American activist, Tarina Hudson. If Mazie had pieced their timeline together correctly, Tarina had met Almondine shortly after the Los Angeles race riots in the early nineties, when her career was just taking off. A page meant for other "H" last names was instead a list of dates and places, including a few hotels. Almondine had used the bottom of the page to draw a picture of Tarina's nude upper body, including a face with luscious lips and inquisitive eyes, and a pair of breasts with tempting nipples. In the drawing she sat in a window with a window box full of flowers below her breasts. It was as if her breasts were sitting amongst the lilies.

Mazie closed the address book and thrummed her fingers on the desk.

What if?

She went to the computer in Almondine's office and Googled Tarina's name. As she suspected, Tarina was in post-production of her new film, a female version of the TV show *S.W.A.T.* Mazie raised an eyebrow, imagining all of those women in black.

She returned to Almondine's address book and spent the next two hours scanning every page for more references to Tarina Hudson. Along the way she picked up a few other interesting tidbits about some used-to-be famous TV stars, but nothing else about Tarina. If she wanted more info, she needed to talk to Almondine, who had seemed less than enthusiastic every time Mazie asked a question about the address book. She groaned again. It was the only way.

She found Almondine in the courtyard, her sketchpad open and a piece of charcoal in her hand. While she seemed to stare at the planter of succulents along the back wall, the picture on the page looked like a busy street in Paris. The buildings toppled over each other, and vendors lined cobblestone sidewalks. Noticeably missing were cars.

Almondine glanced at Mazie and smiled.

"Is that Paris? I've always wanted to go there."

"It is dirty," Almondine said. She pointed to the left corner. "See? I drew a trashcan."

"Oh, yes." Mazie joined her at the table. "Weren't there parts of Paris you loved? What about Notre Dame? Or Saint Chappelle? I've heard it's beautiful."

Almondine's gaze fell to the sketchpad, as if she were closing off a part of herself. She chose a piece of brown charcoal and added detail around the buildings. Mazie listened to the gentle scraping of the charcoal on the linen paper but said nothing.

She'd learned patience and good timing were required when working with Almondine. Few people appreciated silence and listening as much as she did. Sometimes she required an entire minute to formulate an answer to a relatively simple question. Mazie braced herself for a potentially long afternoon based on what she wanted to ask and what she wanted to do to save the Bijou.

Eventually Almondine asked, "Why do you want to go to Paris?"

Mazie shrugged. "I've heard it's the city of love and light. I'd want to go with someone special. When did you visit?"

"The last time was nine years ago."

"You've been more than once?"

"Many times."

"How many?"

"Eleven."

Mazie put her hand to her heart. "Well, even though it's dirty, you must've loved it to return so often."

Almondine replaced the chalk in the box and wiped her hands on her long denim skirt. "The first time I went by myself for inspiration with my art. All the subsequent visits afterward were at the request of a lover, a few different lovers," she clarified. "One in particular wanted to live there but the demands of his life wouldn't allow it. Instead, he journeyed there frequently. Three times I accompanied him."

"Do you think you'll go back?"

She scoffed and waved a dismissive hand. "Never again. It was ruined for me."

"The last time ruined it?"

"*She* ruined it," Almondine said, a sneer on her face.

Mazie glanced at the drawing and noticed window boxes adorned most of the buildings. She thought of Tarina's breasts sitting in the lilies. She cleared her throat and folded her hands in front of her. "Almondine, when you say *she* ruined it, are you referring to Tarina Hudson?"

Almondine's eyes grew wide. She furiously slapped the sketchbook shut and pushed it across the little table that belonged in a French café. In fact, despite some of the overgrown foliage, the entire scene *was* a French café, complete with a French flag tucked into a corner. *How did I miss that?*

Almondine stood abruptly, knocking several pieces of chalk to the ground.

"I'm sorry," Mazie blurted, as she gathered the chalk. "I didn't mean to upset you."

Almondine pointed at Mazie. "Then never utter her name again."

CHAPTER ELEVEN

Addy glanced at her watch as she pulled up to yet another red light. She sighed. Late again. The extra stop for Bianca, combined with her other good deeds—a random stop for Weather, the nanny with COPD, helping Mrs. Hampton read the bus route pamphlet because she never could understand how the transfers worked, and waiting for Luanne and Bus 19 to make its stop at Market and Decker so Addy's regulars could transfer to her bus—cost her time. Overtime, according to the Wilshire Hills Transportation Department. Normally Addy took it all in stride, but today she was experiencing an unusual emotion: annoyance.

She was ticked off that she was running late, and for the first time she agreed with Jackie's summation of the problem. "Addy," Jackie had said, "these people are taking advantage of you. Tell them to grow up and deal with life. They need to figure out their own problems and deal with the bus timetable. They're all adults and you're not responsible for them."

"No, I'm not," Addy muttered as she turned into the bus bay. She quickly initiated her end of shift procedures, avoided dawdling, and deliberately ducked past Jackie's office to get out of the building quickly. She had somewhere to be. On her bike, she pedaled faster than ever, zipping past the pedestrians out for their evening walk. She periodically threw up a hand in greeting to all the walkers she knew, but she kept her mind focused on the road—and didn't let her mind wander.

She was very excited and realized her excitement connected to her annoyance with the day's passengers and their problems. Usually Addy didn't have evening plans. If she stopped at the Bijou or hung out with Jackie, it was completely impromptu. It didn't matter if she was late since she had nothing mentally pushing her forward through the day. But today she did.

Mazie had arranged a special showing of *Dragon Mothers* for the two of them, and possibly Almondine if she wanted to join. The Theater One movie had ended its run at the Bijou, and Mazie deliberately left off a showing of the Theater Two movie so the three of them could watch the documentary alone, after the general public had left.

Addy had never been to a private showing. It was special, and it was nice of Mazie to include her. As the Bijou came within sight, she silently hoped Almondine wouldn't join them. She bit her lip at the realization: she wanted Mazie all to herself. She instantly felt guilty because Almondine had been good to her. No one else would've allowed her to color code the candy or get her own refreshments.

Still, the wish for Almondine's absence lingered. "Then it's like a date," Addy mumbled, as she waved at Tango, sitting in the little ticket booth, compiling the day's receipts. She brought her bicycle through the front doors. It was starting to rain, and Almondine always allowed her to store her bike in the storeroom on nights like these—another nice thing Almondine had done for her.

And you still don't want her watching the movie with you? Then this is a date.

The lobby was vacant, which meant Almondine was probably in her office and Mazie was preparing for the end of the movie in Theater Two. Addy ducked under the concessions stand counter and prepared her popcorn dinner. She was just adding butter when Tango came through the front door carrying the cash drawer.

"Well, that's it for tonight," she said. "Are you excited about seeing *Dragon Moms*? I am." Tango wore a broad smile that Addy would best describe as giddy.

"Oh, I didn't know you were joining us," Addy said, as she deliberately pulled the corners of her mouth up, hoping her smile was convincing. "It's supposed to be a leading contender for the documentary category of the Academy Awards."

Tango grimaced. "Documentary? I didn't know it was... non-fiction. Are you sure?"

Addy saw a light. "Well, yeah. It's about Mormon mothers who support their LGBTQ children, despite their conflicting religious beliefs."

"Oh," Tango frowned. "I thought it was about dragons and baby dragons. You know, like animé?" She looked at Addy hopefully. "Are you sure it's a documentary?"

"Positive."

"Well, after I put the cash drawer in the safe, I think I'll just head over to the card store and play some *Magic*. Can you tell Mazie I'm taking a pass?"

"Sure," Addy said with a nod. When Tango left, Addy grinned. But then she frowned. *Do I want this to be a date—or not?*

"Hey, what's wrong?" Mazie asked as she closed the projection room door.

"Is this a date?"

Mazie swallowed and composed herself before she asked, "Do you want it to be a date?"

Addy bit her lip. She looked away and shrugged. When she glanced at Mazie again, her face oozed kindness, and Addy felt tingly inside. "I'm not sure."

"Um," Mazie said, "then let's not define it. How about that?"

"Okay, but I'd like to know what you intended."

Mazie blushed and smiled coquettishly. "I was hoping for a date." Then she quickly added, "But I just want to spend time with you, so it doesn't matter. We don't even have to sit together."

"No, I definitely want to sit with you." Addy blinked, surprised by her earnestness. "And Tango came by and said she wasn't coming. Will Almondine be joining us?"

"No, she has a migraine tonight so she's gone to bed. It's just us. Okay?"

"Super."

They spent the next two hours learning about Dragon Moms, sharing a tub of popcorn, and occasionally offering editorial comments when the narrator made a point—something Addy never would've done during a regular cinema experience.

But this is a date or a faux-date.

When the movie ended, they clapped and Mazie said, "Stay here while I run up and shut down the system. Don't leave," she stressed, giving Addy's arm a squeeze.

While she was gone, Addy brushed off the popcorn kernels that littered her chest and cleaned up the floor as best she could.

"Thanks for picking up," Mazie said when she returned. "I appreciate it."

"Of course."

"Did you like the film?"

"I did. Did you?"

"I did."

"Yeah."

Addy put her hands on her knees to stop them from bobbing up and down. She stretched her legs and was about to excuse herself when Mazie said, "What's your favorite lesbian movie?"

Addy relaxed and her DVD collection flashed in her mind. "*When Night is Falling.*"

"Oh, that was a good one. I'd say mine is *The Kiss.*"

Addy cocked her head to the side. "I've never heard of it."

"Not many people have. It was French. I saw it in New York. They get a lot of independent and foreign films you can't see anywhere else."

"What was it about? I mean, other than a kiss."

"Actually, that's all it was about. This Parisian woman sets out to find the greatest kiss of her lifetime."

Addy's ears perked. She'd always believed one purpose of her mental vacations was to find a fabulous kisser. "Did she find the best kisser in the world?"

Mazie chuckled. "Well, as you might suspect, she learned it was all about relationships. Anyone can be a fabulous kisser with the right person."

She leaned toward Addy. Her breasts hung over the armrest, and Addy suddenly realized how well-endowed she was. And how close.

"Did you want to practice your singing?"

Mazie recoiled and rubbed her neck. "I don't know, Addy. I don't think I feel like it tonight."

"I'd love to hear you again. I think you have the best voice I've ever heard."

"You do?"

"Yeah. It makes me feel…flimsy."

Mazie laughed and covered her mouth. "Sorry, that wasn't polite. I've just never had that effect on anyone. What does it mean?"

Addy shrugged and clasped her hands together. "I guess it's like relaxed. If I were a cardboard box, after your singing, someone could come by and unfold me."

Mazie seemed to process the image. "Is that a good feeling?"

"It's a great feeling." She stared at the concrete floor. "Sometimes when I'm anxious I'll think about that song I heard you sing. Then I feel better."

Tears pooled in Mazie's eyes. "Thank you, Addy. That's so nice of you to say."

"It's not just nice. It's true."

They stared at each other in the absolutely silent theater until Mazie said, "I'll make you a deal. I'll sing another song for you, but you'll have to do something for me."

"What?"

Mazie reached over and touched Addy's clasped hands. "I'll sing for you, which you know is difficult for me to do, if you'll do something that I think might be rather difficult for you..."

"What?"

"I want you to give me a kiss when I finish."

Addy tensed—until Mazie's fingers gently massaged her hands while she hummed a preview of what she would sing. Each note was like a button popping off a shirt. Addy wanted more. She looked down. Mazie had intertwined their fingers. Heat radiated through her and she felt her heart pounding.

"Maybe I'll take that kiss now," Mazie whispered.

Mazie pulled them together and guided their lips apart. Her tongue roamed inside Addy's mouth, sending shockwaves all the way to her center. She never could've imagined a simple touch could cause such a reaction! Her eyes flew open and she gasped. Mazie pulled away automatically. Addy was certain she'd offered the worst French kiss ever, and Mazie probably thought she was kissing a corpse.

"Sorry," Addy said through clenched teeth. "I haven't kissed a lot of people. I've watched tons of people kiss, mainly women, but I'm pretty sure I have more toes than received kisses. I—"

Mazie touched a finger to Addy's lips. "Don't worry about it." She stood. "I think I owe you a song."

Mazie floated onto the stage. She stared at the floor and her shoulders rose and fell as she took deep breaths. When she looked up, her eyes were closed. The first notes, low and deep, poured forth, and Addy felt all flimsy again. She relaxed into her chair and the notes, an extension of Mazie's beautiful mouth, kissed her everywhere. She stared up at Mazie—for it seemed equally important to see her and hear the song, one she didn't recognize. But it didn't matter. It was as if Mazie took her hand and they traveled the melody together.

The song ended and Addy closed her eyes, trying to hang onto it—to Mazie—as the notes faded away into silence. Her eyes remained closed, but she felt Mazie's presence as she returned to the seat next to her.

Addy sensed the touch before it happened. Mazie's cool fingertips grazed her cheek and cupped her chin.

"I'd like to try again, but if you don't want another kiss, just tell me."

"I want," Addy whispered, but she wasn't sure Mazie heard. She wasn't sure the words were real. She started to say it again, to make sure Mazie knew, but Mazie's lips pressed hers into silence. She wrapped an arm around Mazie's neck and pulled her closer—just like the movies.

Mazie's tongue flicked against her own…and suddenly Addy saw colors. Blues, greens, reds, yellows…all swirling together in a kaleidoscope.

She ripped herself away. "I'm sorry," she managed.

Mazie reached for her. "Addy, stay…"

But she ran out of the theater.

CHAPTER TWELVE

The next morning Mazie decided to walk the twelve blocks to Cammon University for her appointment with Dr. Bertrand. Although she was physically exhausted from lack of sleep, she preferred walking over taking the bus and facing the reason she hadn't slept.

The date had been wonderful, until the moment Addy panicked and ran out of the theater. They'd watched the movie like old friends, and Addy had really enjoyed herself. Mazie was sure of it. Trading a kiss for a song wasn't something she'd planned. It had just happened. She'd so wanted to kiss her again since Addy had frozen the first time.

"Hey, lady! Watch where you're walking!"

Mazie blinked. She was standing in the gutter. A middle-aged man in a blazer had his hand on her arm, pulling her out of the street. She realized she'd attempted to cross against the light. She followed his direction and nodded her gratefulness. He stared at her, clearly wondering if she was a crazy person. When the light changed, she charged ahead, determined to leave her embarrassment behind. Addy apparently wasn't the only one who daydreamed.

She was still a few blocks from Cammon, but she'd deliberately walked to the south, away from Addy's bus route. She wanted to give Addy some time. She'd either take Bus 47 or hoof it home, but she'd have to be much more cognizant of her surroundings, lest she wind up a tire pancake.

Once she was safely on the Cammon University property, she replayed the kiss—and felt a tingle down to her toes. She'd experienced great kisses, and other lovers had described Mazie as terrific in bed, but there was something about Addy's mouth— inviting and willing—on the edge of passionate. She could tell Addy wanted to let go, but she was afraid. Mazie would just have to keep working on her. She smiled as she crossed the lush common grounds and headed into the fine arts building.

She found Dr. Bertrand at her desk, staring out the window while Mozart's *Piano Concerto Number One* played in the background. She hesitated, not wanting to interrupt the professor's solitude.

"Come in, Ms. Fenster," Dr. Bertrand said, her back to Mazie.

Mazie took the leather chair across from Dr. Bertrand's desk. She folded her hands in her lap, feeling a little naked. Dr. Bertrand had asked her to bring nothing, but that made her feel unprepared.

Dr. Bertrand slowly turned her chair, offering a slight smile. "How are you?"

"I'm good, thank you."

Dr. Bertrand leaned back, assessing her answer, furthering her discomfort. Dr. Bertrand continued to stare, and although Mazie attempted to hold eye contact, as she knew she should, she had no idea what to say. So she said the first music fact that came to her mind. "Did you know Mozart was Catholic?"

"Yes." Dr. Bertrand's eyes narrowed. "Are you all right, Ms. Fenster?"

Mazie nodded. "Just nervous." She swallowed and said, "Unfortunately, you make me nervous, Dr. Bertrand. While I know a few facts about Mozart, I know much more about you, and I'm in awe of you." She deliberately closed her mouth and finally met Dr. Bertrand's gaze.

She smiled and said, "Ms. Fenster, I appreciate your kind words, but you need to relax. Tell me how your performance preparation is coming."

Mazie smiled back before apprising Dr. Bertrand of her progress. "Just last night I stood on the Bijou's stage and sang for my friend Addy. I know it's not the same as singing for a room of people, but it was a big step for me."

Dr. Bertrand nodded and picked up a wooden sphere. She rolled it between her fingers while she processed Mazie's announcement. "Indeed. And what are your next steps?"

Mazie outlined her plan to sing in front of a crowd, and Dr. Bertrand continued to nod. "Do you think there could be time for me to practice inside Gallagher Hall? So I'm prepared for the lights and how the stage feels..." She ran out of gas and hoped she hadn't overstepped. Fortunately the professor seemed to mull the request.

"I can arrange that." She reached for her special fountain pen and wrote herself a note. "Is there anything else I can do to support you?"

The question took Mazie aback. "Oh, no, Dr. Bertrand. I believe this is all on me. I have to work through it myself."

Dr. Bertrand actually grinned and chuckled. Mazie blinked, unsure of how to react. Dr. B must have seen Mazie's confusion, for she added, "It's refreshing to have a student accept full responsibility for her actions and her program of study. This younger generation, the Millenials, has a distinct portion of entitled brats. Many of them are quite talented, but I fear their monstrous egos and poor work ethic will land them in a polyester uniform asking customers if they'd like fries with their order." She paused and leaned forward. "I appreciate you May Fenster." She slapped her desk and stood. "Let's take a walk."

Mazie stumbled to her feet and reached for her bag. "Okay. Where to?"

"You want to see Gallagher Hall? You're gonna see it."

Mazie walked double-time next to Dr. Bertrand, who, in addition to her musical accomplishments, apparently boasted several marathon-walking trophies. They zipped across Cammon Commons as Dr. Bertrand lobbed personal questions about Mazie's relationship with their mutual friend, Maestro Larkin, her childhood on the East Coast, and how she knew she wanted to be a singer. Between deep gulps of air, which were necessary to keep up with Dr. Bertrand, Mazie shared her life story, still somewhat shocked that she was in the presence of a noted musical scholar.

"So your parents weren't supportive of you pursuing your musical talent?"

"Oh, they were, but they were pragmatists. They didn't push me to get married, but they pounded the notion that I needed a career to make my own money."

They walked further until Dr. Bertrand asked, "What do they think now?"

Mazie swallowed the lump in her throat. "They're both gone. My dad died in 2010, and my mom died in 2012."

"Any siblings?"

"No. Just me."

When they reached the enormous front doors of Gallagher Hall, Dr. Bertrand extracted a thick bunch of keys from her purse. "I know it's one of these," she murmured.

"Wow, you have your own key. That's cool."

"Oh yes. As much money as I raised for this place, and considering all the asses I had to kiss to get that money, yes, I get my own key." She pulled a shiny silver one from the bunch. "Found it."

They entered the vast lobby that smelled like new carpet and Mazie automatically looked down at the tasteful red and blue swirls. Marble-topped benches lined the perimeter of the space, and a large bar sat in a corner.

Dr. Bertrand wasted no time and charged toward one of the interior doors. She flung it open and marched across the nearest aisle. Mazie stepped inside and halted. She wanted to take it all in. The hundreds of red seats, the enormous sconces that hung like icicles at each entrance, the wide lighting booth that hovered over everything—and the stage. The shiny black floor glistened under the work lights. Stagehands scampered back and forth, carrying lumber, electrical cables, and lights. A few threw a glance toward Mazie and Dr. Bertrand, but they didn't stop and question them. Mazie guessed a few might know the professor, or they assumed anyone who could get through the front door was someone important.

Dr. Bertrand motioned for Mazie to join her in the center aisle. She held up her hands. "What do you think, Ms. Fenster?"

"It's the most amazing place I've ever seen. Did you help design it?"

The edges of a smile crossed her lips. "I did, but mainly this was designed by the previous department chair, Katherine Gallagher. Do you know who she is?"

"Oh, yes. The first female department chair at Cammon, served as the Dean of Admissions for a time, elected President of the Cammon Faculty."

"You've done your homework."

"Yes, ma'am."

Dr. Bertrand frowned. "Ma'am? Who's ma'am?"

Mazie clapped a hand over her mouth. "I'm so sorry!"

Dr. Bertrand winked. "Just messin' with you, May. We know each other well enough now. You can call me Ivy."

Mazie grinned broadly. "Thank you. I'm not sure I can do that, but you can call me Mazie. That's really my name now. I don't go by May anymore."

Dr. Bertrand stared at her. "Why?"

"Well, I left that person behind. She wasn't strong. She wasn't determined. Mazie is. I'm going to get my degree, Dr. Bertrand...Ivy. Yes, I am."

Ivy beamed. "Yes, I believe you are." She gestured toward the stage. Take a look. Commit it to memory. I won't ask you to get up there and sing now, especially with all these strangers around, but you need to keep working toward your goal."

Mazie closed her eyes and absorbed her mental picture. When she looked at Ivy, she knew she had tears in her eyes. "I promise I will."

They left the auditorium through a portal door on the opposite side and came upon a prominently displayed oil painting. "This is Dr. Katherine Gallagher," Ivy said, "or rather, it's her likeness. I don't think it looks much like her, but that's because she refused to sit for the portrait. The university board insisted the namesake of the building be honored, but Katherine wanted no part of it. She's a very humble person. The board forced the poor painter to use an old black-and-white picture from a faculty yearbook."

"It's still lovely," Mazie said. She looked into Dr. Gallagher's eyes. There was a sparkle there. She hoped she'd find her own sparkle as well.

They parted after Ivy escorted her out the front doors. A light rain fell and Mazie smiled. She waved goodbye to Ivy, and she was heartened when she heard Addy's bus turn the corner. She was feeling so good that she knew she could make Addy at least feel okay about their kiss. She took a deep breath and headed over to the bus shelter where she found Kit, the grandmotherly woman she'd met on the bus.

"Hi Kit. I don't know if you remember me—"

"Mazie. How are you?"

"I'm well. I was just visiting Gallagher Hall."

She smiled. "What did you think of it?"

"It was amazing."

They both looked over their shoulder at the Gallagher as Addy's bus roared toward the stop. Kit pointed and said something else, but Mazie couldn't hear her. She nodded and smiled while Kit continued to chatter. As Mazie climbed the steps, she glanced back at Gallagher Hall. Ivy stood on the corner, looking at her with a surprised expression on her face. That's odd, Mazie thought. She smiled at Addy and Addy smiled back, her cheeks flamed red. Everything was okay.

But as the bus pulled away, Ivy continued to stare.

CHAPTER THIRTEEN

Addy's gaze followed Mazie to her chosen seat on the bus. Any passenger looking up to Addy's giant mirror would notice the smile on her face. She'd had some time to process the kiss with Mazie, and more important, the revolting kaleidoscope of color that had followed. She'd realized that was the problem, not the kiss. She'd loved the kiss. Mazie's lips were…Well, she couldn't think of a word to describe them yet. She just knew she wanted to kiss Mazie some more, but the kaleidoscope would have to go. Hopefully a different image would come to her the next time they kissed. Maybe a new box of crayons? All those colors lined up in order. Of course, that wasn't a romantic vision, but the kaleidoscope was a deal breaker.

Addy shuddered and glanced out her side mirrors before she swung the bus onto Hazel Street. Bianca had sent her a text saying she needed to go in on her day off and could Addy please take her to work? Of course Addy had said yes, and at two thirty, Bianca bounded up the bus steps carrying a bag of blue M&Ms, Addy's favorite.

"Thank you," she said, offering Addy a kiss on the cheek.

Addy could feel the heat of a blush at the point where Bianca's lips touched her skin. "You're welcome."

Bianca put a hand on Addy's arm and her smile vanished. "I heard something from someone who rides the creepy guy's bus."

"You mean Pratul?"

"Yeah. And before I tell you, I hope you don't get mad at me, 'cause I think it's my fault."

"What is it?"

Bianca's red lips formed a pout. "Someone at the care center saw me get off your bus. That person rides the creepy bus and hates it. She asked me how I still get to ride the cool bus, and I lied and said you were just doing me a solid—one time. But she must've been suspicious, so she watched to see if you dropped me off again." Bianca hung her head. "I'm sorry, Addy, but she told Pratul. He knows you're not following your route." She wiped away tears. "I'm sorry if you're gonna be in trouble."

Addy patted Bianca's arm, a shiver running down her back. No doubt she'd be fired, but she didn't want to upset Bianca, so she smiled. "Hey, don't worry about it. I'm sure I'll be fine. Go sit down."

Bianca asked, "Are you sure you'll be okay?"

Addy nodded, but she didn't think Bianca believed her as she headed toward the open spot by Mazie.

Addy thought she might throw up. If Pratul reported her, Jackie would be obligated to investigate. Addy couldn't lie to Jackie, and all Jackie had to do was trace the bus's GPS system. While each bus had GPS, reports weren't regularly generated to save the taxpayers' money. Reports only happened when there was a reason, like a bus driver not following her route. Addy sighed. What could her next job be?

Mazie watched Addy's exchange with Bianca closely. It looked like they were sharing a secret. Bianca seemed worried, and although Addy smiled, Mazie noticed the droop in her shoulders. She was upset but wasn't letting on to Bianca. *Because she's in love with her. But she kissed me! And she liked it!*

Bianca shuffled down the aisle and dropped next to her. "Hi, Mazie."

"Hi, Bianca. If you don't mind my asking, is something wrong?"

Bianca let out a long sigh. "I think I got Addy into trouble. One of the other drivers, Pratul, the guy whose bus I'm supposed to take, knows Addy's been making a special stop for me." Bianca threw her chin toward the front. "Addy's acting like it's no big deal, but that's the kinda stuff that gets drivers fired."

"Fired? Addy could lose her job?"

Bianca nodded and started to cry. "And it's all my fault." She wiped her eyes and Mazie handed her a tissue. "I'm so selfish. I never should've asked her." She glanced at Mazie. "I think she kinda likes me, and I took advantage of that."

Mazie bit the inside of her cheek and hesitated before she asked, "Do you like her, you know, like as a girlfriend?"

Bianca shook her head. "I'm not gay. I know Addy is and that's cool. I'm just one of those people that everybody tends to like. Lesbians tend to fantasize about me a lot. Think they can turn me, not that Addy thinks that. Some think I'm bisexual. Whatever." She waved her hand. "I know that sounds snotty, and I don't mean it to be. I just like people and they tend to gravitate to me. I've been hit on a lot by men and women. Truth is, I have a boyfriend. I've been with a couple women, so I guess I'm bi. But I'm with him now, you know? I'm a faithful type of person. He's not happy about the people who call me thinking they're gonna get a date, but I set 'em straight. It's friends or nothing."

"Oh, I see."

Bianca nudged her with an elbow. "What about you? Is there someone special in your life?"

Mazie's gaze automatically flicked toward Addy, and Bianca grinned. "What?" Mazie asked.

"I see how it is."

"Oh...well, I—"

"Don't worry, Mazie. Your secret is safe with me, but does Addy know?"

Mazie shivered again at the question. "Yeah, she knows." She cleared her throat. "Is there anything we can do to help her?"

Bianca leaned back and closed her eyes. "I do my best thinking like this."

Mazie watched the streets zoom by, doing her own thinking. If Pratul was such a tool, then he deserved to be fired more than Addy.

Several minutes passed. Mazie had thought of—and discarded—several ideas such as running over Pratul, pushing him out in front of a bus, having him stoned to death, and worse, dropping him in a vat of hot glue. Nothing seemed feasible.

Bianca sat up straight. "I've got an idea, but I'll need your help."

"Absolutely."

"Let's make a video."

CHAPTER FOURTEEN

By the time Addy had dropped off a glum Bianca, who continued to apologize as she left the bus, Addy had brainstormed three other careers for which she was relatively qualified—baker, census taker, and concessions worker. When she pulled up to the Bijou and Mazie prepared to depart, Addy asked, "Do you think I could ever get a job at the Bijou?"

Mazie looked sympathetic. "Bianca told me about Pratul. Addy, I'm so sorry." She squeezed her shoulder and whispered in her ear. "Don't give up hope yet. You're still my favorite bus driver, and if I have anything to say about it, you'll be a bus driver for a long time."

Addy summoned a little smile and nodded. Mazie was so nice.

As she headed down the steps, Mazie said, "And for the record, I'd hire you in a second at the Bijou if you ever needed a job. Almondine would love it. But you have a job, Addy," she said firmly. "Now, don't forget I'm coming over tonight, right?"

Addy's eyes grew wide. She had forgotten Mazie had made special arrangements with Tango and Almondine to manage the theater for the night so she could go to Addy's and watch old lesbian movies.

Mazie smiled. "You forgot, didn't you?"

Addy nodded.

"Do you still want me to come? I don't have to."

"No, I do," she said sincerely.

"Okay, I'll bring the popcorn, the drinks—and the licorice." Mazie gave a little wink and disembarked.

Addy watched her shapely bottom head inside the Bijou before she closed the doors. She was looking forward to seeing Mazie, and she'd actually spent part of the week readying the tiny house for its first-ever visitor. She'd dusted surfaces that had never felt a rag, reorganized the little cabinet in her bathroom—just in case Mazie was a snooper—and she'd cleaned the baseboards, something she'd never done. The house was spotless. Yet now, all of her excitement about Mazie's visit had been eclipsed by Bianca's news. She might be going home to her clean house unemployed.

For the rest of her shift, she tried to focus on her passengers and Mazie's visit that evening. Every time she heard Jackie's voice on the radio, she gritted her teeth, worried that Jackie was summoning her for a meeting, but the only person who radioed her was Luanne.

"Hey, Addy? Over."

"Addy. Over."

"Um, I have a little problem. It seems I missed a turn, and so I took the very next right, thinking I could backtrack. Unfortunately, it was a one-way side road. Passengers were talking to me, and I got rattled. Everyone was being a backseat driver, and this one guy told me to take an immediate left, which I did. Over."

"And where are you now? Over."

"I'm in a Taco Time drive-thru. Over."

Addy smacked her hand against her head. "You've got the bus in a drive-thru? Does it fit? Over."

"Um, so far. Here's my question. Since we're already here, is it okay if we order some stuff? I'm kinda hungry, and the passengers are asking. Nobody's mad. In fact, a bunch of them are taking pictures with their phone. Over."

Addy couldn't help the laugh that burst forth, one she desperately needed. "Bus Four, I don't think there's a policy about drive-thru etiquette. If you're already in line, why not? Over."

"Okay, thanks, Addy."

Addy heard a chorus behind Luanne shout, "Thanks, Addy!"

"Over and out," she said.

Ten minutes later the radio call she dreaded, came. "Addy, please see me at end of shift," Jackie said.

"Copy."

Addy slumped in her seat. She was about to lose her job.

Jackie faced her, resting her chin in her upturned palm. "What am I going to do with you?"

Addy shrugged. Jackie hadn't bothered to explain the situation and what Pratul had done. It was one thing to bend the rules, but it was another thing when you got caught. Of course, if any of Jackie's supervisors asked Addy if Jackie knew about the unauthorized stops, Addy would say, "Absolutely not!"

"Now that my behavior has officially been brought to your attention, you have to follow policy," Addy answered. "I know that."

Jackie took a deep breath and glanced at her closed office door. "Yeah," she whispered. "But you and I both know Pratul is a complete asshole and a womanizer."

"And he's the reason I did it for Bianca. You know I wouldn't do something like that for myself, right?"

"I know." Jackie pulled out the thick policy binder and flipped through several sections. "Which is why this is going to be painful." She read to herself, her finger trailing across a page.

Addy grew bored and her mind forwarded to the upcoming date with Mazie. She'd show up with a cup carrier, holding the drinks and two boxes of licorice. If Addy were bringing the snacks, she'd pack the popcorn in a plastic bag for the ride over and then transfer it to the bucket before they watched the movie.

She hoped Mazie would wear the beautiful, flowing blue dress Addy liked so much, not only because it was one color, but when Mazie wore it she looked ethereal. The sleeves billowed and the skirt seemed to float when she walked. Addy found the effect mesmerizing. She'd never touched the fabric, although she wanted to. Maybe when they were sitting on the couch watching a movie, Addy would put her arm around Mazie. But the touch might distract Mazie from the movie...*Is that a bad thing?* Maybe they would kiss again. She imagined pressing against Mazie, touching the curve of her breast...

"I'm so glad your impending discipline makes you so happy," Jackie said dryly.

Addy dismissed the image of Mazie. "Sorry."

Jackie opened her mouth, closed it and shook her head.

"What?" Addy asked.

"No, I don't want to know." She paused and splayed her fingers across the binder, studying her cuticles. "Actually, I have to ask." When she looked up, she looked almost embarrassed. "Addy, setting aside whatever we may have personally, or whatever I wish we had...Are you and Bianca involved?"

"No." When Jackie looked at her skeptically, she sighed. "There was a time when I wished we were, but the truth is, Bianca has a boyfriend. She and I are just friends and I was trying to help her."

Jackie stared at her a beat longer and nodded. "Okay, here's what we're going to do. I'm suspending you for the rest of the week without pay. I will conduct a short investigation and make a recommendation to Human Resources, which they may—or may not—take. Do you have any questions?"

"Do I need to clean out my locker?"

"No, this is just a leave. You still have your job, you're still covered under the company health insurance, and," she said pointing a finger, "you're still covered under all policies and procedures adopted by the Transportation Authority. This means if anyone harasses you in any way, you have the right to file a grievance. Understood?"

"Yeah, thanks, Jackie." She stood and pushed the creaky chair away.

"Do you want to have dinner on the barbeque tonight?" Jackie asked. "I don't want you to mope around."

Addy bit her lip and struggled to maintain eye contact. She'd hoped Mazie could slip in and slip out without Jackie knowing. "I'm having someone over to watch a movie."

Jackie's surprise was obvious and Addy could almost see the wheels turning. She swallowed and said, "Well, that explains it."

"Explains what?"

"That stupid expression on your face." She waved her hand. "Go on. Get out of here."

"Are you mad?"

Jackie's face softened. "No, I'm not mad. Now go. Get ready for your date."

"It's not really a date. We're just watching a movie."

"Uh-huh."

"But we might kiss."

"Yup. Got it."

"Does that make it a date?"

"It does."

Jackie returned to her reading and Addy headed to the Bull Pen. It was after six so no one was around. She clocked out, but when she turned around, the driver known as Bump was behind her. She jumped and immediately stepped away. Bump, which wasn't his real name, hung with Pratul. He was highest in seniority and union president. He looked like most of the bus drivers—white, male, overweight, balding, and hairy. Nearly all of the male bus drivers sported facial hair in the winter to ward off the cold, but many of them shaved in the summer. Not Bump.

"Hey, Addy. Sorry if I scared you."

"No problem. Have a good night," she said and charged past him.

"Can I talk to you real quick?"

She looked back, noting how soft his voice had become. He looked nervous and his gaze darted around the room. She was equally nervous, having never exchanged more than a hello with him. She took comfort knowing that Jackie was just down the hall. If he tried anything, Addy could scream and Jackie would come running.

"Sure. What's up?"

He licked his lips and stepped closer so she could hear him as he said softly, "I think the way Pratul treats you is shitty. I heard what he did."

She shook her head. "Well, thanks for that, Bump, but if you think it's wrong, why do you go along with it? Why don't you say something?"

His gaze dropped to the floor. "I know I should, but..."

"But what?" Addy asked sharply. She wasn't in the mood for his pity.

"But nothing," he finally said. "I don't have an excuse. There's just stuff going on that you don't understand."

She crossed her arms. "You know I just got suspended without pay, right? Just because I go a little off route each day to help someone, a woman who's been sexually and verbally harassed by Pratul and doesn't want to ride his bus. Why are you protecting him?" Her heart pounded. She wasn't used to confrontation, but it felt like a rush.

He shuffled his feet. "Hey, I only go—"

"You only detour to your house twice a day to check on your cat."

"She's elderly. She has to have medication." He looked at her suspiciously. "How do you know that?"

"I've heard you all talk. Half the time you guys don't even notice I'm around when you're telling your awful jokes, making your disgusting fart noises...or revealing your secrets. I know lots of things, but I've never told any of them to Jackie."

They stared at each other until Bump looked away. He put his hand on his back and winced. "Can we sit for a minute? My back is killing me." He motioned to a small table in the middle of the room. Once he'd lowered himself into a wooden chair that creaked under his weight, he said, "I'm gonna give you something you can use. You'll never jam up Pratul on sexual harassment. He's way too careful. But there is something else." He leaned over the table and whispered, "Pratul deals oxy out of his bus."

"*What?*"

"He's selling drugs. I should know. Up until yesterday I was one of his customers."

She couldn't believe it. What Pratul was doing was so much worse than her simple policy violations. She thought to ask, "What changed yesterday?"

He mustered a slight smile. "I filed my retirement paperwork at the insistence of my neurosurgeon. My back has been trashed for the last five years. Had an accident out on my ranch. Doc has been watching my liver, and between the booze and the pills, the numbers aren't good. He's forcing me to retire. The only thing that's going to get me some relief and help me kick the pills is surgery. And if I'm retired, I'll have the time to recuperate. It's a big surgery and I'll need ten weeks of rest. No friggin' way I could've taken ten weeks off work, so I just took the oxy to get by until I could retire."

She couldn't believe it. "What should I do? Tell Jackie?"

He shook his head. "No, don't do that. She'll have to follow company policy, and he'll just stop selling for a while." He tapped the table. "You need to think of something else." He pointed at her. "But keep me out of this."

CHAPTER FIFTEEN

Mazie felt like a parent leaving her child with the babysitter as she and Tango concluded a tour of the Bijou. They returned to the concessions stand and Mazie prepared the refreshments she'd take with her to Addy's house. "You have the movie end times programmed into your phone, right?"

"Check," Tango said.

"And you're comfortable with the start and stop procedures for each film, right? Because Almondine really should stay out of the projection booth. She can't figure out the digital projector, and she's never understood how streaming works."

"Got it. Don't worry, Mazie. Just go enjoy your evening."

Mazie took a breath. "Thanks. You know I appreciate you, right?"

Tango smiled and pointed at the licorice. "So you're going on a date with Addy?"

Mazie looked away. "It's not really a date…Well, maybe it's kind of a date."

"You two make a cute couple."

Mazie stopped and faced her. "You think so?"

"Yeah."

Tango looped her arm through Mazie's and escorted her to the emergency door at the back. "Now, go. I've got this. I seriously doubt the Tuesday night crowd will be the downfall of the Bijou."

"I know." Mazie gazed up at the dark wooden crossbeams. "There's just something special about this place."

"There is. Now go."

She got into her little Fiat, praying it started. It had conked out right after she arrived in Wilshire Hills, and she'd finally saved enough money to get the new belts it needed. When the engine rumbled, she smiled.

She managed to drive to Addy's house—or rather, Addy's landlord's house—without spilling their drinks. Addy had told Mazie to text once she arrived, and Addy would come out the side gate, which was closest to the tiny home where she lived. Mazie sent the text and checked her makeup in the rearview mirror before heading across the lawn. She heard music and smelled the distinct odor of grilled fish.

The gate squeaked and Addy appeared, wearing a T-shirt and cargo shirts. She immediately took the bag of popcorn hooked between two of Mazie's fingers. "Hey," she said. "Did you have any trouble finding the place?"

"Oh, no. It was easy."

Mazie followed Addy into a backyard oasis, across a trail of red brick pavers that cut through luscious green groundcover. Flags, signs, and nautical décor—oars and fishing nets—hung from the freshly painted wooden fence. Ahead was a tiny cute green house with white trim. A red rocking chair sat on the small front porch, inviting guests to have a seat. As they climbed the steps, Mazie looked over her shoulder toward a large redwood pergola bathed in soft light where two women enjoyed beers. One oversaw the grill while the other tossed a salad, her back to Mazie. The one at the grill, a dark-haired beauty with serious curves, turned and stared. Mazie offered a smile but didn't think it was her place to call out a greeting. If Addy wanted to introduce her, she would do so.

Walking through the front door introduced Mazie to a completely different side of Addy. She'd known about the color "peculiarity" since the day they met but seeing how it played out in Addy's home was sobering. The interior reminded her of an accessory store where every display was organized by color. Her living room was brown—sofa, drapes, carpet, and furniture. Her DVD collection covered an entire wall but was also grouped by label color. The small kitchen was white with orange accents— orange plates, orange teapot, and orange can opener. Mazie imagined if she journeyed up the ladder to Addy's loft bedroom, she'd encounter a completely different color.

The walls, however, defied the color scheme. Old movie posters were tacked up everywhere, regardless of prominent colors. One theme connected all of them: lesbian cinema. She'd seen some of the movies at a theater, movies like *Boys Don't Cry* and *Claire of the Moon*, but there were several posters advertising movies Mazie had never seen or heard of, and two of the posters displayed topless women. She studied one in which a woman with bare breasts stood in front of another, who was on her knees. The standing woman cradled the kneeling woman's head, practically pushing her face into her crotch. The tagline at the bottom read, For Adults Only.

"Is this porn?" Mazie asked.

Addy looked up from the kitchen where she was emptying the bag of popcorn into the bucket Mazie had brought. "For that era, yes. By today's standards, no. And ironically, it really wasn't a lesbian film, although I like the poster because it projects that."

Mazie strolled along the wall, reading the taglines and studying the various images, noting the posters of the sixties and seventies conveyed an overt tone of smuttiness while feelings of love and beauty emanated from the newer ones. Lesbian film had certainly come a long way.

"How did you get these?" Mazie asked.

Addy finished chewing a handful of popcorn. "I bought a few of them online and others are from a theater. Back home we had one indie film place, and I knew the manager."

"So where's home?" Mazie asked.

"Everywhere," Addy replied with a mysterious smile.

Mazie offered her own smile and said, "I'm originally from Kentucky, but I moved to New Jersey when I was older."

Addy pushed the bucket toward Mazie. "How did you wind up out here?"

"Well," Mazie said, grabbing a few kernels, "it turns out my vocal music coach knows a professor at Cammon. They might've been lovers. The prof at Cammon owed my coach a favor, so she asked the Cammon prof to become my advisor and help me finish my master's."

"That's cool. I wonder what she owed her?"

Mazie laughed. "I don't know, but I think vodka was involved." She glanced at a picture in a silver frame on Addy's beat up end table—an official army headshot of a young man who looked a lot like Addy. She held it up. "Who's this?"

Addy glanced up from her preparations, but only for a second. "That was my brother," she mumbled.

Addy's expression conveyed conflicted feelings, and Mazie thought better than to ask more questions about him. She set the photo down, cleared her throat and asked, "How long have you been a bus driver?"

Addy's face paled at the question. "Well, eighteen months." She looked down and added, "But I might not be for much longer."

"What are you talking about? The passengers love you. Why would you quit?"

"Oh, I'm not quitting. Right now I'm on leave. There's this other driver who hates my guts."

Addy summarized the issues with Pratul, which Mazie knew from talking with Bianca, but Addy also mentioned that Pratul was dealing drugs. "My friend Squeegee is a PI, and she's going to help me. It would be great if I got to keep my job and Pratul lost his."

"You have a friend named Squeegee. Is she a professional window washer?"

"No, that's her roller derby name."

"Oh. I've always wanted to see roller derby."

"Well, we should go some time and you can meet her."

"Are you asking me out on second date?" Addy froze and Mazie worried she'd pushed her anxiety over the edge, so she quickly revised her question. "Come to think of it, I'm asking you out. Addy will you escort me to the roller derby?" She hefted the enormous bucket of popcorn. "I promise I will at least feed you a meal as good as tonight's offering."

They both laughed and Addy said, "I accept. As long as there's licorice."

"Of course."

They carried the refreshments to the coffee table, and when everything was situated—by color—Addy picked up an old VHS tape. "This is my copy of *Therese and Isabelle.*" She cocked her head to one side. "I think the story…I mean…" She shook her head and sprang off the couch. She popped the video into the machine, and as it started she said, "I'll let you decide for yourself."

Once the video began, Addy scooted next to Mazie on the couch. Mazie soon lost herself in a beautiful story of sexual awakening. It reminded her of the moment she realized she was gay—when her high school bestie Laura Smith planted a smooch on her lips at the frosh mixer. They had been friends and lovers throughout high school. Unlike so many other young people, Mazie's coming out wasn't difficult, and her supportive family included Laura in many get-togethers. When graduation came, she and Laura parted friends and still maintained a Facebook connection.

She glanced at Addy who seemed equally immersed in the story. She wondered what Addy's coming out had been like. She obviously didn't want to talk about her past, and Mazie doubted her need for color organization just popped up—literally out of the blue—or red or green. Something must have happened to her. Since meeting her, Mazie had studied up on OCD and learned people were often misdiagnosed and their "peculiarities" were labeled as OCD, when in fact, they were not. Addy claimed not to suffer from OCD and Mazie was going to leave it alone. Besides, everyone had little peccadillos. Addy's seemed rather harmless.

Addy reached for the remote and paused the film. "You're staring at me and not watching the film. You don't like it?" She turned to Mazie with a worried look.

"I like the movie very much. It reminded me of my coming out experience. What was yours like?"

Addy winced. "Not good. Horrible in fact." She leaned back on the couch. "I don't want to talk about it. Can we just watch the movie?"

"Of course," Mazie replied gently. "I didn't mean to pry, Addy. I'd just like to know you better, but I certainly don't want to pressure you into sharing anything that's too personal."

She automatically squeezed Addy's hand. Addy looked down and laced their fingers. When their gazes met, they both smiled. "I like this," Addy said. "I like you."

"And I like you." Mazie brought their joined hands to her lips.

Addy's sudden intake of breath worried Mazie, but she didn't let go. She leaned back on the couch, and Addy followed her lead. She put her head on Addy's shoulder. She sat completely still, waiting for any fallout. When Addy started the movie again, Mazie finally took a breath.

Their hands remained interlocked for the rest of the movie, and Mazie found herself listening to the steady rhythm of Addy's breathing as often as the dialogue. "That was a beautiful movie," she said when Addy ejected the tape.

"I'm glad you liked it," Addy said. "Would you like to see the movie poster?"

"Sure."

"Uh, well, you'll have to climb a ladder. It's in the loft."

Mazie stood and looked at the ladder behind them. "I'm okay with a little exercise." She noticed Addy didn't call the loft "my bedroom."

She followed Addy up the rungs, staring at her buttocks, imagining what it would be like to caress them, kiss them, *spank* them. She was getting hot, and it wasn't because Addy didn't have air-conditioning.

The pitch of the roof made it impossible for Mazie to gracefully step off the ladder, and since Addy's mattress covered almost every inch of the loft, landing on Addy's bed was inevitable. She took a breath to quash her libido, tumbled into the loft and quickly sat up.

"It's a little tricky," Addy said. "I have to be extra careful going down first thing in the morning before my coffee."

"I imagine so."

Mazie scanned the small space—painted in purple. The mattress was covered in purple sheets, and even Addy's alarm clock was purple. There wasn't room for much else except a stack of clothes in the corner. Right above the mattress was the movie poster for *Therese and Isabella*.

Addy stretched out on the bed and pointed at the ceiling. "Did you enjoy the movie?"

Mazie leaned back next to her. "I really did."

"I think it's timeless like *Tipping the Velvet* or *When Night is Falling*."

"What was your favorite foreign film?" Mazie asked. "Other than *Therese and Isabelle?*"

Addy rubbed her chin. "Maybe *La Femme de Amore*."

"I'm not sure I saw that one."

"I guess we'll have to add it to the list to watch," Addy said.

"I guess so."

Addy propped herself up on an elbow. "What movie could you watch over and over?"

Mazie shook her head. "Too many to name. *Desert Hearts*, of course, *A Happy Ending, Imagine Me and You*."

Addy nodded. "I liked those too."

Mazie sat up and faced her. "I'd like to see more movies with you and hear your thoughts. It seems to me we think alike when it comes to cinema."

"I've noticed that. I think it's really cool that you work at the Bijou."

"I love that place. It's historic and relevant."

"Relevant. I like that." She sighed and asked, "Do you think you'll be able to save it? Make enough people think it's *relevant?*"

"I hope so. I'm planning an event."

"What kind of event?"

"Well, can you keep a secret?"

"Of course."

"Do you know Tarina Hudson?"

Addy pointed to one of the posters on her ceiling, which advertised a sci-fi adventure titled *Galaxy Warriors* and starring Tarina Hudson. "She's one of my faves. What does she have to do with the Bijou?"

"She's finishing a movie now—"

"Yeah, a movie version of the old *S.W.A.T.* TV show with an all-female team. I can't wait!"

Mazie clasped her wrist. "Then you're gonna love this. Almondine knows her and I'm pretty sure she and Almondine were lovers."

Addy shot up. "What?"

"It's true. I've been going through a bunch of stuff and I found Almondine's address book. She knows a lot of people." Mazie recounted finding Almondine's drawing of Tarina.

Addy just shook her head. "Wow." She smiled and stretched out next to Mazie. "Thank you for saving the Bijou."

"Well, it's not done yet."

"But it will be."

She stroked Mazie's cheek and Mazie automatically closed her eyes, offering Addy permission to kiss her, touch her, fondle her, whatever she wanted. *Just don't stop.*

She felt Addy's nearness before their lips connected. One kiss turned into two. She desperately wanted to touch Addy everywhere, but she wasn't going to push it. Addy broke the kiss and looked at her seriously. "Remember when you asked me where I go sometimes?"

"Uh-huh."

"It's like daydreams," Addy whispered into Mazie's neck.

"About what?"

"It's embarrassing."

Mazie knew she needed to proceed cautiously. "If you don't want to tell me, that's fine. But I promise whatever you share, I'll take it seriously. I won't laugh or dismiss your feelings."

Addy snorted.

"What?"

"You're not the first woman who's said that."

"And did that other woman—or women—break your trust?"

"That or they never called again because they thought I was crazy. It's happened every time I've told women other than my shrink." She shrugged. "I basically gave up on the idea of having a girlfriend."

Mazie's heart hurt, but she was relieved to know Addy saw a professional. "Hey." She drew Addy's face between her hands and caressed her cheeks. When Addy finally looked at her, she said, "I'm not those women."

"I feel that," Addy whispered. "I really do." Addy's gaze flitted to the side. "They're all about sex. In one I was a cashier at a store. There was this princess in my line… We wound up doing it in the frozen food aisle."

"Really? Oh." Mazie could tell Addy was watching her for any trace of judgment. She licked her lips. "That's really hot."

"You think so?"

Mazie nodded.

"Sometimes I'm in a position of power and sometimes not. Usually I don't know the other woman."

"Usually," Mazie repeated. "Have I ever been in your fantasies?"

"No."

Mazie looked away, dejected. Apparently she didn't rate. "What about Bianca?"

Addy couldn't meet her gaze. She had her answer. She closed her eyes and envisioned herself taking a step away. She took a breath and reached for Addy's hand. Suddenly she saw a different image—taking a step forward. She decided her goal was to be the subject of all of Addy's little mental vacations. She caressed Addy's chin and turned her face so Addy had to gaze into her eyes. "I'm not a psychologist or psychiatrist, and if it makes you feel better, I've seen a psychologist for years, even more so after I got stage fright. I think we're a lot alike. Just know you can trust me, and if you're not ready to trust me yet, that's okay. I'm here when you are."

Addy's look of relief sent tingles through Mazie. Their lips were only inches apart, and Addy closed the distance. Her kiss was hungry. Mazie gave her control, allowing Addy's tongue inside her mouth.

It was a fiery kiss unlike any Mazie had experienced. It was as if Addy could anticipate when Mazie would slightly shift left or right, or when it was the perfect moment to take Mazie's lower lip between her teeth. All Mazie could think about was Addy's lips on her *other* lips. She was so wet, but when she reached for Addy's zipper, Addy gently swatted her hand away.

"Not yet," she whispered.

Another minute of kissing was all Mazie could take. At an apropos moment (as if there was one!) Mazie regretfully and gently pushed Addy away. "I have to stop." Addy seemed bewildered and hurt, so Mazie added, "I'm about to explode, Addy. I want you—bad. But I respect your wishes. Do you understand what I'm telling you? That was the greatest necking session I've ever had. You're like a fifteen on a scale of ten."

Addy slowly grinned. "Thanks."

"How did you become such a good kisser? I've kissed women twenty years older than you, and none of them are as talented. *I'm* not as talented as you."

While Addy didn't disagree, she said, "You're a great kisser."

Mazie buttoned up the front of her dress, which had miraculously come undone during the kissing session. "So what's your secret?"

Addy looked amused and content. "I may not have a lot of experience, but I've done a lot of research. I've studied the kisses in every lesbian movie scene I've ever watched."

"Well, your research has paid off," Mazie retorted. "But tell me what you've learned."

Addy fidgeted uncomfortably. "Well, I have a list."

"Let's hear it."

"Okay." She sat up straight, as if she were preparing to give a lesson. Her formality had the opposite effect on Mazie, who reclined on the bed to listen and learn.

Addy held up her index finger. "First, and perhaps most important, is to read the moment. Is it right for a kiss? And to be clear, I'm not talking about quick pecks or the end-of-the-movie-kisses. I'm talking about the first kiss."

"You mean like the one we just shared?"

Addy's face turned beet red. "Well, technically that was our second kiss." She cleared her throat. "Don't interrupt the lesson, please."

Mazie held up a hand. "My apologies. Please continue."

"Most films get that part right, but there are some where it's just stupid. Like they're right in the middle of a personal crisis or a natural disaster. No one is going to be kissing, at least not passionately."

"Agreed."

"Second factor. Approach. If someone is right-handed, she'll usually lean to the right. Opposite for lefties. Have you ever had the experience where you go in for a kiss, but the other person's head is at the wrong angle? So you shift your head and she shifts her head—"

"And then you just laugh at each other."

"Exactly. And the moment is ruined. That's number two. Number three: contact. The second that both sets of lips touch determines whether the kiss will be long and lingering or a complete crash and burn. Think about the first kiss between Vivian and Cay in *Desert Hearts*. And contact should always start with cradling the upper lip, not the lower lip. Moving for the lower lip makes it seem like you've got vision problems and you missed."

Mazie chuckled. "You've just explained why it didn't work out between me and a college blind date." They both laughed, and Mazie said, "What's number four, Dr. Smooch? And for the record, I've decided that's what I'm calling you."

"I like it," Addy said proudly. "So number four is continuation. This is tricky because the kisser has to read the ability of the person being kissed. Think of it as mouth dancing. You know how in ballroom dancing the leader guides her partner around the floor by gently pushing on the small of her back? This is the same. And it depends on the experience level of the woman being kissed. The kisser may bring in a little tongue action, but if the other person isn't ready for French kissing, the kiss will probably end, or, and this is worse in my opinion, the tongue action will resemble two dogs lapping at a water dish."

"Not a pleasant image."

"Indeed not," Addy said primly.

"What about all the kissing in *The L Word?* I noticed you don't have any TV posters."

Addy scowled. "TV's not the same. There are too many plots and too little time to build up the necessary suspense."

Mazie sat up and faced Addy. She placed a hand on each of Addy's knees and lightly stroked her thighs. "Now that I'm aware of your very important kissing criteria, I'd like to practice my form. I want an 'A' in Dr. Smooch's class."

Mazie knew how cliché she sounded, but Addy laughed and willingly obliged.

CHAPTER SIXTEEN

Had it not been for her date—and kissing lesson—with Mazie, Addy's mood would have been awful. Fortunately she was only mildly glum when her internal alarm clock woke her at five a.m., the time she normally got up for work. She'd just swung out of bed when she realized she had nowhere to go. She remembered she was on leave, and her appointment with Nadine wasn't until eleven thirty.

She'd texted Nadine after Mazie had left, saying she had new information about Pratul. Nadine texted back with some choice adjectives, a few emojis, and several different marks of punctuation. Although company policy forbade Jackie from sharing the details of Addy's leave from the Transportation Department, once Addy told Nadine, Jackie could comment freely to Nadine as a friend. She may have blurred the lines, but neither Addy or Nadine felt compelled to second guess her. Then right before Addy fell asleep, when her mind reviewed the kiss with Mazie, she got a reassuring text message from Jackie. *We've got your back.*

Around seven, Jackie's familiar soft knock sounded on her door. She held two steaming mugs of coffee and she handed one to Addy. "I wanted to check on you before I left. Are you okay?"

"Yeah. It's weird not going to work since I'm not sick."

Jackie leaned against the front porch railing and Addy joined her outside. "You've never missed a day. Perfect attendance for the last year."

"Yeah, and this is a stupid reason to miss work," she pouted.

"Well, maybe you can find someone to spend the day with," Jackie said quietly.

"You mean Mazie, the woman who was here last night."

Jackie shrugged. "She didn't seem to be your type."

Although she wanted to defend Mazie, Addy held her tongue. While she knew she was standing on her own front porch, the property belonged to Jackie. And although she counted Jackie as a friend, Jackie was her supervisor. No matter how hard they attempted to keep their relationships separate, it was complex.

"I'm not sure what my type is. We have fun together."

Jackie started to say something but then bit down on her lip.

"What?"

"Nothing. Forget it." Jackie looked away and sipped her coffee.

"No, I want to know."

Jackie glanced at Addy but quickly averted her gaze. It seemed as if she was embarrassed by what she was going to say even before she said it. "It's just…Do you think… Could this woman possibly be a substitute for your mother?"

The question spewed out of her mouth quickly and it took Addy a moment to process it. Once she did, she turned furious. She slammed her cup on the porch railing and coffee sloshed everywhere. She didn't bother to apologize and retreated inside, slamming the door behind her. She heard Jackie's car start, but before it pulled out of the driveway, Jackie sent a text. *I'm sorry. That was a no-win. If I asked, I offended you. If I didn't ask, and there was truth to it, and you got hurt down the road, I'd be angry with myself. I don't want you to get hurt.*

Addy replied, *Are you sure that's the reason? I'd rather you were angry with yourself.* Jackie's car pulled away and Addy assumed it was the end of the conversation, since Oregon had the strictest laws in the nation regarding texting and driving. Then one more message came through. *I only want what's best for you. I accept that I'm not the right person for you, but if it's not me, it better be somebody worthy of you.*

Addy wrote four different replies and deleted all of them. She finally tossed her phone on the counter and buried her head in her hands. Was Jackie wise or petty? In the course of the discussion the previous evening, Mazie had disclosed she was eleven years older. But what did that matter? Mazie didn't mother her. She didn't tell her to pick up her house. She didn't condescend to her. She treated her as an equal, and while she had more experience in the bedroom, she'd said Addy was indeed the better kisser. Still…

She couldn't think about this now. She needed to focus on getting her job back. She needed to help Mazie pass her vocal performance test and save the Bijou. They could sort out their relationship later, or maybe it would develop organically. She jumped off the stool, suddenly feeling claustrophobic in the tiny house. She decided to use the morning for a bike ride. She could take the wide loop of the Willy, and she'd end up close to Nadine's office downtown.

It had been over a year since she'd ridden all twenty-five miles of the beautiful path, and while the six miles she rode to and from work each day were lovely, it was the outskirts on the north and south side that illustrated the vastly different ecosystems of Wilshire Hills. There were usually a few overgrown sections where the bike path was invisible, covered in hostas and blackberry bushes. The hostas she didn't mind, but the sharp and thorny blackberry bushes, known as the Pacific Northwest Weed, regularly punctured bike tires. She'd learned to carry reinforced gloves and her clippers in her bike pouch, since her phone calls and emails to the parks department had only yielded the empty promise of, "We'll look into it."

The farther she pedaled, the fewer bikers, joggers, and walkers she saw. She constantly glanced left and right, always observing her surroundings. The homeless regularly camped in the bushes or under the trees with thick canopies. Most of them just wanted to be left alone, but she'd endured a few scary encounters with guys who'd stopped taking their meds and were mentally unstable. They would leap out from the bushes and a few had tried to steal her bike.

She was surprised by how many small encampments she found along the way. Their number had doubled, an indication that a growing percentage of the population couldn't find work or a way to participate effectively in the community. She knew Cammon University was partly responsible. Several homeless camps had been closed as Cammon erected more buildings and parking structures to accommodate more students. The higher the enrollment, the greater the university's wealth and need for land.

Up ahead the path disappeared and Addy screeched to a stop in front of several sinewy blackberry branches. Two more inches and she would've been walking her bike to the nearest bus stop and replacing her bike's inner tubes. She grabbed the clippers and gloves and went to work on the jungle in front of her.

Her machete slices effortlessly through the tall grass. The cooing and cackling of birds smothers the crunch of her footsteps. A veil of fog ensures she can't see more than a foot in front of her—and she almost slices off the leg of the Amazonian woman emerging from the mist, camouflaged in a green and brown pelt, ala Tarzan. It covers all of her tasty bits but hardly anything else. She is incredibly tall but curvy at her calves, stomach, and breasts. She is soft and fleshy, not rock hard as Addy would expect. The possibility of a smile lingers on her lips. Addy gazes into her eyes. They are familiar but she doesn't know why.

"Don't move," Addy commands.

She places the machete into the Amazon's cleavage, and with the slightest flick of her wrist the top pelt falls away. Addy slides the cold steel across the dark areolaes. She gasps and her fine nipples stand at attention. The Amazon has no tan lines, and Addy pictures her nude, lying on a flat rock, basking in the sun's rays. She says nothing and stands still. Addy sees the bottom pelt is two pieces, a front and a back, connected by leather string around her hips. The goddess doesn't flinch as Addy's fine blade slices twice—and then the Amazon is naked.

Two steps and she is in Addy's arms. Their lips merge in a steamy kiss while Addy caresses as much slick, wet flesh as she possibly can. When she cups a breast and strokes her nipple, the Amazon moans and breaks the kiss. She pulls Addy to the ground and rolls on top of her. She straddles her and guides Addy's fingers to her wetness. She slides inside and the Amazon moans, "Deeper."

Addy obliges. The Amazon rocks her hips. It begins to sprinkle but as the intensity of the Amazon's impending orgasm builds, so does the rain. The Amazon turns her chin to the dark sky, welcoming the forceful shower that smooths back her long dark locks. By the time she cries out in ecstasy, it is pouring. She looks down at Addy, a sensual smile on her face. Addy gasps. Staring down at her is Mazie.

She was nearly thirty minutes late for her appointment with Nadine. Although she'd left that morning with a straightforward plan—ride the Willy and go to Nadine's office—she'd passed the downtown and rode fifteen more miles. She was completely perplexed by her latest daydream. Rarely did she know the subject of her sexual fantasy. They were usually nameless strangers, beautiful enough to be in the movies. Even Bianca was "movie-worthy," by Hollywood's standards. Mazie was different.

And Jackie's question rattled in her brain. *Could this woman be a substitute for your mother?* It was a ridiculous question. Growing up, Addy had a horrible relationship with her mother, with Addy running away as often as possible. When Addy's "peculiarities" started around the time she turned fourteen, the school principal tried to convince her mother to get her help, but her mother refused. And she had her reasons.

Once Addy had her high school diploma, that very same principal paid for a bus ticket for her out of West Virginia. Addy remembered standing in front of the large electronic board at the bus terminal, reading all the cities where she could go.

She picked one the farthest away—Portland, Oregon. Portland immediately soured for her. It was the new "it" place to move, full of hipsters, crowds, and noise. If Addy had known this, she never would've gone there. She got a job in one of the million local coffeehouses that existed on every corner and rented a decrepit room from a creepy cigar-smelling guy, a room that took all of her tip money.

She met a woman outside a theater one night and they went on a few dates, but when the woman—Lydia—invited her home after a make out session in Lydia's old Toyota Camry, and Addy declined, Lydia squealed out of the parking lot, nearly running over Addy's feet. Although she was attracted to Lydia, there was a wall of anxiety, and the thought of climbing it gave Addy more anxiety. As she watched Lydia's taillights disappear into the night, she vowed not to date again until she conquered the wall.

She decided to leave Portland once she had a place to go. One day she overheard a coffeehouse hipster mentioning Wilshire Hills, a town south of Portland. She spoke of it with disdain in her voice. "Yeah, it's beautiful, and it's got the university, but it's so slow and quiet."

It sounded perfect to Addy and she left a week later. Then she met Jackie. And Dr. Pfeiffer, who was slowly helping her climb the wall.

She smiled as she rounded the corner to Nadine's office. She'd prepared an apology, but it was all for naught. She found a note tacked to the front door: *Addy, had to go. Not much to tell yet. See you tonight. Jackie has the deets. Bring gfriend. Couldn't see much of her since you hurried her inside, but I like what I saw!*

Addy sighed. She read the message again. While Mazie wasn't her girlfriend, she liked the word and wondered what it would feel like to have a real relationship. She wanted a girlfriend who treated her well and understood patience. Maybe Mazie was that person. She turned her bike toward the Bijou and decided to find out.

CHAPTER SEVENTEEN

Mazie was uncomfortable. Deception wasn't one of her talents, and while Pratul certainly deserved what was coming to him, she struggled with her decision to be a participant. She reminded herself that it was for Addy, and she'd do just about anything for Addy.

She and Bianca had met the day before and made a plan to catch Pratul sexually harassing Bianca and perhaps some other female passengers. Bianca's friend Norman was a gadget guy and designed surveillance equipment. He'd given Bianca a book with a hidden video camera and microphone. Mazie's job was easy. All she had to do was board the bus, sit within ten feet of Pratul, and hold the book up to her face. She'd look like she was engrossed in her reading, when in fact, she was filming Pratul. Bianca would get on a few stops later wearing a microphone. Hopefully she'd be able to record Pratul's advances while Mazie filmed incriminating body language. Then Bianca would get off at her usual stop, but Mazie would remain on the bus for several more stops to catch footage of Pratul's behavior with other passengers. She wouldn't have the benefit of audio, but maybe he'd violate another bus policy. Whatever they could collect would hopefully be enough to save Addy's job.

She couldn't help but smile when she thought of their date the night before. She'd so wanted to rip off Addy's clothes, but she tamped her libido because she could tell Addy wasn't ready. But on the drive back to the Bijou, thinking of the steamy movie and the kissing session on Addy's bed, her libido busted out of its puritanical prison and she couldn't find her vibrator fast enough.

She wanted Addy, which was why she was standing at a bus stop at seven in the morning. She was alone since the stop bordered a strip mall not yet open for the day's business. She zipped up her jacket to fend off the crisp Oregon wind, a reminder that winter was approaching.

She heard an engine roar and Pratul's bus came around the corner. She took a deep breath and plastered a friendly smile on her face as it stopped in front of her. She'd never ridden with Pratul, so she knew he wouldn't recognize her, but she needed to stay calm and not act suspiciously, something bus drivers were trained to observe, according to Addy.

As she boarded with her bus pass in hand, he said, "Well, good morning. I don't usually have such beautiful women boarding my bus this early."

His sliminess washed over her, but she managed to say, "Thank you for the compliment. I live in Albany but I work in Wilshire Hills. My car is dead and a friend said she'd drop me at a bus stop on her way out to the coast." Mazie told the lie with ease. She and Bianca had brainstormed a cover story for Mazie which would explain why she was standing in front of a shopping mall when nothing was open.

"Sorry to hear about your car," Pratul said. "Where do you work?"

"Centerpoint Mortgage Company over on Skypoint Street."

"Yes, I know it well."

His gaze traveled up and down, and Mazie felt gross from his stare. She'd chosen the same blue dress she'd worn to Addy's house, but she'd not bothered to secure the plunging neckline with a safety pin. Pratul was getting a little show as Mazie put away her bus pass.

"When will your car be fixed?"

"Oh, hopefully today. The mechanic said he'd call, but who knows? I could be on the bus for a week, I suppose."

"How fortunate for me," Pratul leered. "I would never wish you bad luck, but I'll be happy to help you turn a negative into a positive."

"Thank you," Mazie said. "How might you do that?"

His gaze swept over her once again and landed on her cleavage. "Let me think about it."

She flashed a sexy smile and chose a seat a few rows back.

"Don't want to sit too close," he said, looking at her through the large mirror. "I see."

"I wouldn't want to distract you."

"Oh, you've already done that. What's your name?"

"Vivian. Vivian Bell." She'd chosen the name of one of the main characters in *Desert Hearts*.

"Vivian," he said slowly, almost as if it were a dirty word.

Mazie shivered, suddenly aware the bus still idled. He watched her intently as she removed the book from her shoulder bag and opened it. She'd also practiced the motions necessary to aim and focus the camera lens before enclosing it behind some real book pages. Anyone sitting behind her would just think she was reading.

Pratul didn't leave, even after Mazie shut down the conversation and focused on her book. Another minute passed and Mazie's heart pounded. The camera was recording, and although Norman had assured them there was plenty of memory for hours of filming, she wished Pratul would go. The sooner Bianca got on and off and Pratul committed whatever transgressions he might, the sooner they would be done with this and Addy would have her job back.

A Pontiac Firebird pulled up next to the bus. The driver got out and trudged up the stairs. He was a chunky Hispanic man in a Mexican wedding shirt and dark blue jeans. Over his shoulder was a small backpack. "Sorry, I'm—"

"How may I help you, sir?" Pratul interrupted. "Are you lost?"

The man looked oddly at Pratul, before noticing Mazie and her book. "Yes, I saw your bus here, and I was hoping you could help me. I'm looking for Starbird Lane?"

Pratul checked his watch and said, "I have one more minute before I must leave. I'll show you on a map. Don't you have GPS?"

The man seemed to think a beat too long in Mazie's opinion, as if he were making up a story. "My phone's dead. That's part of my problem."

"No worries," Pratul replied. "Customer service to our community is one of my job expectations." He actually turned and winked at Mazie, who thought she might be sick.

Pratul withdrew a map and opened it across the console beside him. They spoke in low voices for a few moments, until the man said, "Oh, okay. I see where I need to go. Thank you. Have a nice day."

The man left and the Firebird sped off. When she glanced back at Pratul, he was watching her.

"We go now," he said.

Ten more passengers got on and off at the handful of stops Pratul made before Bianca boarded. He knew his regulars and often shook hands, gave high fives—even hugs—to the various men and women who came and went. Two men brought him gifts, a candy bar and a power drink. Mazie was impressed with his demeanor—until Bianca climbed the steps. Mazie inserted the earpiece Norman had provided so she could hear the conversation. When Pratul saw Bianca, the slimy gigolo act returned. "Well, well. Haven't seen you in a while. Why did you stop taking the bus? I missed you." He made kissing sounds and touched her elbow tenderly.

She jerked it away. "No way, Pratul. Not gonna happen."

"I think you should give us a chance, especially if you want that dyke to keep her job. I know why you haven't been on my bus."

"Are you serious? You're telling me that if I do...whatever with you, you'll let up on Addy?"

"Think about it. You. Me. Maybe some chocolate sauce."

Bianca looked disgusted and turned away. When she passed Mazie to take a seat in the back, she mouthed, "Yes!"

Mazie nodded. Hopefully what they had recorded was enough.

Addy spent the rest of the day sitting at home and watching three of her favorite lesbian classics, *Cloudburst*, *The Gymnast*, and *The Incredible Adventures of Two Girls in Love*. She'd texted Mazie and said, *How would you like to go to the roller derby?*

Mazie replied with, *Wow! That was quick. I'll just need to ask Tango to play Assistant Manager again. I'm sure she will.*

When Mazie knocked on her door around six, Addy felt a rush of butterflies. She'd thought so much about Mazie in the last twenty-four hours that her brain had almost worn her out. She couldn't picture her face anymore. It was a relief to see her in her jeans, V-neck T-shirt, and leather jacket. She looked incredibly sexy.

Mazie looked equally happy to see Addy. "Hey."

"Hey. Come on in."

When Addy shut the door, Mazie moved closer. Addy automatically wrapped her arms around Mazie's waist. "I have a confession," Mazie said.

"What?"

"I've thought about you a lot today, and I'd really like to push you against the front door and smother you with kisses just like they do in the movies."

"You would?"

"Uh-huh. What would you think of that?"

"I, um, well…"

"Can we try it?"

Addy couldn't believe it. Mazie wanted to touch her and kiss her. She wanted to do the same to Mazie. What was stopping her?"

Then Mazie's smoldering, sexy face went away and was replaced by a sad, sorry face. "Hey, it's okay if you don't want to. I understand. It's not like I'm one of those movie fantasies."

"It's not that…"

Mazie cocked her head to the side.

"I can't explain it yet. Please be patient. I just need to figure this out."

Mazie nodded slowly. "I can wait."

Addy swallowed. *She'll wait for me. Maybe she's the one.* Her throat was dry and her heart thrummed in her chest. She couldn't tell if she was ecstatic, afraid or both.

She must've looked afraid, because Mazie wrapped her arms around Addy and whispered, "It's okay."

"Thank you." She decided she needed to call Dr. Pfeiffer. Thank goodness Jackie had helped her fill out that insurance paperwork.

Mazie stepped away and tapped the side of her head. "Okay, my mind, like a parachute, works best when it's open. I'm ready to see roller derby."

Addy laughed. "That's a really good saying."

"I can't take credit for it. My sophomore English teacher had it on her wall. I've never forgotten it."

Addy opened the door. "We're supposed to meet Jackie at her car. She's got the tickets. I think you'll really like her."

Mazie looped her arm through Addy's. "I'm sure I will."

But when they arrived at the car, Jackie wore her serious expression, the one Addy only saw when the big bosses of the transportation department visited. They thought women couldn't be tough, so Jackie gave them something to think about. She shook Mazie's hand and was courteous but not friendly.

Addy looked at her curiously but she didn't seem to notice. They got in the car, and Mazie immediately illustrated her good manners, thanking Jackie for the invitation.

"It wasn't me," Jackie said sharply. "This was Nadine's doing." Her gaze flicked to the rearview mirror. As the newcomer, Mazie had offered to sit in the backseat. Jackie didn't suggest that Addy should join her, so Addy sat in the front with Jackie. "Addy said you've never been to the roller derby."

"No, I've just never had the opportunity."

"Too good for it?"

"Jackie," Addy scolded.

"What?"

Addy quickly offered Mazie an "I'm sorry" look, and Mazie nodded slightly. She seemed perfectly calm, but Addy thought she might have a heart attack. Her best friend and her possible girlfriend didn't like each other. This could be bad.

Jackie made everything worse by refusing to answer any of Mazie's polite questions. Instead, after a long silence, Addy answered the question for Jackie, who would then correct Addy. The conversation gave Addy a headache. Something was definitely not right with Jackie. She wouldn't even sing along to her favorite songs. Perhaps she was shy in front of people she didn't know, but nothing had ever kept Jackie from belting out the chorus to "Natural Woman," when either Aretha or Carol King started to sing. But today Jackie left Aretha hanging.

Completely fed up, Addy turned to Jackie and said, "What's wrong?"

Jackie frowned. "Nothing."

"Something's wrong."

"Nothing's wrong," she said through clenched teeth.

"Please stop lying."

"Damn it," Jackie spat. "Now you made me miss my turn."

"Just go in the other entrance."

"It's always blocked."

"Not always."

"Most of the time," Jackie insisted.

Addy pointed. "See?"

Jackie didn't reply but instead peeled into a space, barreled out of her seat, and slammed her door shut. Addy had never seen Jackie this way. Addy rushed over to Mazie, thinking she might need some protection, but Mazie held up her hand and stepped in front of Jackie, who looked like she might slap her.

"Jackie," Mazie said softly, "Addy mentioned you once had feelings for her, and while it's absolutely none of my business, I completely understand, and I respect your feelings. I hope you can respect mine. I hear you're an awesome person and supervisor. Addy's said so many wonderful things about you.

She's very lucky to have you in her life, and I feel honored to be invited tonight."

Jackie didn't seem to know what to say. A tear leaked out the side of her eye, and she quickly rubbed it away. She just stared at Mazie with a look that defied expression.

"Can I just add," Mazie said, "that if this evening gets brutal, like in the Australian film *Starcrossed Jammers*, I might throw up."

Jackie burst out laughing, and soon Addy and Mazie were laughing as well. Jackie crossed her arms and looked at Mazie thoughtfully. "I wanted to hate you but I can't."

"Is that a compliment?" Mazie asked.

"It is," Addy said. She threw an arm over Jackie's shoulder and took Mazie's hand. "Let's go watch some women kick ass."

CHAPTER EIGHTEEN

After they purchased beer and popcorn and found their seats, Addy and Jackie gave Mazie a short lesson on roller derby. "There are five on a team, one jammer and four blockers," Jackie started. "The goal of the jammer is to get past the opposing blockers two times in a two-minute period."

"Our friend Nadine is a jammer," Addy said. "She's an awesome skater. Completely fearless."

"How does a team win?"

"When somebody dies," Jackie said casually.

"What?" Mazie exclaimed.

Addy laughed. "She's kidding. There might be a little blood when somebody throws an elbow, but nobody dies."

"Oh, that's good." Mazie said.

The teams burst onto the rink and a flurry of women took a lap.

"That's Nadine," Addy said, pointing to a tall woman whose helmet bore a star on each side. "Her roller derby name is Squeegee."

Nadine towered over most of the other players. When she saw Jackie and Addy, she offered a little salute.

"I know her," Mazie said.

"You do?" Jackie asked.

"I think so. Is she a CPA?"

Jackie eyed her suspiciously. "Yeah. Why do you need a CPA?"

"I don't, but Almondine does. Nadine is helping us save the Bijou."

"That's great," Addy said. "I feel a lot better knowing she's involved. You and Nadine can probably convince Almondine to make the changes she needs to make."

"I hope so," Mazie said. "Almondine can be awfully stubborn."

Jackie and Addy laughed. "Ain't that the truth," Jackie added.

Nadine made another pass. When she looked over at them, she peered at Mazie and waved frantically, a look of recognition on her face. Mazie smiled and waved back.

The buzzer sounded and the teams went to huddle. Addy leaned back in her chair and put her arm around Mazie. When Mazie smiled at her she asked, "Is this okay?"

"Absolutely." Mazie put her hand on Addy's knee. Addy looked away, her cheeks a bright shade of red.

The bout began. Addy explained the strategy, and Mazie quickly realized there was more to roller derby than violent skating. She learned about J-block, passing the star, and ending the jam. Since Squeegee was the jammer for the Yellow Jackets, she was the focus of the action until she passed the star to her blocker, Ninja. Nearly two hours later the battered and bruised teams left the rink. Only a little blood had been shed when one blocker walloped her opponent and went to the penalty box.

"What did you think?" Addy asked Mazie as they gathered their things.

"I enjoyed it. Watching the teams circle the rink is rather hypnotic."

"Truth," Addy said. "Once I came to a bout and I was exhausted. Even though it was super loud, I still managed to fall asleep!"

They laughed and headed toward the exit. Mazie glanced behind her. "Where did Jackie go?"

"Right before the last jam she caught some woman's eye. I'm guessing they found a place to hook up."

"Here? At the roller derby?"

"Oh yeah. Definitely at the roller derby. Everybody's hyped up, watching all these women in tight shirts and little shorts crash into each other. That's why the line into the women's restroom is always long."

Mazie had to admit her libido kicked in after the first tumble—toned arms and legs intertwined and breasts jiggling left and right.

"Let's go find Nadine. Are you up for getting a beer with her?"

"Sure. I'd like to ask her how she manages to perform in front of all of these people."

"Perform?" Addy asked, puzzled.

"Well, there's clearly a lot of ability and athleticism involved in this sport, but the women were getting the audience involved. That's performing."

"Huh, I never thought of it like that, but you're right."

They waited by the locker rooms with the rest of the crowd until the players emerged. Many had exchanged their colorful uniforms, protective gear, and helmets for shimmering silk blouses, stiletto pumps, and makeup. Mazie was impressed that these women, who'd just spent two hours hurling epithets and elbows, looked good enough now to be seated at Noisette, Wilshire Hills' premiere French restaurant. She felt guilty about ogling the women while holding Addy's hand, but the guilt evaporated when she saw the dumb grin on Addy's face. She was enjoying the view as well.

Nadine was the last to emerge, her arms open for a hug. "Hey girl!"

Addy slipped into her embrace, and when she saw Mazie, her eyes grew wide. "I know you. Get in on this hug."

Mazie obliged, and when they broke apart, Mazie said, "I was surprised to see my CPA mowing over the competition."

Nadine stuck a hand on her hip and pointed at Mazie. "Girlfriend, I mow over the competition in all of my jobs, and in every way imaginable."

Mazie stared at her, mystified. "What other jobs do you have?"

"You're looking at the best private dick in all of Linn County," Addy said.

"No, no," Nadine corrected. "We don't ever use the word *dick* to describe me, not since the surgery."

Addy held up a hand. "I stand corrected."

Mazie immediately thought of her cloak-and-dagger antics on the bus with Bianca. She'd not yet watched the movie they'd made of Pratul. If it turned out horribly, perhaps Nadine could help them.

Nadine looked around. "Where's Jackie?" When Addy looked uncomfortable and rubbed the side of her neck, Nadine's aura of happiness melted away. "I see." She sighed and blew her bangs off her face. "Well, I'm starving. Where should we go?"

"How about our usual? The pizza place around the corner?" Addy suggested.

"Sure," Nadine said unenthusiastically.

As they exited the rink, Nadine looked over her shoulder, and Mazie guessed she was still looking for Jackie.

"Hey Nadine, have you had any luck with your investigation?"

"What investigation?" Mazie asked.

"Nadine is hunting for dirt on Pratul. If we can get something on him, then he'll leave me alone. Maybe all I'll get is a letter in my file for going off my route. But if he keeps picking on me, I'm sure he'll get me fired."

Mazie imagined Addy was thinking about her daydreams. If Pratul knew she sometimes took a mental vacation while operating the bus, he could move for her dismissal.

"I've not found anything yet, Addy, but I'll keep looking."

Addy looked glum, and Mazie squeezed her hand. "It'll be okay."

She nodded and smiled.

As they walked to the restaurant, Nadine asked Mazie several questions related to the Bijou's financial situation and Almondine's actions. She finally said, "Did she agree to host an event?"

"Yes, sort of," Mazie replied.

Both Addy and Nadine looked at her quizzically and she explained Almondine's connection—and possible relationship—with Tarina Hudson, the actress.

"If you could get a premiere at the Bijou, it will put you on the map," Nadine said. "Do whatever you need to do to make it happen. Even if it's underhanded and deceitful. Almondine makes decisions slower than a slug. If I hadn't pushed her to purchase a state-of-the-art sound system two years ago, what few customers she'd still have would feel like they were watching a movie from the inside of a tin can."

They all laughed and Nadine opened the front door of Frank's Pizza. Again, she looked behind them as if she were waiting for someone.

"I'll go place the order and get drinks," Addy volunteered.

"No, it's my turn," Nadine said. She pointed to a bench. "Sit. And we have matters to discuss." Her tone was cryptic and piqued Mazie's curiosity.

Addy did as she was told, and Mazie said, "I'm going to hit the restroom. Be right back."

Mazie caught up to Nadine who was in line to order. "I need to talk with you—without Addy."

"What is it?"

"You know about Addy's suspension, right?"

"Yes, I'm working on it."

Mazie sighed. "That's great. Do you know the bus rider Addy was helping, Bianca?" Nadine nodded. "She and I did our own detective work today and made a video of Pratul hitting on her."

"You did? Where is it?"

"I have it. I just haven't had a chance to review it."

"Does it have video and audio?"

"Hopefully, if everything recorded correctly."

"Yes, it can be tricky. I can help you with that, and I'm dying to see what you captured." Nadine paused. "We could meet after pizza, unless you and Addy have other plans."

Her voice dripped with innuendo and Mazie blushed. "Well, actually I need to be back by eleven to help close the theater."

"Okay, I'll meet you there at eleven thirty."

"And I don't want Addy to know," Mazie added. "Not yet. I don't want her to get her hopes up."

Nadine squeezed her arm. "I understand." She looked over her shoulder. "Oh, look who finally got here."

Jackie slid in next to Addy and chatted with her while Nadine fumed. Mazie said, "I'm sensing some tension between you and Jackie. Is something wrong? Is there something I can do?"

Nadine's expression quickly shifted and she batted her eyelashes at Mazie. "It's nice of you to offer, but the problem is between me and Jackie." She lowered her gaze to the floor, and Mazie thought she mumbled, "I suppose it's really just my problem."

They returned to their table with a little plastic number and beers for the four of them. Jackie jumped up to give Nadine a hug, but Nadine quickly took the chair opposite Addy. Jackie leaned down and whispered something to Nadine, who remained as stiff and unresponsive as a mannequin.

The pizza arrived after an awkward fifteen minutes. Addy tried diligently to keep the conversation going, first praising Nadine for a terrific bout at the rink, and then talking about movies they had all seen. Mazie continually answered her questions so they didn't hang in the air, and Addy seemed oblivious to the situation, or she was so caught up in her favorite topic that she didn't care.

"Seriously, the best sex scene was in *When Night is Falling*," Addy said.

Mazie wiped her fingers on a napkin. "I'll agree that was one of the best, but my personal favorite is still *Tipping the Velvet*."

Addy nodded. "That was near the top of my list." Addy reached for another slice and asked, "What about least plausible plot?"

"Oh, so many there. I hate any movie where there's a professed lesbian character who goes back to her husband," Mazie said.

Her response got a chuckle from Jackie, who said, "You mean you don't like women who can't make up their mind?"

"I just don't think those women are lesbians. They're wannabes." She noticed the table had gone silent, and she worried she'd stepped in a topic landmine. "Look, I'm fine with bisexuality, but just call it, you know? Be who you are and not a poser."

"Interesting. I've known a few posers." Jackie shot a glare toward Nadine.

Mazie closed her mouth. She'd walked into a trap, and now she wanted to back out slowly, which would best be accomplished by saying nothing.

"A woman has every right to change her mind. That's what bisexuality is all about," Nadine said.

"That's not the same as straight women who experiment," Addy said.

"True," Nadine conceded, "but sometimes that experimentation leads a woman to shift her thinking about her own label. And the choices nowadays!" Nadine's face grew animated and she threw up her hands. "I love that we're breaking out of the old molds."

"Yeah," Addy agreed. "It's pretty cool."

Mazie bit her lip and slowly raised her hand. "Um, I'm showing my age here, but I don't get a lot of it. It's like a foreign language to me. What's Cis? And what's with the pronouns? Can I just be 'she' or am I required to pick another one? It's like someone changed the secret handshake and didn't tell me. Can't I just like someone and not worry about a label?"

She glanced at Addy, who wore a goofy expression. "Yes," was all she said.

Nadine leaned across the table and planted a surprising kiss on Mazie's cheek. "Miss Mazie, if everyone thought like you there wouldn't be a need for labels."

Mazie knew her face was bright red. "Thank you, Nadine."

"I don't get any of it," Jackie said, tossing her napkin on the table. "To me it's just gamesmanship. Everybody should just be straight up." Nadine laughed heartily and slapped the table. Jackie scowled. "You find that amusing?"

"Coming from you, yes," Nadine said. "You're not straight up at all, at least not with yourself."

Mazie was beginning to feel as though she was in a lesbian movie. She expected Jackie to say something like "explain yourself," but instead, Jackie just stood. "I'm going home. Any of you bitches want a ride, the train is leaving now."

The three women looked at each other, puzzled. "Jackie, chill," Addy said. She held up her third slice of pie. "I'm still eating. Can't we wait five more minutes?"

Still glaring at Nadine, Jackie said, "I'll meet you at the car. Five more, Addy, but then I'm gone."

After Jackie left Mazie turned to Addy and Nadine. "Um, explain?" Addy kept chewing, and motioned to Nadine, who sighed and fidgeted with her lovely gold necklace. "I like that," Mazie said.

"Thank you, Ms. M." Nadine waved a manicured hand at her. "I think that's my new nickname for you."

Mazie smiled. "I like it." She touched Nadine's hand. "What's up with you and Jackie? You two seem like best friends one minute and enemies the next. Is that frenemies?"

Nadine blinked several times, and Mazie could tell she was trying not to cry. "We're best friends and we both want more. But that would mean Jackie has to accept that I'm bisexual, in addition to being transgender. Jackie is biased against bisexuals. She thinks they should all just make up their mind. Her lack of acceptance is standing in our way. I've told her that as a bisexual, I might find I need more than just her. I'd never pick another woman over her," she said quickly, "but I might, *occasionally*, need a man to satisfy me. She can't see being with someone who is also with a man. We're at a standoff. So she has quickies or one-night stands, and I pine for her. And yes, once in a while I'll go to a straight bar and pick up a man." She pointed and said, "But I never go to Lolly's and pick up a woman. Never. I may be many things, but I'm not a hypocrite. Until she and I come to some conclusion about our relationship, I'm true to her."

Mazie nodded. "So the two of you have slept together?"

"Of course. That's how we know we're so right for each other. We're great friends, but the sex sealed the deal. No other woman could please me the way Jackie does." Mazie shifted uncomfortably and Nadine asked, "What are you thinking, Ms. M?"

She gazed at Nadine tenderly. "There's another way to look at this, but I don't think you'll like it, and you can probably guess what I'm going to say."

Nadine looked away. "Yes, I know."

"Well, I don't," Addy said, her mouth full. "Enlighten me."

Nadine's gaze went from Mazie to Addy. "I believe your delightful, prospective girlfriend believes that bisexuals have a greater challenge in relationships. We not only have to resist temptation from half of the proverbial fish in the sea, but from *all* the fish." Her gaze returned to Mazie. "Did I summarize correctly?"

"Yes, far more eloquently than I would have."

"That makes sense," Addy said, wiping her lips with her napkin. "She's not opposed to your bisexuality. She just wants you to be faithful."

Nadine rolled her eyes. "Leave it to you, kid, to call me an asshole—without really calling me an asshole."

Addy looked puzzled, and Nadine and Mazie laughed.

Mazie yawned. It was one thirty a.m. She and Nadine had spent two hours on Mazie's laptop, attempting to connect the audio to the video of Mazie and Bianca's surveillance of Pratul, but nothing worked.

"I don't know what happened," Mazie said. "I know she had it on, because I heard her through my earpiece."

Nadine patted her cheeks to keep awake. "There's not always an easy answer, Ms. M. I'll take this home and fiddle with it, but I think you and Bianca are the ones who got *stung* in your sting operation."

CHAPTER NINETEEN

"So you like this woman. How much? Think about that for a minute," Dr. Pfeiffer said to Addy before she turned and prepared for her croquet shot. With decent form and a smooth stroke from Dr. P., the blue ball sailed through the wicket and kissed Addy's green ball, knocking it further away from the next wicket.

This was how their sessions normally went. Addy hated the idea of sitting in Dr. P's home office on a couch while she extracted memories and fears from her conscious, subconscious, and any other cerebral crevice that might provide insight into her complicated psyche. So after their first session, which they both agreed was a dismal failure, Dr. P had looked for an alternate meeting place. They'd tried walking in the park (too distracting for Addy), kayaking on the river (too difficult for Addy, who couldn't steer her kayak and talk at the same time), and finally croquet in Dr. P's backyard, the winner. They played very slowly and with few rules, allowing Addy time to think about Dr. P's questions between shots but without the baggage of remembering the nuances of the game. And Dr. P's sprawling one-acre backyard guaranteed confidentiality.

"Well," Addy said, "I like her so much that lately my daydreams have changed."

Dr. P raised an eyebrow. "How so?"

"She's in them." Addy recounted the carnival dream that began with Bianca but ended with Mazie.

"Interesting," Dr. P said, preparing for her next shot. She tapped the ball just hard enough to line it up with the next wicket. Addy marveled at Dr. P's hand-eye coordination. Of course, Addy had never played croquet until she met Dr. Pfeiffer, and although still wasn't very good, she knew she was improving. Perhaps someday they would follow all the rules.

Addy set up her next shot and Dr. P asked, "Have you had any other dreams about her?"

"One. She was an Amazonian warrior, and I was about to make love to her." Addy tapped the ball with too much force and it sailed past her intended stopping point.

"And do you think the extinction of your daydreams and your increased involvement with Mazie are related?"

Addy shrugged. "Maybe. I think it's possible, don't you?"

"Oh, yes. We've previously connected your dreams to anxiety. You're nervous about your health coverage from Meritain, so Princess Meritain appears. Pratul catches you violating rules at the sauna. I don't even need my advanced degrees to see that one."

"No," Addy laughed.

"I hope they're related. A strong romantic relationship can indeed lessen our fears. We have someone we completely trust to confide in, help share the load, and who listens to us. Does that describe your relationship with Mazie?"

Addy felt the butterflies in her stomach. "Yeah, we talk about a lot of things, especially movies."

"How are you feeling about the suspension?" She pointed at the mallet Addy tapped against her foot. "I'm guessing you're nervous."

She stopped tapping and shrugged. "A little. I don't think they'll fire me because I broke the rules. I did it for a good reason. But I'll probably get a letter in my file."

"Do you think it's okay to break rules you don't like?"

"No, I think it's okay to break rules that are wrong, or it's okay to break rules that are wrong for certain people."

"Explain."

"It was wrong to make Bianca ride the bus with Pratul because of what he was doing to her. And since there wasn't a way to make him stop, all I could do was make it better for her."

"Do you break other rules for other people, or is it just people you have a crush on?"

"I don't have a crush on Bianca anymore, but I've bent some of the other rules to help passengers."

Dr. P stroked her chin. "Well, at least you're consistent." She whacked her ball through the last wicket and it came to stop just inches from the colorful peg in the middle of the course. She pointed to the rattan table surrounded by four matching chairs. "Can I infer the color issue is still as strong as ever?"

Addy's keys, which were on a blue keychain, sat next to Dr. P's blue purse. The two coffee mugs they'd carried out from the house—both red—sat next to each other. All by itself sat her backpack, the only lime green object. Addy nodded and looked down.

"I think it's time, Addy," Dr. P said gently. "We've talked about hypnosis for over a year. If we're ever going to tackle this, we have to explore the cause. I believe you don't remember when this color fixation started. It's obvious you've completely blocked it out. To help you move to a healthy mental state, we need to go back. Are you willing?"

"Yes," Addy whispered.

"Good," Dr. P replied. She tapped her ball against the center peg, essentially "winning" the game. She looked up and smiled. "I'm proud of you, Addy."

Before Addy left Dr. P's house, she made an appointment for hypnosis. For only the second time, they would meet in Dr. P's office, which still intimidated Addy, with all of Dr. P's degrees hanging behind her desk, the books with long scientific titles, and the seashell collection Dr. P kept on top of a bookcase. Unfortunately, none of the shells were grouped by color. Addy would need to make sure she sat with her back toward that bookcase, or she'd never be able to concentrate on anything.

Addy decided to walk up a few blocks and take the bus— her bus—to the Bijou. She missed her regulars, and since it was late morning, several of them should be on the bus or boarding soon.

As she approached the stop near Gallagher Hall, she saw Kit sitting under the shelter, knitting. When she recognized Addy, her face lit up in a smile. "Addy!"

Addy offered a hug and said, "Hi, Kit. How are you?"

"I'm fine." Her face hardened. "The question is, how are you?"

"I'm okay. I'm just waiting for my supervisor to conclude the mandatory investigation."

"Well, they better find the right conclusions, or I'll be having a word with the Wilshire Hills Transportation Department. Yes, I certainly *will*." She returned to her knitting with renewed vigor, and the needles clickety-clicked against each other. "I can't believe they would suspend the best driver they have. Absolutely ridiculous. When I worked at Cammon, some of the professors attempted similar shenanigans with women. It was a different time. When I was in charge, it didn't happen. Imagine that, huh?"

"I had no idea," Addy said. "Sexual harassment must've been really bad in the past."

"Oh, yes, but we didn't call it that. It was just boys being boys." She winked and added, "You did the right thing by Bianca. Just remember that."

"I will."

The bus pulled up and Addy motioned for Kit to get on first. Addy climbed the steps behind her, and Kit announced, "Look who I found!"

The whole bus cheered, including Addy's substitute driver, Wilma. She stuck out her hand and Addy shook it. "I'm praying for you, Addy. I'd love to take this route permanently, but you've earned it."

"Thanks, Wilma. Everything going okay?" she asked.

"It's fine, but every regular who gets on asks, 'when is Addy coming back?' I always tell 'em soon."

"I hope so."

She scanned the passengers and saw Mazie waving at her. Kit approached Mazie, who sat next to Weather and held Coda and Huxley. Kit asked for the seat and Mazie moved to a row near the back with two empty seats. Addy quickly joined her and gave her a hug.

"What are you doing on the bus?" Mazie asked.

"I was playing croquet."

Mazie raised an eyebrow. "Really?"

"Uh-huh." She bit her lip, unsure how Mazie would react when she learned Addy saw a shrink. Mazie continued to stare expectantly, so Addy whispered, "My therapist and I play croquet at her house."

Mazie's surprise was evident, and Addy wished she could take back the words until Mazie said, "Wow, your therapist plays croquet with you? How cool. I wonder if mine would consider something like that."

"You have a therapist?"

"Actually two. I had one back home and I started seeing a new one when I moved here. She's over on Jefferson Street."

Addy gasped. "My therapist is on Jefferson Street. What's your therapist's name?"

"Dr. Tingle." They both laughed and gazed at each other. Mazie looked concerned and said, "How are you doing? Is it weird to ride the bus?"

Addy sighed. "I like Wilma, and she asked me if I do anything special, so I told her about dropping off Weather and the kids wherever they need to go."

"That's good." Mazie looked toward Kit and the kids. Huxley was reading a book to Kit. They couldn't see Kit's reaction, but Addy was certain it was a look filled with love. "Why does everybody move so Kit can sit with Weather and the kids?" Mazie asked.

"Those are her grandchildren."

"They are?"

"Uh-huh. Kit and her wife aren't welcome in her son and daughter-in-law's house, so Weather arranges times for them to meet on the bus. Sometimes they get off together and sometimes they don't."

Mazie looked astounded. "This is the only way she sees her grandchildren? That's horrible."

"Shh," Addy said as Mazie's voice turned shrill. "It is horrible, but for now it's all they have."

"Why?"

"Kit came out much later in life. After her husband died in the eighties, she fell in love with another female professor at Cammon. Her fifteen-year-old son didn't take it very well. He got a lot of grief in high school. He went away to college and fell in love with this ultra-religious woman. They ended up coming back here because he's a religious studies professor. Kit got him a position at Cammon. But the wife won't see Kit or allow her in their house. Kit's son is a wuss and goes along with it."

"Does he know Weather is secretly bringing the kids to see her?"

"I think so, but I'm not sure."

"How awful that must be for her." She turned to Addy and planted a kiss on her cheek.

Addy felt the butterflies and knew she was blushing. "What was that for?"

"Because you're one of the best people I've ever met, Addy Tornado. I'm very proud to know you."

Addy sat up straighter. "Thank you, Mazie Midnight."

Mazie took Addy's hand and squeezed it. They stared at each other and Addy suddenly went to a different place. She saw the two of them in a field. A puppy ran toward them. They were on a blanket having a picnic. The puppy jumped into Mazie's arms and licked her face. Addy laughed and threw her arms around both of them.

"What are you thinking about?" Mazie asked. "You looked far away."

Addy blinked. "Yeah, but I wasn't. Not like other times. I was…just imagining the future."

"And that was different?"

"Completely."

Mazie leaned closer. "Was I in it…your future?"

"Yes."

CHAPTER TWENTY

Since Addy couldn't go to work, Mazie invited her to help at the Bijou. They found Almondine sitting in her office chair, her hands clenching both sides of her head—and groaning.

Mazie knew she couldn't be upset by the financials because she'd already had her red-bottom-line migraine for the current month. This had to be something else. "What's up?" she asked nonchalantly. Mazie had learned the best way to pull Almondine out of a funk was to ignore her dramatic urges.

She raised her head and said, "Just listen."

She pushed the message button on the oldest answering machine Mazie had ever seen. After much whirring and clicking the mechanical voice said she had two messages and the first one had come in at two-fourteen in the morning. When the recording began, Mazie heard the obvious sounds of traffic. The caller was in a car.

"Hey, this is a message for Mazie Midnight. Like your name, girlfriend. This is Tarina. You called and asked if I could do my premiere at the Bijou, where, apparently, the woman who walked out of my life without any warning, without a note, a fax, a singing telegram, or any facsimile of a goodbye, is the owner."

"She's so dramatic," Almondine interjected, and Mazie had to stifle a laugh.

"I've thought about your proposal for the last few weeks, and I've spoken with my manager as well as the film's producers. My manager knows if it's something I want to do, I'm gonna do it anyway, so he was chill. But the producers said no way in hell—until I explained who owned the theater, and if they want me to be in the obvious sequels to this movie, they needed to comply. Because if I don't want to do something, no amount of money, prestige, or promises is gonna move my ass. Tarina has other options."

Almondine waved her hand and leaned back in her chair. "Always so stubborn," she muttered.

Mazie's heart started to pound. Tarina was going to say yes!

"So, I'm gonna say yes," she continued, "but I've got some demands. I—"

The tape automatically cut out and a long beep sounded. "End of message," the mechanical voice said.

"Wait!" Mazie cried.

"Don't worry," Almondine said. "Tarina will always have the last word."

More whirring and clicking and the traffic sounds returned. "I got cut off, probably because Almondine is too damn cheap to use real voice mail. You've still got that ancient answering machine, don't you Deenie?"

"Deenie?" Addy asked.

Almondine frowned at the nickname.

"Anyway, here are my demands before the freakin' thing cuts me off again." Mazie immediately grabbed a pad of paper and a pen. "I want a room at a nice place for two nights. I expect a bottle of pinot gris from a great Oregon winemaker—you pick—and most important, what I want...is an apology and an explanation. From you, Almondine. Mazie, let me know if this is gonna work, and then my people will reach out." The mechanical voice told them it was the end of messages.

Addy and Mazie looked at Almondine. Her eyes were closed and she was pale. "I cannot do this," she said with a long exhale. "This is too much."

"What's too much?" Mazie asked. "Apologizing? Explaining yourself? What if it saves the Bijou?"

Almondine swiveled so her back was to them. "It was so long ago."

Mazie marched behind the desk and stood in front of her. "I get that, Almondine, and I imagine between now and when Tarina visits, you have some reflection to do. But she's an A-list celebrity who's agreed to premiere her movie at our little theater. Here. At the Bijou. We'll have people from all over Oregon coming for that. Everyone will know about us. As a historic landmark, we can accept donations, we'll get bigger films, and we will, once and for all, solve the financial difficulties."

Almondine said nothing, despite Mazie hovering over her, arms crossed, for nearly a minute. She looked shell-shocked, and Mazie imagined whatever had happened to their relationship had devastated both of them, perhaps in different ways. But they were stuck. Almondine was alone, and as far as Mazie knew, Tarina didn't have a significant other. Mazie felt a knot in her throat. She never wanted this to happen to her. She glanced over at Addy, who stared at her with an odd expression.

"You think about it," Mazie said. She stormed away, grabbing Addy's hand and pulling her out of the office.

Once the door was closed, Addy said, "Wow. This is just a wow day for a lot of things."

Mazie touched the wall as the room spun, or at least she thought the room might be spinning. Addy moved beside her and rubbed her back.

"Are you okay?" Addy asked.

Mazie shook her head. "I don't ever want to be Almondine. I don't ever want a love that strong to die."

Addy pulled them together and kissed her deeply. "Me either."

Mazie knew she could say important words and mean them, but she worried it was too soon. Both of them had issues lying on their respective tables—Addy's color issue and Mazie's stage fright. They needed to finish working on themselves before they could be good together.

A knock sounded at the Bijou's front door. Mazie checked her watch. It was ninety minutes before the first show, which meant thirty minutes before the doors opened.

"Who could that be?" she asked.

"Maybe it's FedEx?"

Mazie shrugged and headed for the door, which was equipped with an old-fashioned peephole. She twisted the level and a tiny door opened. It was Nadine. Shoot! She'd forgotten Nadine was coming back this morning to play with the footage and see if she could retrieve Bianca's audio of Pratul. She'd naturally invited Addy to the Bijou, forgetting her clandestine meeting with Nadine.

"Good morning," Nadine said. "We've got to talk."

Addy stuck her head up near the peephole. "Hey, Nadine. What are you doing here?"

Nadine looked surprised, but Mazie just sighed and shrugged. There wasn't any way to keep this from Addy. Nadine had a box in hand and headed straight for Theater One. "We need to view this in private," she said.

They followed her to the small stage at the front of Theater One. She opened her laptop and connected an external drive and a thumb drive. Once all the cables were connected and the laptop was powered up, she turned to Mazie and Addy and said, "I think you're about to get your job back."

"I am?" Addy jumped up and down and fist-pumped the air. Then she looked quizzically at both of them. "How? Why?"

Mazie put an arm around her shoulder. "Well, I wasn't going to share this with you until I was sure it would help… Bianca and I did some surveillance yesterday. We got on Pratul's bus separately, and I taped him making sexual advances to her."

"That's great!" Addy cried.

"No," Nadine disagreed. "That's not so great. That part didn't go well. Something happened to the audio, and it went into the great vortex of unexplainable technological problems.

Mazie, what Pratul said wasn't captured on the audio, so basically we have a silent movie."

Addy sighed and leaned against the stage. "Well, it was worth a try. I've been thinking about other things I can do—"

"No, no." Nadine waved a hand. "I didn't say the whole effort was a bust. No, no, not at all." She tapped her keyboard and the movie started.

After thirty seconds of Pratul looking at his cuticles, Addy said, "Why isn't he driving? Why is the bus sitting at Stop Two?"

"So that is weird, right?" Mazie asked.

"Definitely," Addy said. "He's got a schedule to keep."

"When I got on, he said some flirty things to me, and I took my seat, but the bus didn't move. I thought maybe he was waiting for a regular, but then this Pontiac Firebird pulled up next to the bus." The film showed the man with the backpack climbing up the steps. Mazie pointed and said, "That guy got on and it was strange. He mentioned being lost and needing directions."

"Watch closely," Nadine instructed.

The three of them saw the man set his backpack next to the console while Pratul opened a map and pointed at locations. The man thanked him and left. Pratul closed the door and started to drive.

"He didn't take the backpack!" Mazie exclaimed.

"Ding, ding, ding," Nadine said. "We have a winner." She paused the film and pointed to the backpack that sat next to Pratul. "He left it."

"Why?" Addy asked.

Nadine held up a hand. "Oh, all will be made clear, young Skywalker."

Addy chuckled at the reference. Mazie could tell she was giddy at the prospect of keeping her job.

"Now," Nadine continued, "I'm fast forwarding to two stops later. Pratul left the backpack alone, Mazie, probably because you were the only one on the bus, and he was worried you'd get suspicious if he moved it. I'll tell you, this guy is good. But watch what happens three stops later."

Pratul opened the door and quickly moved the backpack from his right side to his left, which was obstructed by the wall that separated the driver from the passengers. He occasionally looked over his shoulder and greeted some of the passengers, but he remained hunkered down, his back to the front door, at least thirty seconds after the last passenger boarded.

"He's not moving again," Addy said. "I know I probably shouldn't talk about being late, but he's just as bad."

Mazie leaned closer. "I remember thinking something similar, wondering who he was waiting for."

"He wasn't waiting for anyone," Nadine said. "Watch."

Pratul sat up straight, and he set a water bottle and an apple on the console next to him.

"He's making it look like he reached into his lunchbox," Nadine commented. "But he didn't just get out his lunch. Watch what happens at the next stop."

The ride continued uneventfully to the next stop. Five passengers stood to disembark. As they left, Pratul shook each hand.

"Watch this last man," Nadine said, tapping a figure on her computer screen. "The short guy."

Just before the young guy reached him, Pratul turned away and coughed. The young man slowed, as if he wanted to shake Pratul's hand. When Pratul turned back, he clasped the young man's hand in both of his before the young man disembarked.

"He gave him something," Mazie said. "It was a handoff."

Nadine smiled proudly. "Mazie, darling, I'd love for you to be my assistant. Between your steady videotaping skills and keen eye, we could make a great team."

"Really?"

"Really." She pointed at her. "Think about it."

Mazie glanced at a grinning Addy. She'd never considered a career as a private eye. Then she remembered this wasn't about her and turned serious. "So what did he give the guy, and how does this help Addy?"

Nadine minimized the video, tapped a few keys and three pictures appeared on the screen. "I won't bore you with the other twenty-six minutes of footage you captured, Mazie, but Pratul's coughing fit and the two-handed handshake happen thirteen more times. Here's what we know."

Nadine expanded the first picture to full screen. It was a picture of the guy with the backpack. "I took this movie to the narcotics division of the Wilshire Hills Police Department, who immediately involved Portland PD. This man," she said pointing at the photo, "is Gus del la Cruz, a known drug supplier." She tapped on the second photo, a close-up of the short, young man. "This is Bill Wambucher. His street name is Jump. He's a dropout and a user. He's also already got two strikes against him for possession. Detectives picked him up early this a.m., and not so surprising, he was high and holding. He was more than happy to work a deal, rather than get a third a strike. Here's how Pratul's scheme works. Every Wednesday Gus meets Pratul at Stop Two." Nadine looked at Mazie. "You were a surprise. They didn't expect you to be there, so Pratul improvised as a helpful bus driver giving directions to a lost citizen. Del la Cruz leaves the backpack, which has Pratul's order for all of his customers."

"So Bump was right," Addy said.

"Who's Bump?" Mazie asked.

"He's the guy who told me Pratul was dealing." She sighed. "This is just unbelievable."

"I know, honey," Nadine said sympathetically. She clicked the third picture, a blow-up of the apple sitting on the console. "According to Jump, this is Pratul's signal that he's open for business. His customers know that when they disembark, they shake his hand. They give him cash folded into a tiny square—no more than two bills—and he gives them a baggie of Oxy, all under the guise of extraordinary customer service—a handshake."

Addy stamped her foot. "He actually got a commendation for that stupid handshaking. Made it sound like he knew his regulars better than anybody else."

"Oh, he knew these people," Nadine interjected. "But it didn't have anything to do with customer service on the bus."

"What happens next?" Mazie asked.

Nadine checked her watch. "I imagine right about now they're checking Pratul's bank records. About lunchtime he'll be quietly relieved of duty and taken to jail. They hope he'll roll over on Gus. It's always about the big players. If we don't cut off the supply and just put the low-level scum like Pratul in jail, we never stop the cycle. I'm sure he'll cut a deal for Gus to get a more lenient sentence." Nadine beamed at Mazie. "You and Bianca are freakin' heroes."

Addy fell back in her seat glumly. "I don't understand how this helps me with my job."

"I talked with Jackie this morning. The Wilshire Hills Transportation Department is just as concerned with public relations as any other business. They want to completely wash their hands of anything having to do with Pratul. According to Jump, he's been buying from Pratul for nearly two years. The fact that nobody caught on is disconcerting, to say the least."

"Is Jackie going to be in trouble?" Mazie asked.

Nadine shook her head. "Doubtful. She wasn't the one who promoted him, and she's only been his supervisor for the last year. She had no reason to suspect him. He was very good at staying under the radar." She paused and smiled at Addy. "Anyhoo, according to Jackie, whatever complaints he issued will be thrown out. The most that'll happen is you'll get a stern warning, but she thinks you'll be back on your route by tomorrow."

Mazie whooped and threw her arms around Addy. Nadine joined the celebratory hug and they all jumped up and down.

"I can't believe it!" Addy shouted, almost in tears. "Thank you so much, Nadine."

"You're welcome, but I'm not the person who made the movie." She nudged Mazie's shoulder. "That would be this one."

Addy and Mazie gazed into each other's eyes, and Mazie felt the butterflies fluttering faster than ever. "Thank you," Addy said, before she pulled Mazie into a hug and a deep kiss. Who cared if Nadine saw? Mazie thought she heard Nadine say something about becoming a private investigator, but she wasn't sure and didn't care. In that moment, all she wanted was Addy's touch.

CHAPTER TWENTY-ONE

Addy was on a high for the rest of the day. The kiss with Mazie was the best of her life. Then she got the best phone call of her life—from Jackie. She confirmed that Addy should be back at work tomorrow morning. She would have a Letter of Reprimand in her file, but that was as far as the Transportation Department would take the issue. Jackie had personally sought out Bianca at work and introduced her to her new driver, Addy's friend Wilma.

While Addy was sorry the ever happy and cheerful Bianca would no longer be on her bus, she was happy for Wilma and relieved she no longer had to violate such an important department policy. Of course, there were still a few other policies Addy intended to bend, like making random stops on the route to pick up her elderly passengers or helping Weather deal with her COPD by stopping as close to her destination as possible.

Jackie also recounted Pratul's arrest. He had pulled up to Stop Nineteen. Jackie, Wilma, and three fine members of the

Wilshire Hills Police Department boarded the bus. He was read his rights, handcuffed and escorted off the bus to a police car. Wilma picked up the radio and announced she'd be finishing the route and was proud to be their new permanent driver. Thunderous applause followed, and Addy realized a lot of passengers saw through Pratul's act and knew he wasn't sincere about customer service.

The evening proved to be equally as wonderful. She stayed at the Bijou and helped Mazie run the concessions stand using their new protocol—saying the names of the patrons they knew.

"Nice to see you, Carlos," Mazie said as she handed him his popcorn, drink, and candy.

Carlos smiled and said, "Gracias, Miss Mazie."

Addy realized Mazie had learned more than fifty percent of all the customers' names. "You could be a bus driver," she said once the concessions area cleared and everyone was in the theater watching the movie.

Mazie kissed her cheek. "You are so sweet, Addy."

Addy offered a shy smile and shrugged. "Thanks."

Mazie pulled her into the janitor's closet and closed the door. "I'm finding it harder and harder to watch you and not touch you," she whispered. "It's just like *Desert Hearts*, where they are constantly tortured by each other's physical presence, but they can't do anything about it."

Before she could agree, Mazie kissed her and plunged her tongue deep into her mouth. She caressed Mazie's buttocks and pushed her against the wall. Mazie unbuttoned Addy's shirt and cupped her breasts. Their pelvises ground against each other. And suddenly Mazie stopped.

"What?" Addy cried out. "Don't you want—"

"I do," Mazie said. She buttoned up Addy's shirt and looked around. "But not here." She cupped Addy's face and said, "I don't want your first time to be in a disgusting closet, like we're hiding. Surrounded by mops and the smell of disinfectant."

Addy nodded. She stroked Mazie's soft cheek and stared into her eyes. She could look at those eyes every day for the rest of her life. For the first time she felt truly loved, even though they hadn't said the words yet. She finally got it.

"You look like you want to say something," Mazie asked gently.

She licked her lips. She wanted to explain. It was like puzzle pieces. They were all on the table, but… "The words aren't in the right order yet. Is that okay?"

Mazie nuzzled her nose against Addy's. "It's absolutely okay. You let me know when they line up correctly."

"I will."

Mazie sighed. She checked the time on her phone and stuck it back in her pocket before giving Addy's hands a squeeze. "Okay, it's time."

Addy grinned. "This is gonna be great." She flung open the closet and they headed back to Theater One.

"I hope so," Mazie said nervously. "I feel like Sally Field in *Norma Rae* when she stood on the table in front of everyone and gave that speech."

Addy opened the door to Theater One. "You'll be better than that."

They crept down the side aisle as the final scene of the movie concluded. The music swelled and the screen faded to black. Some patrons clapped while the credits rolled. A few gathered their things and left, but many stayed through the credits, not because they were curious to know the identity of the set designer, but because prior to the movie, Addy had shared that there would be a special short performance after the feature film, and this performance was included in the price of their admission. Of course, most people loved getting something for free, so Addy guessed a lot would stay—and she was right.

Once the credits finished, she immediately jumped on the stage and pulled a microphone from the wings. "Thanks to all of you for hanging around. My friend Mazie Midnight would like to share a special song to end your evening at the Bijou. Please help me welcome Mazie Midnight."

The crowd politely applauded as it would for any performer who had yet to prove herself. Addy handed Mazie the microphone, and to her own surprise, kissed Mazie on the cheek, which incited a collective, "aww" from the crowd. Addy hustled into the second row, moving to the center aisle. Here she could see Mazie, but more importantly, Mazie could see her—and focus on her if the stage fright overwhelmed her, as it had the night before, and the night before that.

This was Mazie's tenth attempt at singing "It Had to Be You." Addy took heart that each night Mazie had sung a few lines more than the night before. The audience was always kind when suddenly the beautiful notes disappeared, like someone had abruptly turned off a CD player. Mazie would mumble a heartfelt, "I'm sorry," and flee from the stage. She'd run out the back door of the Bijou, unable to confront the sympathetic eyes of the patrons. Undoubtedly amongst the moviegoers was a strong contingency of patrons who could never stand in front of a crowd and do anything.

As Mazie crooned the first line, Addy was lifted on a magic carpet ride that traveled across the tops of the notes. Addy had heard the song so many times that she knew what came next, but ironically she hadn't memorized the lyrics—except for those first few words. The magic carpet transported her away from the Bijou, Mazie beside her. She was wearing the blue dress Addy loved, her cheeks rosy after they kissed and her lips bright red from the silky lipstick she reapplied throughout the day. As long as she sang, their carpet floated on air, soaring skyward with the highest notes, picking up speed with the beat. They held hands, kissed, and touched as the song grew bolder, stronger. As she sang the final notes, the carpet coasted across a shimmering sea, and glided to rest on a sandy beach.

The last notes. The end. Mazie had done it!

Roaring applause brought Addy to her feet. Everyone was clapping. Mazie was bowing as tears rolled down her cheeks. She'd sung the entire song. She blew a kiss to Addy, who realized she was crying as well.

Addy wanted to climb on top of the Bijou and scream, "Mazie Midnight is the greatest singer in the world!" But she knew the citizens of Wilshire Hills who were at home, although they might agree, wouldn't be pleased to hear such a communication this late in the evening. Most were asleep, and those who were awake were probably enjoying *The Jimmy Fallon Show*. No, she'd wait until an opportune time.

Addy's heart was ready to burst. She'd never known she could *feel* this happy for another person. Maybe it was just another way she loved Mazie. Maybe love wasn't a one- or two-theater movie house. Maybe love was a multiplex.

After three more bows and another thank-you, Mazie replaced the microphone in its stand, raised her chin and trotted down the center aisle stairs with pride. She immediately looped her arm through Addy's and they slowly made their way toward the exit. People stopped and thanked her for such a lovely performance. She shook hands with all those who reached out, basking in the glory of her triumph.

Once the crowd had exited and the Bijou was quiet, another round of clapping ensued. Almondine stood outside her office shouting, "Brava! Brava, Mazie Midnight!"

Mazie ran to her and threw her arms around her. Addy couldn't hear what they said, but no doubt it was high praise from one performer to another. Almondine pulled Mazie against her and kissed the top of her head the way a mother would do for a child. Well, the way most mothers would—not Addy's, but most.

Almondine said a few more words to her, squeezed her hands and kissed her cheek before retreating upstairs. Mazie stared at Addy and took a deep breath. Then she flew back into her arms. She whispered, "Thank you. Thank you for believing in me. Thank you for your help. I'd never have been able to finish that song without you, Addy."

"Yes, you would," Addy disagreed.

"No." She held Addy at arm's length and said, "I watched you the entire time while I sang. At first I thought you'd gone away to some other place—"

"No, I didn't. I—"

"I know. I realized you were still with me because your eyes were closed. You were swaying in time to the music, and it was like you were dancing in your seat. I knew it was real."

"It was."

Addy pulled Mazie against her and kissed her passionately. She knew she was ready to be with Mazie, and a collage of sex scenes played in her mind. She doubted she would be as skilled as anyone in the movies, and she doubted Mazie would proclaim her as the best lover she'd ever had, but she could tell Mazie loved her enough to make it all right.

But she ended the kiss and pulled away.

Mazie looked confused. She touched Addy's cheek. "Not tonight? You don't want to stay."

"I do," Addy said quickly. "I really do, but…Tonight is about conquering your stage fright. You did it. I want that to be the memory of tonight. We'll make a new memory of our first time."

Mazie offered a lazy smile. "Well, there was the action in the janitor's closet."

"Yeah, but that was just the preview. That wasn't the feature."

Mazie nuzzled her earlobe and whispered. "I like the way you think, Addy Tornado."

Addy whimpered when Mazie said her name, and her knees slightly buckled. Too much more and she was sure she'd melt into a puddle at Mazie's feet.

"But let's be clear," Mazie continued. "When we finally make love, it'll be a double feature—at least."

CHAPTER TWENTY-TWO

Addy awoke to Mazie's singing. She bolted upright in bed, thinking they had slept together, but when she glanced at the pillow beside her, she realized it was all in her head. She had replayed Mazie's wonderful performance. She sighed, both grateful and remorseful that Mazie wasn't with her. She scratched her head, contemplating what it would be like to have Mazie snuggled against her. She'd never spent the night with a woman. She pushed the notion away and focused on Mazie's performance the night before.

Addy had managed to sneak a few glances at the Bijou audience while they watched Mazie. Everyone seemed equally enraptured by her voice. It was the most beautiful performance of "It Had to be You" Addy had ever heard, the perfect marriage of a voice in the right key, singing the right notes. Mazie's voice never strained. She hugged the song with both arms, somewhat similar to the way she'd hugged Addy in the janitor's closet...

She grinned and a blob of toothpaste landed on her sock. Smiling and teeth brushing didn't go together. And now, apparently, neither would her uniform and her socks. She'd just soiled the last perfectly matched pair of clean socks she had. She'd be forced to go with a backup pair. Normally such a shift could make her very nervous throughout the day, thinking her feet didn't match the rest of her outfit, but today she didn't care. She hummed "It Had to be You" as she ate her plain yogurt and checked the news on her phone. She was excited for her work day, grateful to have the suspension behind her—and Pratul gone. It would be much different walking through the Bull Pen. Some of the guys would probably be upset with her, since she imagined they would figure she was the reason he was fired. But they would know the truth once the trial began. A secret that big in little Wilshire Hills wouldn't be kept.

She took the time to pack a lunch since she would actually have a lunch break now that Bianca rode Wilma's bus, free of harassment. The "oven mitt" had officially lost its thumb. She grabbed her bag and was headed toward the door when her phone rang.

She stopped with her hand on the doorknob. There was only one person who called her this early in the morning. Her mother. She was calling "to chat," which was a tremendous understatement to describe the verbal tongue lashings Addy received during their calls. But what if it were something else? What if Cousin Ike was hurt? What if their ramshackle house had burned down? What if her mother was just calling to acknowledge her recent birthday?

She took a deep breath and debated answering. "Hello, Mama."

"What took you so long? Thought I was going to wind up on voice mail, and you know how I hate that shit."

"I know. I was leaving for work."

"On Sunday? Buses run on Sunday?"

"It's not Sunday, Mama." She bit her lip. Three hours ahead meant it was only nine a.m. in West Virginia, and her mother was obviously drinking.

"Aw, hell. It's not Sunday. Well, good. That means I didn't miss church. You know how I feel about church," she said, laughing hysterically. "Guess I won't get to heaven this week."

"I doubt it matters, Mama."

"Figures, coming from you."

She closed her eyes. She refused to be baited. She set her lunchbox on the table and dropped onto the sofa. She rubbed her forehead, hoping the action might bring Mazie's voice back. "It Had to be You" had played so clearly just a few minutes ago, but it had disappeared, smothered by Lorene Tornado.

"Well, what's going on?"

"Nothing. Just on my way to work. It's six. I can't be late."

"Of course not. Wouldn't want to displease the Man. Be late once and you're out."

She didn't bother to correct her. Dr. Pfeiffer called it transference, and they had discussed (at length) Lorene's inability to separate her own life, where she had indeed been fired from a job for being late once, from Addy's. Dr. Pfeiffer had explained Lorene believed she was in competition with Addy, jealous that Addy had escaped the darkness of their West Virginia life. She distinctly heard the burp of a pop top as her mother opened a beer.

"Pretend you're me," Dr. Pfeiffer said. "You're the counselor and your mother is the patient. Hear my voice and perhaps you won't lose your own."

Addy closed her eyes. Her mother was blabbering about the idiot Congress trying to end her disability benefits, the neighbor down the road and his yapping dog, and, her favorite topic, Oren, Addy's dead brother.

"He visited me last week in a dream. Did you know that?"

"No, Mama. I didn't."

"Know what he said?"

"No," she whispered, but she knew what was coming.

"He said it was your fault."

She closed her eyes but it didn't prevent the tears. She wiped them away only to have more drip down the front of her shirt. She smacked her forehead. Where was Mazie's voice? Where was Dr. Pfeiffer? *Pretend you're me.*

"I doubt he said that, Mama. Oren knew how much I loved him."

"Ya think so? Well, he loved me more."

"Of course he did. You were his mama and gave him life."

"That's right!" Lorene shouted. Addy heard slurping as her mother lubricated her throat with the Schlitz. "So why did he leave? Why'd he have to go and get shot? Those damn ragheads! The president oughtta dump a fuckin' plane full of nukes on those godless countries!"

"Just let her play her tape," Dr. Pfeiffer had said. *I can do that.*

"It shoulda been you! What kind of god takes the world's greatest son and leaves a skinny-assed lesbian, one who runs off and abandons her mama?"

"I have to hang up now, Mama. I can't be late for work," she added, which was certainly the truth. She didn't want to be late on the first day back from suspension. How would that look to Jackie? She wondered if somehow her mama knew about the suspension. *How could she?* There were times during her childhood when she was certain her mama had a sixth sense. Of course, that was before Oren's death, before Addy came out (or rather, was forced out), before...before...*that.*

"Mama, I'm hanging up now." When Lorene didn't reply, Addy checked the display. Her mother had hung up.

When she arrived at work—late—she had no recollection of riding the six miles. It was her mother's version of hypnosis. Lorene had the ability to suck every thought—everything, especially the good things—from Addy's brain. She was a powerful emotional vacuum cleaner, and all Addy could hope was that after these horrible phone conversations, her mother received some sort of spiritual and emotional lift. Perhaps, as Dr. Pfeiffer had suggested, a peephole—not a door or window because that would be too much to expect—of Lorene Tornado's heart opened, and for a few minutes she saw goodness and optimism.

Hopefully her mother felt better after those conversations, because Addy lost the rest of the day, sometimes multiple days. She couldn't help but believe everything her mother said. Oren had died because of her. She was a terrible daughter for leaving her medically frail, alcoholic, and bipolar mother alone. It didn't matter what Dr. Pfeiffer told her. She was an awful person.

Dr. Pfeiffer had suggested she not answer the phone. Addy tried that once, but Lorene, on medical disability, had nothing but time. In a single day she'd called two hundred and forty-two times.

Addy traipsed past Jackie's office, not offering a cursory glance to see if Jackie cared that she was tardy. Addy doubted she would care any time soon.

She sauntered through the Bull Pen and clocked in. Laughter erupted from one of the nearby break tables and someone called out to her, "Isn't that right, Addy?"

She turned toward the voice, a younger, bald guy whose name she didn't know, but who had bragged about going to the white supremacist march in North Carolina. She said nothing, trying not to engage.

"I said, 'isn't that right?'"

She shrugged. "What? I wasn't paying any attention to you. Who are you?"

A few of Baldy's friends chuckled, and his grin transformed to a scowl. "I'm Clovis. And I said, muff divers don't own any razors. They like hair everywhere. That's how you know your date's a lezzie." His grin returned, begging for her to respond.

She laughed. "Lezzie? Who the hell uses *lezzie* anymore? You been talkin' to your grandma? Is she the one who gives you dating advice?" A few more chuckles emerged from Baldy's tablemates and his grin cracked. "Does she wipe your ass too? And what kind of name is Clovis? Definitely a name for a guy with a tiny penis. Is that the common trait for you and the other Hitler youth?"

His face turned red. "Shut up, bitch."

"Who's gonna make me, *Clovis?*" She stepped into his personal space and sniffed. "Just what I thought. You smell like a coward."

"Fuck you!"

He pushed her and Addy stepped back calmly and put her hands in her pockets. He pulled back his hand to punch her, and his tablemates grabbed his arms and restrained him.

"Bitch!" he shouted.

Jackie rushed into the room and yelled, "What the hell?"

Devoid of compassion, empathy, and wisdom, a different Addy Tornado responded. "Clovis told me lezzies don't shave or own razors because we're muff divers and we like a good bush." She shot him a look. "Have I got that right, Clovis?" The men looked away and said nothing, too embarrassed to continue the harassment in front of their lesbian supervisor. Addy shook her head, disgusted. She unbuckled her belt.

"Addy, what are you doing?" Jackie asked.

"I just thought I should check," she said, unzipping her uniform pants and pulling them open slightly.

"Addy!" Jackie hissed.

"I don't think my bush is any bigger than any other woman's. Clovis, I believe your research is flawed."

She zipped her pants and sauntered out of the room, Jackie close behind. When they reached her office, she pulled Addy inside and slammed the door shut. "What the hell was that? Are you *trying* to get fired? Your suspension just ended!"

Addy's lip trembled. The bravado had worn off, but she didn't feel like herself. She knew it was her mother talking, like a poison she ingested over the phone. It was in her and it would just have to wear off in time.

Jackie paced. She stopped and turned. "Your mother called, didn't she? Whenever you get like this—whenever you turn into a bitch—it's because of her."

Addy simply nodded. Jackie knew bits and pieces about the interactions between Addy and her mom, and she'd certainly been on the receiving end of the painful backlash. Jackie waved a hand. "Get out of here," she mumbled. "But Addy, you've got to keep it together with the passengers. Please don't make me suspend you again."

Addy headed out to the bus bay. After a rather apathetic precheck that would have displeased the safety inspectors, she left the depot. Normally the sunrise, the promise of a new day, and the awakening of her town was enough to improve her mood. But not today. She offered pleasant smiles to everyone who boarded, and when a few of her observant regulars inquired if she was all right, she offered believable reassurances. Like most strangers, they only asked the question to be nice. They didn't really want the truth. Addy could see that now. Her mother always helped her see how things were.

During her lunch break she left a message with Dr. Pfeiffer's service, telling Dr. Pfeiffer she was canceling the hypnosis appointment. Once she hung up she stared at her phone. "I don't need it."

CHAPTER TWENTY-THREE

After Mazie replied to Tarina Hudson's phone message, assuring her they would meet all of her needs, including an apology from "Deenie," she received an official acceptance from Dewan Bird, Tarina's publicist. He explained that from now on Mazie would work with him exclusively, and she should no longer phone Ms. Hudson. Mazie disliked Mr. Bird's heavy-handedness, but she imagined a lot of people wanted something from Tarina Hudson.

He explained that what would happen at the Bijou was a "soft" premiere. While the Bijou would indeed be the first theater where *S.W.A.T. 2018* was viewed, he would control most of the guest list. Mazie pushed back slightly, although she knew she had zero bargaining power—but she could be persuasive. She convinced Dewan to give her thirty tickets, three of which were allocated for herself, Almondine who was to sit next to Tarina per her request, and Addy. Tango would serve as the stage manager and handle guest issues with Mazie's support.

Mazie knew something was wrong with Addy when she told her they would watch the premiere with Tarina and Almondine. She'd expected Addy would be over the moon since Tarina was one of her favorite actresses. Yet all Addy replied was, "Cool." She also became less available, which Mazie didn't notice at first since Dewan emailed her a fifty-item to-do list after their one phone conversation. Running the Bijou, stressing about her performance, and crossing off Dewan's to-do list kept her moving from morning to night. She had to secure lodging for Tarina and her entourage, handle all of the local publicity, and plan the after-party, since Dewan insisted all premieres were followed by a party. Each item encompassed ten more to-dos, and Almondine was of minimal help, too lost in her anxiety about seeing Tarina again. Fortunately, Tango was a lifesaver and did anything Mazie asked.

Noticeably missing was Addy, but for good reason. Two days after their little hookup in the janitor's closet, Addy had texted Mazie that she was studying to become a trainer. This involved attending several after-hour classes, perusing all the training videos and eventually passing an exam. Mazie congratulated her with several emojis, and while she was thrilled that Addy was moving up in the transportation world, she would miss seeing her. Still, she hoped they could find an hour here and there over the next few weeks before the premiere. She wanted some more lessons from Dr. Smooch.

But whenever she found a sliver of time and fired off a spontaneous message, asking for a brief face-to-face, Addy either didn't reply in time or didn't reply at all. It was like a tiny itch Mazie ignored rather than scratch, and inevitably the premiere planning and her own anxieties hijacked her mind and she wound up back in the whirlwind. And once the publicity began, she was inundated with requests for tickets from the townspeople and strong-armed by the Wilshire Hills elite, all of whom promised to help the Bijou after the premiere was over.

Who should get the extra tickets? Mazie texted to Addy one afternoon.

??? was Addy's reply.

Mazie smirked. Addy must be busy with passengers. Usually she was so helpful. She texted back, *No idea? What about the mayor? She should probably get one, right? But does her husband get one too? Maybe I could say something about this being an official event. What do you think?*

IDK!!!

Mazie stared at Addy's terse reply and knew something was seriously wrong. Three exclamation points. A punctuation mark Addy detested because it was so overused and often implied rudeness. And Mazie certainly thought it was rude in this text. Addy wasn't rude to her. Ever.

She hadn't seen Addy for nearly three weeks, and she wondered if she really was studying to become a trainer, or if, for some reason, she was avoiding Mazie. Maybe the hot and heavy action in the closet had been too much for her. Maybe she realized she wasn't attracted to an older, somewhat dumpy, over forty woman? Mazie thought about phoning Jackie, but she didn't know her well enough and it would be uncomfortable since Jackie might still be crushing over Addy.

She decided to call Nadine, who she'd already tapped to be in charge of premiere security. Although Mazie didn't have time to do anything except finish the to-do list before Tarina arrived, she found twenty minutes to meet Nadine for a brief coffee at First Espresso.

Nadine was already there when Mazie blew in. She pulled Mazie into a hug and whispered, "How are you?"

"I'm okay," she said.

Nadine gestured to the two cups on her table. "I know how busy you are, so I took the liberty of ordering for you."

"Thank you," Mazie sighed.

"What's up?"

"I'm worried about Addy." She showed Nadine the text and explained her anxieties. "Maybe she's just stressing over the trainer's test? I know she's been studying like crazy at the library."

Nadine peered over her cup. "No, she hasn't."

"What? She told me she was going to the library each evening and studying the policies and procedures manual. That's why she hasn't been at the Bijou lately."

Nadine shook her head slowly. "I hate to break it to you, but I've been there for the past week, surveilling one of the librarians. Her husband thinks she's having an affair, which she is. But that's not the point. I've been all over that building, and I've never seen Addy."

Mazie rubbed her eyes. She felt a migraine coming on. "I scared her off. That has to be it."

"What do you mean?"

Mazie gave Nadine a sanitized version of the tryst in the janitor's closet. "Almost immediately after that, we didn't see each other. I just didn't realize it was happening because this whole premiere thing has swallowed me. I don't have time for anything else."

"What about practicing for your test?"

Mazie looked away and shook her head.

Nadine dropped her cup noisily into the saucer and Mazie jumped. "No. That is unacceptable. Your test is in less than a month. You have to be ready."

She had nothing to say. She'd put the test on the back burner to save the Bijou—for Addy and Almondine. It was an easy excuse not to face her fears.

Nadine wiped up the coffee that had sloshed out of the cup and said, "It will always be something, Mazie. There will always be a reason why you can't do what you most need to do and don't want to do. Always. Now, I will find out what the hell is going on with Addy. You promise me that starting tonight you will resume your singing in front of Bijou audiences after the show."

"I don't know—"

"Yes, you do." Nadine took her hand. "Listen to me. People are talking about you. They're talking about the little added performance Bijou theatergoers are experiencing after the last show. They love your singing. I can't imagine how disappointed some people must have been these last few weeks, staying all the way through the credits, especially the really boring ones, only to learn you weren't going to perform." Mazie knew she was right. A few people had come up to her and complained. She'd figured they were just being nice and told them she had terrible laryngitis. "Okay, I'll put it back in my schedule. You find out what's going on with Addy." She circled the rim of her empty cup, wondering if she'd be able to sing, or if, as she suspected, all of her forward progress had been erased and her stage fright had returned.

Mazie's worries were confirmed that night. Nadine breezed in to catch the end of *Dragon Moms*, giving Mazie the "I've got my eyes on you" signal as she ducked into the theater. Mazie crept down the side aisle as the credits rolled, and when the screen went dark, she ascended the stage. A decent percentage of the moviegoers had stayed back, and they offered supportive applause when she took the stage. She glanced at a beaming Nadine—before her gaze settled on the empty seat in the fourth row, the one where Addy usually sat. She tried to picture Addy and her smiling face. She tried, but she couldn't.

She must've stood there awhile, lost in her own thoughts. Only when she heard the shuffling of feet, did she blink and see the last moviegoers slipping out the exit. Only Nadine remained in her backrow seat. Mazie started to cry, and Nadine's long-legged stride ensured she got to the stage before the cries turned to sobs. She held Mazie close and whispered affirmations in her ear, none of which mattered at the moment.

Eventually Mazie pulled away and took a deep breath. Nadine offered her a tissue and she blew her nose. She scanned the empty seats. "I don't know what to do."

Nadine squeezed her hand and winced. "I have good news and bad news about Addy."

"She hates me?" Mazie thought she might throw up.

"No," Nadine said quickly. "The good news is that Addy's issues have nothing to do with you."

"Then what's the bad news?"

Nadine put her arm around Mazie's shoulder and led her off the stage. "Let's go get a drink. A stiff drink. I'll tell you a story about Lorene Tornado."

"Who?"

"Addy's mother."

CHAPTER TWENTY-FOUR

Addy shuffled across Jackie's backyard, her lunchbox flung over her shoulder. *Another day, another dollar.* That's what her father used to say when he'd come home. She'd been so young when he left that she couldn't picture his face, and her mother had destroyed all the photos that contained any likeness of him. Consequently, she made up her own version of his countenance. He looked like Gregory Peck in *To Kill a Mockingbird*.

She grabbed a yogurt from her fridge and made a PBJ before she settled on her couch. She nibbled on her dinner and glanced at the TV. Sitting next to it were three movies, the ones she wanted to watch with Mazie—*Big Eden, Cloudburst* and *The Russian Doll*.

A part of her wanted to drop her dinner and return each movie to its appropriate spot in her color scheme, but doing that would mean Mazie might never come back. She probably wouldn't. Addy wasn't good enough for her. Lorene Tornado had reminded her of that. Besides, Mazie was slowly slipping away, establishing her own career, planning the premiere and preparing for her test. She didn't need Addy anymore.

Addy finished her dinner and perused her DVDs. She found one starring Tarina Hudson, *Love Hurts.* If that's what she felt for Mazie—or had felt for her—then the producers got it right. She popped in the film and dropped back on the couch, yawning.

She sees her from across the crowded lobby. The violet-colored evening gown bedecked in tiny rhinestones shimmered every time she greets someone. Women and men lean closer to kiss her cheek, smell her perfume and touch her.

Addy so wants to touch her. She adjusts her red bow tie, worn especially for this occasion, and smooths her pressed white Oxford-cloth shirt. Another customer approaches the concessions counter, a B-list actor who she has seen in several Grey's Anatomy *episodes. She retrieves his order, her gaze returning to the goddess in the evening gown.*

"She's a hottie. Am I right?" the actor asks.

Caught. They both look in her direction and Addy says, "Yeah. She's amazing."

"I hear she's taken."

Addy shrugs. "Doesn't matter. I'll never have her."

He nods and walks away, leaving her to gawk. Of course, since the room is filled with Hollywood A, and B-listers, most will never indulge in movie refreshments for fear of gaining weight, although Addy guesses her Diet Coke syrup will soon run low. So she stands at the counter, humming to herself.

"You wouldn't happen to have a hot dog, would you?"

She turns to the far side of the counter—and there she is. The shimmering and glimmering beauty is addressing her. The look on her face is one of near desperation. From that look, Addy doubts she's had anything to eat in the last twelve hours. She offers an alluring smile, and Addy is tempted to leap over the counter and into her arms.

"Do you?" she asks again.

"No," Addy says. "I'm sorry. I could run into the office and get you my peanut butter and jelly sandwich? Would you like that?"

Ms. Shimmering sucks in a sigh. "That would be wonderful." She scans the lobby, no doubt looking for whoever might be looking for her. "Where is it? We need to hurry."

Addy ducks under the counter, grabs her hand, which feels like silk, and hurries to Almondine's office. She throws open the door and heads to the little fridge behind Almondine's desk. She retrieves her lunch bag and says, "I can also offer you one of the manager's strawberry-banana yogurts if you prefer?"

She doesn't reply but Addy smells her perfume. She is close. Her hands leisurely trail down Addy's buttocks to her thighs. Addy closes her eyes and remains hunched over the refrigerator. She doesn't want to stand for fear that the amazing touch will end.

One hand slides between her legs and cups her crotch. Ms. Shimmering places her palm right over Addy's center. She whispers, "This is all we have time for. Ride my hand."

Addy slams the fridge's door shut and clamps both sides of the box. She brings her hips up and down, softly moaning as the intensity grows. Ms. Shimmering grabs Addy's waistband with her free hand, guiding Addy's rhythm to a perfect climax that comes too fast.

Her heart still racing, Ms. Shimmering says, "I'll take that PBJ now."

Addy blinks, leaving the shore of passion and drifting back out into the sea of reality. She is a nobody. She is working the concessions stand at the Bijou, and the beautiful woman hovering over her will never want her for more than a quickie. Addy grabs the sandwich from the fridge, and when she looks up at Ms. Shimmering, her eyes behold two large breasts.

The sandwich drops out of her hand and lands on the desk. Somewhere Addy hears drums, and the beat matches her pounding heart.

"Since I'm eating your sandwich, I thought you might like something else to munch on," Ms. Shimmering suggests. She pulls apart the two pieces of bread and licks a dollop of peanut butter and jelly from the slice in her left hand.

"Hmm. That hits the spot," she says.

Addy so wishes they had more time. Ms. Shimmering reads her mind and smiles. "Don't worry, baby." She holds out the slice once more and dabs her nipples in peanut butter and jelly. She closes the sandwich and takes a bite. "Hmm," she says again.

Addy just stares at the beautiful brown nipples. While the peanut butter stands at attention, gravity draws the jelly toward the floor.

Between bites Ms. Shimmering says, "You better get to work. Any of that jelly gets on this dress, my manager will be handing you the dry-cleaning bill."

Addy drops to her knees and realizes she is too short to reach the perfect mounds of flesh. The jelly dangles, threatening to drop onto the length of dress near the floor. Addy pops up, leans her ass against the desk and opens her mouth—just as the jelly drips off Ms. Shimmering's breast. It lands squarely in her mouth.

"Hmm," Addy says. Her tongue circles one nipple and then the other, ensuring there will be no dry-cleaning issues. Then she works on the peanut butter. Ms. Shimmering's nipples are at full attention, and Addy caresses both of them—first with her tongue and then her teeth.

"Oh, my," Ms. Shimmering says between bites. She presses her free hand against the crown of Addy's head. "Don't be gentle, baby. I like it rough."

Addy sucks ferociously until Ms. Shimmering goes rigid and gasps. She drops into Addy's arms, her legs too wobbly to stand. She whispers into Addy's ear, "Best damn PBJ I've ever had."

Always a considerate lover, Addy asks, "Do you need to use the manager's private restroom to wash up? I've done quite a number on your chest."

"And everywhere else as well," she chuckles. She stands, her legs strong again, and examines her gorgeous breasts. The peanut butter and jelly are gone, but the aroma of peanuts linger. "No, I'm fine."

She pulls up the halter, hiding her breasts away. She places her index finger under Addy's chin and pulls her gaze upward. Their eyes meet, and for the first time, she sees the distinct contours of her face— her broad nose, doughy cheeks, and the slight hint of wrinkles around her smoldering eyes. Mazie.

"Addy?"

A confused and hurt Mazie stands in the doorway. How can this be? She glances back at the face that hovers above her. Also Mazie, but this one brims with lust.

Pounding. Someone was pounding on her door. She jumped and saw Nadine waving. When she opened the door, Nadine offered a worried look. "I've been out there for three minutes."

The drums. "Sorry," she said. "Come in." She headed for the couch but thought to ask, "Do you want anything? Water? Juice?"

Nadine waved her off and took the chair across from the couch. "I'm only staying long enough to give you an update."

"An update on what?"

"Mazie's singing progress."

"Oh?"

"Since you stopped coming by the Bijou, she hasn't been practicing."

"What?"

"She stopped altogether. I know it's because she's completely stressing over the premiere thing, but she also lost her muse."

Addy shook her head. "Who was her muse?"

Nadine sighed. "Addy, you are her muse. I pressured her to practice a few nights ago and she couldn't do it. You weren't sitting in your seat, and when she tried to sing, no words came out."

Addy wiped a hand across her face. The premiere was a week away and Mazie's performance was only two weeks after that. "If she can't sing for the Bijou audience, she'll never be able to perform at Gallagher Hall."

"I know." Nadine took a deep breath. "What I'm about to say will make you very upset. I'd like you to resist the urge to throw something at me, or at least don't throw anything at my face." She touched her cheek and added, "We have team photos later this week."

"Okay," Addy said slowly. "What?"

"I told Mazie about your mom and how you were lying about studying to be a trainer. I know you haven't been to the library."

Rage pushed up from Addy's gut. Nadine had no right to disclose information about her family. She balled her fists together. She wanted to lash out.

"Nuh-uh," Nadine said, waving her index finger. "You promised."

"How could you tell her all that stuff!"

"She had a right to know why you've become completely unavailable—to all of us."

"I have not," Addy said, even though she knew it was true.

"You've withdrawn. You go to work and you come home and sit here and watch movies. You don't hang out with me and Jackie—"

"Grilling season is over. You aren't outside anymore."

Nadine shook her head. "Seriously. You don't know where the back door is? You've never learned to knock?" Addy looked away and Nadine said, "And you haven't been to the Bijou so Mazie's fear returned. I thought you agreed to help her."

"I did…" Addy wrung her hands and started to pace in front of Nadine. Mazie made her so happy, but she wasn't entitled to be happy. At least that's what her mother believed.

When she passed in front of Nadine again, Nadine pulled her into a hug. "You need to banish your mother, possibly forever."

"Impossible."

"Why?"

"I'm all she has. If I don't answer her calls, she just keeps calling."

Nadine offered a dismissive gesture. "Pfft. We've all got a friend or relative who's tried that tactic. Don't answer and eventually she'll get the message."

"You've had somebody call you two hundred and forty-two times in one day?"

"What?" Nadine looked incredulous. "You can't be serious."

"Oh, yes. My mom has nothing in her life and she doesn't work. She has no friends or family except me. After I got mad at her once, she called me for eight hours straight until I finally picked up."

"Sounds like Lorene Tornado is aptly named. Why don't you turn off your phone?"

"Can't do that. I need to be available if there's an emergency on the route."

Nadine shook her head. "You should share this with Mazie. She can help you. Don't shut her out. The two of you are an adorable couple, and she doesn't have a problem with your color…thing. You just need to go for it, Addy."

Addy crossed her arms. "You sure can give it, but you can't take it."

Nadine stared at her manicure. "What do you mean?"

"You tell me to go for it, but have you ever told Jackie how you feel about her?"

"It's not the right time, and we're not presently discussing my mercurial love life."

"Oh, yes, we are. If we're talking about not going for it, then we're talking about both of us. I'm afraid I'm not good enough for Mazie. There. I said it. Now what about you, Nadine? Why aren't you with Jackie?"

She didn't reply. She wiped away a single tear, dug through her Chanel bag for a tissue and blew her nose daintily. Eventually she looked up and said, "It might be hard to believe, but some of the most open-minded people can't fathom falling in love with someone who is transgender."

"She's told you that?" Addy couldn't believe Jackie would be so judgmental.

"Sort of, yes."

"What is 'sort of?'"

Nadine paused and said, "We've had a couple of necking sessions in the past, and one time we consummated our relationship, but I knew she was uncomfortable, so I pulled away. And there were interruptions. The timer went off in the kitchen, somebody knocked on the door—usually you."

Addy grinned. "I thought so. Once or twice I came in and you both looked a little hot and bothered."

The corners of Nadine's mouth turned up. "Yeah."

"And you've always been the one to stop it, right?"

"Well, yes, but—"

"Have you ever thought she might think you're not interested? You know like in *Better than Chocolate*? Where Judy doesn't think Frances is interested in her because she's transgender?"

Nadine threw up her hands. "How did we get here? We're talking about you helping Mazie prepare for her performance! You promised."

Jackie knocked on Addy's door and opened it. "Hey, why are y'all yelling? What's going on and why am I not included?"

"Addy has abandoned Mazie."

"I have not!"

Nadine ignored her and said, "They haven't seen each other in weeks, and Addy has been lying about why she's not going to the Bijou. Consequently, Mazie has stopped practicing for her performance test."

Jackie looked stricken. "Oh, no." Then her expression turned stony. "You still can't shake that phone call from your mother, right?"

Addy nodded.

"Have you told Dr. Pfeiffer? When is she hypnotizing you?"

"She's not. I canceled the appointment."

Jackie sighed. "Oh, Addy, please rethink that. You're not doing it for anyone but yourself. That's not about Mazie. You need to get to the bottom of your anxieties, and Dr. Pfeiffer can help you do that. You trust her, don't you?"

"Yes, but what if my mother is right?"

"About what?"

"About not being good enough."

"You are," Nadine interjected.

"Wait. Good enough for who?" Jackie asked. "You mean Mazie? Are you worried Mazie will leave you?"

Addy looked down, feeling as small as a speck of dust on her hardwood floor. She whispered, "Yes. And then I'll just be anxious again. And Mama will be right."

No one said anything and the silence went on long enough for Addy to hear the ice maker drop a tray of cubes into the ice bucket.

Nadine cleared her throat. "Addy." She looked up. "There's no guarantee about anything in life, but you never know until you try. You choose most of your own landmark days. You make your own life significant." She turned to Jackie. "Jackie, there's something I've been wanting to share with you for a long time. I haven't done so because…I was afraid of your response. I was afraid of your rejection. Like Addy is afraid to talk to Mazie, I've been afraid I'm not good enough for you. Mostly, I was—I *am*—afraid of your prejudice." Nadine took Jackie's hands and brought them to her lips. "I'm in love with you. You're my best friend. The most beautiful woman, inside and out, that I've ever met. And you're sexy as hell. I wonder if you might feel the same about me?" She squeaked out the question and dropped Jackie's hands.

Jackie chuckled and rubbed her temple. "Oh, jeez." Then she started to laugh hysterically.

Addy and Nadine exchanged puzzled looks. Addy asked, "Why are you laughing? This isn't funny. Nadine just poured her heart out, probably as a lesson to me." She smiled at her. "Thanks, Nadine."

Nadine reached over and kissed the top of Addy's head.

They both frowned at Jackie, who couldn't stop laughing. She ran a hand through her hair and sighed loudly. "Nadine, I'm not laughing at you or making fun of your declaration. I didn't think you liked me…like that. I know there was that one time, but the other times I got you on the couch always ended with you running out of the room."

"That's because we kept getting interrupted—"

"No," Jackie disagreed. "Not true. Well, yes, once, but the other two times, you pulled away. I just assumed…" She shrugged. She let out a moan that bordered on a scream.

Nadine sunk to the couch, shaking her head. "All this time…" She swiped a few stray hairs behind her ear. "So, am I too late? You and that woman from the rink the other night sure got cozy fast."

"Oh, no," Jackie said. "You don't get to do that. You can't judge my decisions when you haven't been honest with me." She hovered over Nadine and slid her hands into her back pockets. Addy thought she looked sexy as hell. "What do you want right now?"

Nadine's gaze traveled the length of Jackie's body. "You."

Jackie offered a seductive smile. "How fortunate for us both. That's my answer as well."

Nadine held up a finger. "What about her?" she asked, pointing a finger in Addy's direction.

Jackie shrugged and smiled at Addy. "A part of my heart will always be with Addy, as a friend." She roughly pulled Nadine up and into a sizzling kiss. Addy was reminded of so many great movie kisses—*Elena Undone*, *Amore de Femme*, and *A Perfect Ending*. She blinked and realized their kiss was morphing into much more, as Nadine's hand was already under Jackie's T-shirt.

Addy coughed. "Hmm. Excuse me? My house."

Nadine broke the kiss and said to Jackie, "Hold that thought." She looked at Addy. "We're leaving now, going off to start our new life together, riding off into the sunset, just like they do in the movies. What are you going to do, Addy?"

CHAPTER TWENTY-FIVE

Tarina Hudson's arrival in Wilshire Hills was just hours away, and the premiere was the next night. Mazie was knee-deep in last-minute preparations, finalizing orders with the caterer for the after-party, checking in with the rental company, which was bringing a real red carpet, theater lights, scansions, and backdrops to create a Hollywood-like premiere atmosphere. She gave Almondine a pep talk nearly every hour, as she fretted—almost cyclically—about seeing Tarina, the money spent on the premiere, and what she'd wear.

Acquiring the film proved the most laborious task, as their film booker and the distributor went through extra hoops to ensure its security—physically and virtually. If *S.W.A.T.* wound up on the Internet as a result of the premiere, all of Mazie's hard work would be for nothing. Her name would be mud to the production company, who would spread the word throughout the film industry that the little Bijou theater couldn't be trusted.

They had finally decided to send the hard drive that contained the movie via special courier. Mazie would sign for the film and immediately upload it to the Bijou's system while the courier waited. She'd check to make sure the film played and return the hard drive to the waiting courier.

Then Addy texted her. *Having an emergency. Please be at the bus stop at 12:05. IMPORTANT!!*

Mazie moaned. She was desperate to see Addy, but she had so much to do, and the courier would arrive in two hours. She wondered if Nadine might be staging some sort of intervention. She'd not kept her promise to Nadine. She hadn't returned to the Bijou stage. She'd not been practicing, and she'd ignored two texts from Dr. Bertrand—Ivy. She'd deal with all of it, and the possibility that she'd fail once again, after the premiere was over. Then she'd ponder whether she'd used the premiere as a convenient distraction from her goals.

She sighed and replied to Addy, *Ok. I'll be there, but I only have a few minutes. Sorry.*

Addy gave a thumbs-up and Mazie dove back into her preparations, setting her phone alarm for their meeting. When it sounded a few hours later, she dropped the to-do list on the concessions counter, grabbed her bag and headed for the bus stop. A minute later Addy's bus rounded the corner and stopped in front of the Bijou.

Mazie chugged up the steps and looked toward the seats. The bus was empty.

"Hey," Addy said with a smile.

She looked so cute and Mazie realized how much she'd missed gazing into her soft brown eyes. She couldn't help herself. She threw her arms around Addy and kissed her passionately. And much to her great pleasure, Addy kissed her back equally as hard.

"I've missed you," she said, loud enough to be heard over the hum of the bus's engine.

"I've missed you, too," Addy replied.

"Why is the bus empty? I mean, I'm glad it's empty because I get to do this..." She drew Addy in for another deep kiss. "But isn't this a regular work day?"

"It is. But I'm technically on lunch and helping a friend."

"Who? What's going on?"

"You'll see."

Addy climbed out of the driver's seat and led Mazie to the first seat of the first row. "Sit here." Then she pulled out a karaoke microphone and handed it to her. "You'll need this."

Mazie stared at the microphone. "Why—" The speaker was on, and she jumped at the sound of her own voice. She put a hand over the microphone and stared at a grinning Addy. She couldn't help but laugh. "What are you doing? I'm behind, Addy," she whined. "I've got so much going on to get ready for this thing."

"I know. This won't take long. I want you to close your eyes and start singing. And I want you to promise me that no matter what you hear, no matter what the bus does, you keep your eyes closed and *you don't stop singing*. Okay?"

"Okay."

"Promise?"

She nodded. "Addy, I promise. Can we just hurry this along, whatever *this* is?" she said as nicely as she could.

Addy grinned and climbed into the driver's seat. She looked back at Mazie. "Start singing and close your eyes now."

Mazie did as she was told. She sang "As Time Goes By," and they pulled away from the stop. Her voice echoed throughout the empty bus, and she was surprised at how true and confident she sounded. She impressed herself and wished more people— like her committee—could be on the bus to hear her.

The bus started and stopped twice more, and she heard the swoosh of the air doors, but didn't hear anyone board. She thought this private concert for Addy, although unorthodox and ill-timed, was a great confidence booster. Maybe after the premiere she would start practicing again. She crooned the big finale to the song—and heard thunderous applause.

She whirled around to see the full bus. They were applauding madly. Kit, Bianca, Mrs. Gelpin, Weather and Coda. Evn the young texter guy wasn't texting but listening. Little Huxley smacked his hands together. Someone yelled, "Bravo!" and jumped up. Soon the entire bus followed. Mazie looked back at Addy and mouthed, "Thank you."

"You're welcome." She motioned for Mazie to bow, and when the crowd returned to their seats, Mazie held up the microphone and said, "I can't tell you how much it means to me to see you all here. This is a very special memory."

"You can thank Addy," Mrs. Gelpin said. "She's the one who planned it yesterday."

Everyone applauded again, and Addy waved, unable to speak with passengers while the bus was in motion.

"Sing us another one," Kit called.

"Only if you all join in," Mazie said. The group shouted their agreement. "Hopefully you know the words to this one. It makes me think of my childhood in Kentucky."

She launched into "Take me Home, Country Roads," the John Denver classic. By the time they had returned to the beginning of the route, the final chorus was ending. She looked over at Addy. Tears ran down her cheeks, but she was holding it together as the bus cruised to a stop. Addy wiped her face and met Mazie's concerned gaze. She smiled as she opened the door and waved to everyone as they disembarked.

Kit, Weather, and the kids stopped in front of Mazie. Kit took her hands, "You have the voice of an angel. That's the highest compliment I can pay you."

She put her hand over her heart. "That means so much to me coming from you, Kit. Thank you." She wrapped Kit in a hug. "Thank you for being a part of this."

"You're welcome, dear. I'll see you soon," she added with a mysterious look before walking away with Coda in her arms.

Everyone else insisted on shaking Mazie's hand and complimenting her on the performance. She watched the passengers disperse, some walking through the park, others going to cars they'd parked in the mini-mall lot. It was clear everyone had made an effort to be at Bus Stop 2 at a certain time—and Addy had arranged the whole thing. She gazed at Addy, who seemed content to lean against her huge steering wheel, watching Mazie bask in compliments from the passengers. Mazie couldn't name all of the feelings inside her, but she knew they equated to love. She so wanted to say the words, but it wasn't time—yet.

Instead she smothered Addy with kisses, but realizing Addy was on break, she pulled away quickly and said, "I know you have to get back to work and so do I, but this meant so much to me. You went to a lot of trouble." She stroked her cheek and stared into her kind eyes, thinking she might dissolve into a puddle at Addy's feet.

Addy whispered into her hair, "I just wanted you to see that you can do it. You can sing to a crowd. You can pass your test."

Mazie hugged her tighter and replied, "I'm starting to believe you."

They chugged back to the Bijou in relative silence, as Mazie didn't want to disobey the placard that read, "Please don't distract the driver." Only after Addy came to a full stop did Mazie jump out of her seat and into Addy's lap. She doubted there was a specific policy about making out with the driver on her lunch break.

"Did you hear about Nadine and Jackie?" Mazie asked between kisses.

Addy smiled. "I did. It's about time."

"Yeah. And in a few hours Tarina arrives, and I guess we'll see if sparks fly between her and Almondine again."

Addy looked at her cynically. "Do you think after all this time they could get together again?"

"Of course. It's just like in *Tipping the Velvet*. Nan Astley is away from Kitty Butler for years, and then they find each other again." She kissed Addy sweetly. "Fate is the most powerful friend of love."

"I like that," Addy said.

"Come back after work and have dinner with me, Almondine and Tarina. I'm begging you. If I'm wrong and fate stays away, I'll have a catfight on my hands and I'll need reinforcements to help break it up."

"Okay. I brought a change of clothes. I'll be here around six thirty."

She climbed out of Addy's lap and kissed her on the cheek. "I loved today," she said before disembarking the bus. She looked back at Addy as the doors whooshed closed. She thought Addy mouthed the words, "I love you," but she couldn't be sure.

Normally she would've played those last moments over and over in her mind, just like the ending of a movie, but she had too much to do.

An hour later the limousine service called and said they were on their way to the Portland airport to pick up Tarina and her small entourage. Hiring the limousine had been a point of contention for Almondine, who wondered why a cab or Uber wouldn't do. Mazie insisted that Hollywood bigwigs would be dissatisfied with that choice. The limo would take them to the hotel and then bring Tarina to the Bijou.

With only a few hours left, Almondine chose to have a meltdown. Suddenly nothing was right. She wanted to redo all of Mazie's work. The posters were in the wrong place, there wasn't enough VIP seating, the bathrooms weren't clean enough, and it was just foolhardy to have the Bijou playing its regular fare the day before the premiere. When Mazie reminded Almondine it was she who wanted to be open the day before their big event, insisting they needed the ticket sales, Almondine denied ever saying such tripe.

Nadine arrived just in time. Mazie was ready to walk out, but Nadine, a master of chaos control, took over and sent Mazie to complete the minor details, while she went with Almondine to select her outfit for Tarina's arrival and dinner.

At seven o'clock sharp, the limo driver texted Mazie that he was two blocks away, and just as Mazie read the text, the car pulled around the corner and glided to a stop. The three of them—Mazie, Nadine and Addy—were there to greet Tarina, but Almondine insisted she wasn't ready. Mazie suspected she wanted to make an entrance, a la Norma Desmond from *Sunset Boulevard*.

Tarina didn't bother to wait for the driver to let her out. She opened her own door, a smile on her face. She wore a close-cropped Afro accentuating her beautiful eyes and wide smile. She was petite but compact, and her large breasts struggled to remain contained in her tank top. She wore jeans and white high-tops and projected an earthy attitude. Mazie couldn't understand what Tarina and Almondine could possibly have in common, but she knew opposites attracted, like in *Imagine Me and You*. Her face looked just like Almondine's drawing in her address book, and judging from Tarina's physique, Mazie imagined her breasts looked equally good.

"Which one of you is Mazie?"

Mazie raised her hand and Tarina pulled her into a bear hug. "Bring it in. Thanks for doing all of this."

"You're welcome," Mazie croaked. "And it's an honor to meet you."

"Pfft," Tarina said. "I'm just an actress who got lucky." She held out her hand to meet Nadine and Addy, and then she looked around. "Okay, where is she?" She pointed to the front doors. "Is she inside? Insisted on making an entrance?"

"I think she's very nervous," Nadine said.

Tarina's look softened. "Yeah, I get it. When she walked out on me in Paris, I knew she loved me." She shrugged. "Well, let's get to it."

They headed inside and Tarina made a full three-sixty turn as she admired the lobby. "This place is way cool."

"Thank you," Mazie replied.

"I'll go find Almondine," Nadine offered.

"No need," Almondine said, emerging from the office.

She'd chosen white flowing harem pants and a turquoise tunic that brought out her green eyes. She'd put her long steel-gray hair into a tight bun, and the overall effect made her look much younger.

"It's wonderful to see you, Tarina."

"Deenie," Tarina said.

Mazie heard hope, forgiveness—and a little lust—in the way she said her name. Tarina made no movement toward her.

Whereas she'd immediately hugged the three of them on the curb, with Almondine she was tentative, quiet and possibly unsure of what to do or say.

"How long has it been?" Almondine asked.

Tarina rubbed her chin. "Since Paris? I'd say nine years, eighty-eight days, and fourteen hours."

Almondine's stoic face blossomed into a smile. "Not that you're keeping track."

"No, of course not. How about a tour? This place is fabulous."

"It is. I'm very proud of it."

With Mazie's assistance, they toured Theater One, the projection room, and the stage. Tarina was impressed with the old Wurlitzer organ hidden behind the enormous movie screen, and Mazie was surprised when she sat down to play. Rachmaninoff filled the building, and Mazie imagined it could be heard on the street. Tarina was clearly a woman of many talents.

"Let's go out to the courtyard," Mazie suggested.

As Tarina walked through the doorway, she abruptly stopped. "Are you kidding me?"

Mazie smiled, assuming Tarina was impressed with the wonderful French motif Almondine had chosen. But Tarina's scowl telegraphed displeasure.

"Is something wrong?" Mazie asked.

Tarina stared at Almondine. "Nobody knows, do they? These three lovely women have no idea what you've done here." She made a sweeping motion toward the courtyard. Almondine looked off into the distance. Mazie shook her head and Tarina nodded. "Let me check something." She went to the center of the courtyard and squatted beside a bistro table. "Uh-huh, just what I thought." She stood and pointed. Mazie, Addy and Nadine huddled to see *A+T* scrawled on the edge in black marker. "I can't believe this!" Tarina exclaimed. "I instantly recognized this whole scene, but how did you get this?"

"Friends," Almondine said simply.

"I'm sorry," Nadine said, "but what are you talking about? Ms. Hudson, what's the significance of the table?"

"Just call me Rina, please." She crossed her arms and gestured with her chin. "This is the table Almondine and I sat at when we visited our favorite French café, Ines. One day we were being ridiculously childish, and we claimed the table as our own, branding it with a Sharpie marker. We sat here...maybe a hundred times." Her gaze swept the courtyard. "This whole space looks like Ines." She touched the table as if she couldn't believe it was real, and then she sat down in the chair and faced the scrawl. "Deenie," she managed before she covered her eyes and the tears flowed.

The emotion pulled Almondine from her reverie. She immediately sat down next to Tarina and wrapped a protective arm over her shoulder. She whispered in her ear and Tarina shrugged.

Mazie glanced at Nadine and Addy. The tour was over. As the three of them retreated to the lobby, Mazie threw a parting glance toward the couple. Almondine had recreated the café she had shared with Tarina to make her feel closer. Somehow she'd acquired the table where they had sat when they were lovers—from France. She'd gone to enormous trouble, just as Addy had with the bus performance. Mazie's heart crackled with emotion. It was certainly a day of grand gestures.

CHAPTER TWENTY-SIX

"I don't think Almondine got much sleep last night," Mazie said the next morning on the phone. "I know I didn't," she grumbled.

"Did Tarina have a sleepover?"

"*Sleep* would be quite the overstatement. I think absence must really make the heart grow fonder."

"Not always," Addy said quietly. Wishing she could retract the comment the minute she said it, she changed the subject. "So how will today go?"

"This was supposed to be a soft opening, but word has gotten around, and apparently, according to my booker, bigwigs from the production companies, the distributor, the studio, as well as Tarina's co-stars will be here. I'm still trying to find some lodging for a few of the minor actors. I think they'll wind up in Salem. Every hotel and motel room within a twenty-five-mile radius of the Bijou is full. And other stuff keeps cropping up. It seems every time I answer a phone call, it leads to more work."

"Well, I called you, but I won't make you do anything for me."

"You're the one person I'd do anything for."

Addy smiled. "Yeah, I'd do anything for you too, so let me know if you need help today. I'll be by right after my appointment with Dr. Pfeiffer."

"Are you nervous?"

"A little."

"Well, I've known a lot of people who've been hypnotized and it was successful for most of them." When Addy didn't reply, she added, "I'm sure it will be fine."

"Yeah." Desperate for a change of subject, Addy said, "Are you going to get a chance to rest before tonight?"

"If I'm lucky I'll get a short nap before all of this starts. Maybe Tarina and Almondine will go out for a romantic nature walk, or at least, back to Tarina's expensive hotel room we're paying for."

Mazie shared more of her day, and Addy closed her eyes, picturing Mazie talking to her while they sat at one of the little French bistro tables—in France. Mazie had become her greatest fantasy and someone she'd trust with anything.

They said their goodbyes and Addy cleaned her house until it was time to go to Dr. Pfeiffer's house. She headed over at one forty-five for her two o'clock appointment, trying not to take a mental vacation as she cruised through downtown Wilshire Hills.

Dr. Pfeiffer greeted her warmly and they headed through the living room toward Dr. P's office. While most of the room was painted in a neutral tone called Siesta, her gaze was drawn to an accent wall, which in Addy's mind, didn't fit. An unsettling memory emerged. The first time she'd ever come here at Jackie's urging, she'd nearly walked back out. Fortunately, she'd liked Dr. Pfeiffer, and Dr. P was willing to meet her someplace else—rather than repaint the wall as Addy had suggested during that session. *When I leave today, maybe I won't be so bothered by it.*

The office was exactly how she remembered it the one time she'd been inside—tastefully decorated in earth tones with dark wood. Dr. Pfeiffer motioned to a chaise lounge.

"This is one time when a lot of patients prefer to lie down. You don't have to. You could sit in a chair instead." Addy settled on the lounge, lacing her fingers behind her head. Dr. Pfeiffer pulled a chair close to her and gazed into her eyes. After a few minutes of small talk and Addy apologizing for canceling the original appointment, Dr. Pfeiffer told her to close her eyes and take a few deep breaths. "The only way this will work, Addy, is if you really want it to work. Do you want to be hypnotized?"

"Yes," she said firmly.

Dr. Pfeiffer led her through a series of breathing activities and questions, none of which Addy thought were important to her color peculiarity. When she finally asked, "Addy, what is your favorite color?" Addy knew they were moving forward.

"My favorite color is black."

"Why?"

"'Because it's all of the colors."

"I see. Now, I want you to listen to the sound of my voice. Let your mind float away, like it's on a cloud...Focus on your breathing. Hear the air going in and out. Feel the expansion of your lungs. I want you to think about the picture you showed me, the one you keep on your refrigerator."

"Yes."

"You're a little girl and you're wearing a plaid shirt, but I know you don't like plaid now, correct?"

"Yes, it's too busy."

"But did you like that shirt?"

"I loved that shirt. It was my favorite."

"What happened to it?"

"Can't say."

"Can't say or won't say."

"Both."

"And you've kept the picture, despite the plaid shirt."

"It's the only picture I have from my childhood...with my mother."

"Where were you when that picture was taken?"

"Beckley."

"West Virginia?"

"Yes."

"Who was living there?"

"Me. My mom. My brother Oren. And Ted."

"How old were you?"

"Fourteen."

"How old was Oren?"

"Seventeen."

"Who was Ted?"

"He was the renter who lived above the garage."

"So you lived in a house?"

"Yes, we rented the house and Ted was already there."

"Did you like Ted?"

"Not at first. He seemed creepy. He was always watching me and Oren playing out front. He'd stand at his window and look out at us."

"What changed to make you like Ted?"

"He saved me."

"From who or what?"

"Oren."

"How did Ted save you?"

"He followed us into the woods behind our house."

"Why did you go into the woods?"

"Oren made me go. He was mad."

"Why was he angry with you?"

"We were playing horseshoes and I threw one way off. It hit him in the leg."

"Did he yell?"

"Yeah. It musta hurt."

"Was your mother at home?"

"No, she was at work, I think. Or she might've just been out."

"So Oren got very mad. What happened next?"

"He grabbed me by the arm. I started yelling that he was hurting me, and he said it couldn'ta hurt worse than his leg."

"Then what happened."

"He dragged me behind the house and into the woods. Called me names like dyke 'cause I dressed in flannel shirts. He…punished me."

"How?"

"He was smokin' by then. He lit a cigarette and burned me."

"Where?"

"My arm."

"Is that when Ted showed up?"

"Not the first few times. I don't think he wanted to get involved, but then he finally did, and Mama kicked him out."

"How did he get involved?"

"After he followed us, he told Mama what Oren was doing, but Oren called him a liar… Then Mama told me to prove it. I looked at Ted, and I could tell he really wanted me to tell the truth, but when I looked at Oren, I saw how bad things would go for me if I got him in trouble. Mama was going to kick Ted out anyway. He'd already told her he wanted to go to the police, so she knew he'd cause trouble for her, which meant more trouble for me.

"So I lied and told Mama that Oren wasn't doing anything bad. That's when Mama kicked Ted out of the house. He shook his head and went and packed. Before he left, he told me I should report Oren to the police. I nodded, but we both knew I wouldn't do it. I was stuck for a few years more, but fortunately, Oren enlisted in the Army on his eighteenth birthday."

"Between the time Ted left and Oren left, that was about a year?"

"Yes."

"And did the abuse continue?"

"Yes. Anytime I pissed him off, so like once a month."

"Did your mother know?"

"She had to. She did the wash and she saw all the holes in my flannel shirts."

"Did you keep wearing them?"

"For a while. Oren would pick a color and that'd be the spot he burned the hole."

"While you were wearing the shirt."

"Yes. Eventually I got other shirts. I told Mama I didn't want to wear flannel anymore. I think she connected it to what Oren was doing, but she didn't want him to get in trouble. The school had already called once when the nurse saw a hole."

"So your mother took you shopping."

"Yeah, she wanted me to buy these cheap T-shirts, but there were all these colors. It was like flannel to me…I insisted on shirts that were all one color."

"Is that your first memory of hating colors mixed together?"

"Yes."

"Did the abuse stop after you bought new shirts?"

"Mostly. I'd learned not to say anything to Oren to make him mad, but I think the new shirts were more girly, and he thought they were more appropriate. But he still burned me sometimes. I think he liked hurting me."

"And you continued to separate colors?"

"Yeah. I remember my mother used to make this medley of frozen vegetables. I started putting the peas, the limas, and green beans together, and the carrots and corn by themselves. Oren thought it was hysterical. Mama knew something wasn't right, but she wasn't going to bring it up. She knew it was tied to Oren, so she didn't want to know."

"Did she ever ask to see your scars?"

"No. But I remember we always had a giant bottle of rubbing alcohol. She made a point of telling me that if I ever had a burn or a cut, I was supposed to swab it in rubbing alcohol. I'm sure she realized that if any of the burns got infected, I'd have to go to the hospital."

"So she didn't see them, but she knew they were there."

"Well, she saw them once, or at least, she saw some of them one night when she'd worked late. She came home and found Oren on the front porch drinking and smoking. That's what he always did when he got really mad. She came into the house and I was going to take a shower and wash the dirt off the newest burn."

"Where was it?"

"Under my left breast. So I got in the shower, and a few minutes later she barged in and threw open the curtain. She stared at me, and her face turned white. Then she walked out."

"Did anything change once she saw the evidence of his abuse?"

"He enlisted soon after that. I remember the day she practically forced him to go down to the recruiting station. I don't know for sure because they were whispering, but I'm pretty sure she blackmailed him. She told him if he didn't leave, she'd report him to the police, and she'd find Ted to back up her story."

"Why do you think she forced him to go?"

"She didn't want him to get into trouble."

"Do you think it could've been because she wanted to protect you?"

"No, that wasn't it. When Oren died in Iraq, she blamed me. She said I'd driven him away. It was all my fault that he was gone. She always says that…"

"Addy, I think we've gone far enough today. I'm going to count to three and you'll come back. One, two, three."

Addy blinked and noticed her face was covered in drying tears. Dr. Pfeiffer handed her a tissue, and she blew her nose. She jumped up. "One second, please." She flung open the office door and rushed to the living room. She turned to the accent wall—and felt the familiar anxiety. *It's still there.*

She returned to the office and dropped on the sofa. "I thought the hypnosis would solve my problem. It didn't work."

Dr. Pfeiffer looked at her sympathetically. "Addy, this is a process. When we start hypnosis, it's like going into a dark room. Sometimes it takes a while for our eyes to adjust and see things clearly. This is going to take more than one session. I think it's going to take many sessions." She leaned forward and took her hand. "Hypnosis is just one part of the work we need to do. You'll reveal and remember the past, but then you and I will need to spend time making sense of it, what happened then and how it's affecting you now."

"And then I won't freak out about colors?"

"I hope so."

"Me too."

CHAPTER TWENTY-SEVEN

Mazie glanced at her watch for the third time. It was nearly seven o'clock and Addy still wasn't there. A huge crowd of Wilshire Hills residents had shown up and lined the streets, hoping to stargaze, obtain autographs and take photos of their favorite movie icons. Mazie saw Kit and Weather behind the gold ropes and waved. They waved back and gave her a thumbs-up. Kit mouthed, "Where's Addy?" to which Mazie could only shrug. It was a good question and Mazie was getting worried.

She sent her a text, but she knew if Addy was riding her bicycle, she couldn't answer. *And what if she's sitting on a bench in Warren Park, on one of her mental vacations?* Mazie banished the thought. Addy knew how important this was to her. She'd be here.

At seven-ten the limos pulled up, and the shouts and cheers began. The publicists ordered the limo arrival to ensure the biggest star—Tarina—arrived last. The first few limos were filled with the people who financed the movie, directed it and wrote it. The cheering increased when members of the supporting cast got out of the fourth and fifth limos. When the last limo door opened and Tarina emerged, the crowd erupted. She spent fifteen minutes walking the ropes and talking with fans, taking selfies, and signing autographs. Mazie smiled from her perch in the projection room. Tango had the lobby covered, and from up here Mazie could see everything perfectly—and keep an eye out for Addy.

As Tarina made her way into the lobby, the crowd dispersed. They couldn't get into the theater tonight, so they left for other pursuits. Then Mazie saw Addy down the street. She'd been unable to breach the immense crowd, but once she saw an opening she jumped on her bike and headed around to the back. Mazie raced down the stairs to greet her.

"I'm sorry," she panted. "I was in the park thinking about my appointment and I lost track of time. Then I couldn't get through the crowd. Did you know the sidewalk is packed all the way to the university? I would've been here sooner—"

Mazie kissed her. "I know. And I want to hear all about the appointment later, but right now, let's get this done." She wiped some sweat from Addy's face lovingly. "Run up to my room and take a quick shower. I'll meet you in the lobby."

Addy nodded and grabbed her backpack. Mazie walked the lobby perimeter and sidled up to Tango who said, "It's all good. Take a look at Tarina and Almondine."

The two women had their arms around each other and appeared to be holding court as they answered questions from the press. Mazie couldn't hear the questions or their replies, but she had a suspicion Almondine's life was about to change significantly. It was just like *Notting Hill* with Julia Roberts.

"Mazie," a voice said.

Mazie turned to Dr. Bertrand, who wore a gorgeous tuxedo. On her arm was a beautiful Latina woman wearing a flowing green dress. Mazie was certain if there was a "Best Dressed" contest for couples, they would win.

"Dr. Bertrand, I didn't know you'd be here."

"The distributor of the movie is a friend, and you're supposed to call me Ivy," she said, wagging her finger. Mazie nodded through her blush. "This is my wife, Anna." Mazie shook her hand as Tango appeared next to them. They took the hint, and Ivy said, "Have a wonderful evening." She squeezed her hand and glided away with her wife.

"It's time," Tango said.

She sounded some chimes and filtered through the lobby, alerting the VIP crowd to take their seats. Mazie followed her into the theater, glancing back, looking for Addy. She'd looked harried and somewhat upset. Mazie imagined the session with Dr. Pfeiffer had been difficult, but she knew it was necessary. And while she didn't know much about hypnotherapy, she imagined there would be more sessions. Addy would come through it stronger, just as Mazie would come through her performance test.

With that thought, her smile was natural as she assisted the guests with finding seats and ensuring the VIPs landed in the reserved seats near the front. She glanced at Almondine, sharing a whisper with Tarina. Their fingers were lazily laced together, and Mazie felt a rush of sheer joy for her friend. Almondine deserved happiness.

Once everyone was seated, Tango ducked out and headed to the projection room. She dimmed the house lights and the excited chatter decreased until everyone was attentive to the screen. There were no previews, but there was a message from the producer.

Tango, who had a great voice, announced, "Please welcome Ms. Elaine Frunsman."

While Mazie had no idea who Elaine was, many in the crowd knew her and cheered. She thanked everyone who made the movie possible, calling out many names individually, while the audience politely clapped. Mazie looked at the back. Two chairs had been set up at the doors, one for her and one for Addy. Tango would stay in the projection booth, and Nadine and Jackie, who stealthily wandered the event and had escaped Mazie's detection, would keep an eye on the lobby, along with the hired concession temps.

Where was Addy?

Mazie cast a nervous glance at Ms. Frunsman before she slipped out to the lobby and up the stairs. She burst through the door to her room—and her feet halted at the sight of Addy. She wore a bra, her dress shirt in her hand. Mazie's jaw dropped as her gaze traveled across the red, scarred, and angry skin of Addy's back, shoulders and chest. Addy froze for only a moment before covering up, but in that moment, everything was clear to Mazie—Addy's reluctance to become physically involved, her mind's retreat into the world of cinema romance, and, Mazie imagined, her "color peculiarity." She could only imagine who could've hurt Addy in this way, and if she ever met him…And she was absolutely positive it had to be a "he."

"I'm sorry you had to see me," Addy muttered as she buttoned her shirt and stuffed her other clothes into her backpack. "I'll go now."

Mazie realized she was sending Addy all the wrong signals. She rushed to her and put a hand on the backpack. "No, you can't leave."

"But you looked completely disgusted," Addy said in a small voice Mazie had never heard.

"No!" Mazie insisted. "I was surprised and then *furious* at whoever would do this to you. You of all people…" She wiped the tears streaming down her face, not caring how smeared her carefully applied makeup became. "You're the kindest, most gentle person I've ever met, and I'd love to hire a complete badass to take out the scum who hurt you. Somebody like Ripley from *Alien*, or Sarah Connor from *Terminator*, or Wonder Woman or…even Evelyn Couch, the Kathy Bates character from *Fried Green Tomatoes*."

"Tawanda!" Addy whisper-screamed. They both giggled and Addy pulled Mazie closer. "I'd just take Mazie Midnight."

"You've already got her."

Their lips naturally came together and Mazie no longer cared about the movie screening, the Bijou, Almondine, her test—anything. She wanted Addy desperately.

"Let's go to bed," Mazie said between kisses.

Addy stepped back and shook her head. "I want to, but we can't. You're responsible for all of this, and I don't want anything to go wrong. You've worked too hard."

"But Tango—"

"No," Addy insisted. "Not Tango. This is your baby." She kissed her forehead. "Besides, as you might imagine, I still have some more work to do with Dr. Pfeiffer on all of this."

Mazie nodded, suddenly very aware there was much to say and this wasn't the time. "Will you keep me in the loop?"

"Of course."

The movie proved to be quite exciting, and Mazie loved sitting in the back with Addy, holding hands, sharing a bucket of popcorn and some whispered commentary about directorial choices. When the movie ended and the credits rolled, the crowd cheered their favorite tech people, and a few actually stood and waved to the crowd. It was something Mazie had never seen, and she thought it was delightful to see the crew so acknowledged.

Just as the credits finished, before anyone could move, Tango's voice announced, "Please remain seated. It is my pleasure to welcome Tarina Hudson."

The crowd cheered as Tarina took to the stage. Mazie and Addy looked at each other, surprised. Mazie wondered what Tarina was up to, since Tango obviously knew something Mazie did not.

Tarina grabbed two microphones from Nadine, who appeared from stage left. "Thanks, Nadine." Tarina looked out at the crowd as the movie screen rolled up into the ceiling, revealing the enormous old organ.

"What's going on?" Mazie said to Addy through clenched teeth.

Addy shrugged and Mazie was comforted that she wasn't the only person in the dark, but her anxiety soared. This would surely delay the after-party and that would upset the caterer.

She was about to jump up and take control when Tarina shielded her eyes and said, "Mazie Midnight, are you back there?" Mazie froze and Tarina said, "Get your bootie up here, girlfriend."

The crowd cheered as Addy escorted a stunned Mazie to the front. Addy passed her off to Tarina, who said, "Now, I hear you're a singer. I thought we could do a duet with my love, Deenie, on organ." Mazie looked stupidly at Almondine, who wore the broadest grin Mazie had ever seen. She whipped out a quick eight bars that brought the crowd to their feet.

"I'm sure you know this song, Mazie," Tarina said.

She belted out the opening verse of "Ain't too Proud to Beg," and Mazie tried to hide her terror, knowing she'd eventually have to sing. She pictured herself back on the bus with Kit, Weather, Mrs. Gelpin—and Addy. Then she joined Tarina in the chorus. When Tarina pointed, Mazie took the second verse, her gaze straying to Almondine ripping up the keys, Nadine and Jackie dancing in the wings, and Addy clapping her hands in time with the music—like the rest of the crowd. Mazie sang to Addy through the chorus, and then Tarina joined her for the last verse. They wailed on the ending, and Mazie felt the resounding applause shake the Bijou to its foundation.

She and Tarina bowed. She basked in the crowd's praise. She'd dreamed of such a reception, and she could only hope her performance test went as well. Kit clapped furiously, Dr. Bertrand held her camera out as if she were filming a movie, and her wife applauded politely. Tarina pulled Mazie into a strong hug and whispered, "You rocked it, girl."

"So it was the two of you?"

The after-party was pushing three hours when Mazie finally learned who had set up the impromptu concert after the premiere: Nadine and Jackie.

"Well," Nadine said with an air of condescension, "once I told my new friend Rina, that's Tarina to the rest of you, about your stage fright, she said to me, 'Oh, we'll take care of that.' And she did." Nadine laughed heartily and everyone joined in.

"This is a terrific party, Mazie," Jackie added.

"Thank you." She gazed at her new friends, so grateful she'd moved to Wilshire Hills. "Thanks to all of you."

"We need to talk," a stern voice said.

Mazie turned and stared at Ivy Bertrand, who wore an unreadable expression. "I need to see you in my office tomorrow morning at nine a.m."

CHAPTER TWENTY-EIGHT

Addy's emotions hit a wall as the after-party slowly unraveled. She was positive she'd run the entire spectrum of emotions since early that morning. As if she were in a funhouse, she'd experienced emotional shocks every few hours, not knowing what was around the corner and how she'd feel about it, including the sheer elation of seeing Mazie singing with Tarina.

She slouched down in her balcony seat and threw her legs over the railing. Theater One boasted a tiny balcony, but Almondine didn't open it because insuring it would've been too costly. Consequently, it was a storage place with boxes set on many seats and in the aisles. It was also a quiet place to be alone, away from the hubbub of the after-party that struggled to end, even though it was nearly midnight. Addy needed a few hours of sleep, in accordance with policy 14.2 of the Wilshire Hills Transportation Policy Manual, which stated that all drivers would be well rested before they drove.

"Can anyone join this party?"

She sat up. Mazie stood at the top of the stairs. "Well, you certainly can."

Mazie took the seat next to her and kicked off her heels. She put her legs up over the railing on top of Addy's loafers.

"You have cute feet," Addy said, putting her arm around Mazie and pulling her as close as possible. "It's hard to believe that just a few hours ago you were bringing the house down."

Mazie laughed. "It was good, wasn't it?"

"Yes," she managed. Addy hoped her gaze told the story of her heart. She'd never loved anyone the way she loved Mazie.

They gave up on words and their lips took over. Addy explored Mazie's neck, nibbled her earlobe, and when she grew frustrated by the seat that separated them, she dropped to her knees and wiggled between Mazie's legs. Her lips returned to Mazie's cleavage. She only hesitated for a second, but then Mazie, her fingers burrowing in Addy's hair, guided her to a nipple, which she sucked ferociously. Mazie moaned and sank deeper into the seat. Addy's lips danced across her chest to the other breast.

"Don't want this one to feel neglected," Addy said.

"No," Mazie moaned.

Laughter erupted as the doors to Theater One flew open and the sounds of the party floated in with the intruders. Addy jumped up and returned to her seat, while Mazie adjusted her "girls."

"Well, well," Addy said. "We're not the only ones making out in the theater."

They watched the couple, who looked more like one person than two, settle against a pillar in the shadows.

Mazie leaned over the balcony. "Who is it?"

"I can't tell," Addy said. "It's too dark."

"Ouch!" one of the pillar people exclaimed.

Addy chuckled. "I know that ouch. That's Jackie and Nadine."

Mazie leaned closer and whispered, "We should probably get back. I want to make sure the temps close out the concessions correctly, and frankly, I've lost the mood." She rose and Addy followed.

"Do you think you could get back in the mood?" Addy couldn't hide her disappointment as they crept down the winding stairs that led back to the lobby.

Mazie turned and pushed her against the staircase wall. She pressed herself against Addy and stroked her buttocks. They stared at each other and Mazie said, "To be clear. This has been a fantastic evening and I'm not ready to end it."

"Me either," Addy agreed.

"And," Mazie said between kisses, "as much fun as it was to sing with Tarina, and despite the fact that it was clearly a turning point for me regarding my performance ability, it's not going to be the only climactic moment I have tonight."

"We don't have to do this if you're not ready," Mazie said gently. They were sitting on the edge of her bed, holding hands. The Bijou was finally quiet and everyone had left, including Almondine and Tarina, who were taking advantage of the expensive hotel room.

Addy looked at her tentatively and Mazie smiled, but then Addy looked away, troubled. "I guess I'm not sure you'd still want to…after what you saw." Her voice was thin as air and reflected her fragile state.

Mazie took Addy's cheeks between her palms and stared into her eyes. "There is nothing that could turn me away from you. You're all I want."

Addy blinked several times, like a toy whirring to life. "I am? Really?"

Mazie gasped. "Why are you so surprised?" She bit her lip and took a deep breath. "Here goes. You're the most wonderful person I've ever met. I want to spend each day learning more about you, caring for you, letting you care for me, watching movies at the Bijou, eating popcorn, defending you, cussing out your mother if necessary, and…a whole lot of other stuff." Addy's face brightened, giving Mazie the courage to add, "I love you, Addy. I think this is as close to a movie ending as we're gonna get."

Addy jumped up. "I love you too!" she cried.

They both laughed and Mazie pulled her back on the bed. "Come here, silly."

The pronouncement seemed to give them permission. Addy's kisses were confident, and Mazie let her take the lead, still unsure how far Addy wanted to go. She was pleasantly surprised when Addy stroked her thighs.

"I have a confession to make," Mazie whispered.

Addy looked up from her work. "What?"

"I'm not wearing any underwear."

A sexy smile pulled at the corners of Addy's mouth and she went in search of confirmation, which she found when she caressed Mazie's buttocks, situating herself between Mazie's legs. She shifted her hips until she was on top of Mazie, grinding their pelvises together. Mazie moaned at the contact. Addy bit down on Mazie's lower lip and broke the kiss. She lifted herself up and drew circles on Mazie's thigh, slowly inching up the fabric of Mazie's dress, exposing more flesh.

"Your skin is so soft," Addy whispered.

"And you're so beautiful," Mazie said, lost in the kindness and vulnerability of Addy's eyes.

Mazie slid her leg between Addy's thighs so she could straddle her. "I want you to have some fun too."

Addy grinned. Two fingers entered Mazie at the exact same time Addy's tongue returned to Mazie's mouth. They found a slow, easy rhythm. Addy rode Mazie's leg while she tantalized her center. Addy went deeper and Mazie moaned. The kiss eventually broke, each lost in her own pleasure. Mazie cried out first but Addy followed shortly after.

They held each other tightly, listening to their galloping heartbeats and the soft sounds of affection, satiation, and nearness. Addy had buried her head in Mazie's shoulder and was humming. Mazie stroked Addy's spiky black hair and kissed her temple, remembering that first day when she saw Addy sitting in the bus seat, her hat askew on the top of her head.

Somehow Addy had managed to unzip her dress and unclasp her bra, both of which now sat at ridiculous angles on her limbs. She wiggled free of her clothes with a little help from Addy—until she was completely naked. Addy wasted no time, stroking her shoulders, her breasts and her belly.

Mazie laid a hand on the buttons of Addy's dress shirt, making her intent clear and asking permission without words. Addy nodded and Mazie pulled them together for another kiss while she parted the shirt. The pads of her fingers found scars everywhere she touched. She steeled herself. Now was not the time to pity Addy. Or become angry at her assaulter. *Just love her.* She pressed against her—hard. Addy moaned in pleasure as Mazie discarded each item of clothing—her shirt, her bra and her dress pants. They fell back on the bed, Addy's boxers the only scrap of clothing between them.

Mazie broke the kiss and said, "Addy, open your eyes and look at me." Addy obeyed. "I want to make absolutely sure you're with me and not off somewhere else in your mind—in a frozen food aisle, a carnival, wherever. Are you here?"

"Yes."

Mazie's gaze drifted to the scars on Addy's shoulders. She kissed each one, looked back at Addy and saw tears pooling in her eyes. "I love all of you. Every bit of you." She didn't wait for a reply as she dragged her lips southward, offering Addy's nipples the same attention Addy had given to hers. They hardened immediately and Addy sighed.

Addy spread her arms out like a bird who'd been set free. With each kiss her anxiety seemed to decrease. When Mazie's lips reached the waistband of Addy's boxers she said, "Uh-oh. Look what I found."

"Off," Addy managed to say.

She lifted her hips and Mazie yanked the boxers down, masking her hesitation at what might be revealed. Fortunately, there were no scars. Addy's limbs were like liquid, and when Mazie parted her thighs, Addy's wetness glistened. Still, she had to ask.

"Are you ready? It's okay to tell me to stop."

"No!" Addy yelled. She pulled herself up on her elbows. "Don't you dare." She grinned. "But I want to watch."

"Please do," Mazie replied.

She lowered her head, inhaling Addy's scent and fanning her desire. She flicked her tongue against the softest skin, carefully avoiding Addy's throbbing center. Mazie glanced up. Addy's head was thrown back and her mouth was open. Mazie knew it wouldn't take much to send her over the edge, but she wanted to make it last as long as possible. She slid one finger inside and Addy's legs tensed.

"Oh," she whimpered.

Her hips rocked in time to the rhythm of Mazie's finger—then two fingers—sliding in and out. Addy groaned. Mazie knew she was close. She flicked her tongue against Addy's center as she plunged deeper. Addy came in an instant. Her legs quaked, and when she cried out, Mazie plunged inside again. And again. Eventually Addy stilled and Mazie crawled into her arms.

"Will it always be like that?"

"I certainly hope so," Mazie said.

"You know what?"

"What?"

"That was better than in the movies."

CHAPTER TWENTY-NINE

Mazie arrived at Ivy's office promptly at nine. She hoped she looked more awake than she felt. She and Addy had fallen asleep around two thirty, but when the alarm went off at five so Addy could get home and change for work, Mazie was grateful she could go back to sleep once she gave Addy a ride home. She yawned and tapped her cheek, trying to wake up, but it was futile.

"What you see is what you get," she murmured and knocked on the door.

"Come in."

When Ivy looked up from her desk, she frowned. "Did you get any sleep last night?"

"I did," Mazie said, sliding into a chair, "but I think the last few weeks came crashing down on top of me." That was only a partial untruth. The premiere had been a huge success and Mazie's stress level had decreased significantly. The Bijou received a much needed shot of publicity as magazines and social media were already calling about "the quaint little theater" in Central Oregon.

Ivy smiled. "It was a lovely evening."

"Thank you."

Ivy leaned back and crossed her legs. "The movie was good, the after-party was fun, and the mini talent show your friends planned was amazing."

Mazie shook her head. "I had no idea they were doing that."

"I could tell," Ivy said.

She winced. "I hope I wasn't off key?"

"Nope."

"Out of time?"

"Not at all."

"Poor stage presence?"

"Definitely not." Ivy offered a knowing look. "That's how you got stage fright. You psyched yourself out, didn't you? Somebody you trusted told you that you weren't any good."

Mazie nodded. "My ex-lover."

"Shame on her. She's lucky I don't hunt her down and smack her around." When Mazie's eyes widened, Ivy waved a hand.

Mazie nodded again. She folded her hands in her lap, wondering why she'd been called to Ivy's office if it wasn't to be dressed down for a poor performance. Ivy must have sensed her unease, because she reached into her desk, pulled out a folder and handed Mazie her Program of Study. "You need to sign this and file it with the Registrar's Office."

A storm brewed inside Mazie. "You're ending my program? But after last night, I know I can—"

"Mazie, look at the bottom."

Under the box that listed the requirements of the program was the place for signatures. On the left were Mazie's and Ivy's signatures from September, indicating what was agreed upon at the start of the semester. On the right were the spots for signatures upon completion of the program. Mazie's spot was still blank—but Dr. Bertrand had signed.

Mazie looked up slowly. "What does this mean?"

"It means you're done."

"But the performance isn't for another two weeks."

"And what do you call last night?"

Mazie shrugged. "A surprise?"

Ivy waved a finger. "No, that was more of a performance than any other student will experience this semester. Of course it's not easy standing on the Gallagher Hall stage, I'll admit that, but to be pulled up from the audience to sing an impromptu duet with one of the most talented—and beautiful—actresses of our time, and sing in front of some of the top power brokers in Hollywood...That's more pressure than we could've ever manufactured with our little performance at the end of each semester."

"But the whole committee wasn't present. Won't they object?"

Ivy waved her phone. "You can thank technology. I sent them the video I recorded last night, and they all agreed you've fulfilled the requirement for your vocal performance seminar." Ivy smiled. "Congratulations."

Mazie was still troubled. "But the policy states that no outside performances can count toward the performance requirement for the Master of Music."

Ivy's smile evaporated. Apparently she hadn't thought of that. Mazie, of course, had memorized every line of the course curriculum for vocal performance.

"Yes, that's true," Ivy conceded. "The policy does state that. Hmm, what to do?" The smile returned. She picked up her keys and headed for the door. "Follow me."

Ivy walked briskly out of the music building and Mazie struggled to keep up with her. "Where are we going?"

"Well, if we want an exception to a policy, then we should probably ask the person who wrote it in the first place."

Mazie was confused, and her complete exhaustion made it impossible to understand what Ivy Bertrand was saying or doing. Was this something she'd cooked up with their mutual friend, Maestro Lamond? Mazie tried to formulate coherent questions, but her synapses weren't firing, and she struggled to keep pace with Ivy.

They crossed the street to Gallagher Hall, and once again Ivy pulled out her thick ring of keys. This time she quickly found the one she needed and led Mazie around to the other side of the lobby. They headed up a flight of stairs to a wing of administrative offices. Ivy waved to the receptionist and went down a long hallway. One door was open and Mazie peered inside. Each office had a marvelous view of the Cammon Commons.

The corridor ended in front of a large white door. A gold nameplate read *Dr. Katherine Gallagher, Professor Emeritus.*

"Why are we here?" Mazie asked.

"You'll see," Ivy said before she knocked softly.

"Come in," a voice called.

Mazie blinked at the woman who leaned against a filing cabinet, smiling. She knew her, but she didn't recognize her— until she spoke.

"Mazie, dear, it's good to see you."

"Kit?"

"Yes," she said warmly, reaching for Mazie's hand. "I don't quite look like I do on bus day, do I?"

Mazie shook her head. Kit wore a herringbone suit, a white silk blouse and pumps—a far cry from the khakis and printed cotton shirts she modeled when she met Weather and the kids. "You're Katherine Gallagher. Oh, my."

"I am. And I've had the good fortune to hear you sing not once, but twice."

Mazie's eyes widened as she remembered the day on the bus with Addy and all of the passengers singing "Take Me Home, Country Roads." She bit her lip. "Why didn't you tell me who you were when we first met?"

Kit snorted. "I don't put on airs, and I don't like people who do." She pointed at the chairs. "Please sit down."

Kit went behind her desk, navigating stacks of files, sheet music and books. "Sorry for the mess. I don't get up here every single day." She plopped into the leather chair that seemed three times too large for her. She looked at Ivy. "Do you have something for me to sign?"

"I do. We're asking you to make an exception to the rule that states all candidates must perform in the Gallagher Hall music night. The committee believes Mazie's performance last night was far more rigorous and demanding than the music night ever could be."

She handed Kit the folder containing Mazie's precious Program of Study, the piece of paper that would indicate whether or not she received a Master's degree in Vocal Performance. More importantly, it symbolized that Mazie Midnight had achieved her dreams.

Kit read it and smiled. "I will gladly make an exception." She stared at Mazie. "Your performance last night was incredibly inspiring."

"I remember seeing you, but I didn't see your name on the guest list."

"I was actually the 'plus one' for my wife, who is the president of the university."

Mazie's jaw dropped. "Oh, my." She blinked. "Sorry, I didn't know that."

"No need to apologize, dear. But thank you for such a wonderful performance. We both enjoyed it very much."

Mazie was about to humbly tell Dr. Gallagher everything that had gone wrong in her estimation, but Ivy touched her arm and said, "Just say thank you."

Mazie took a deep breath. "Thank you."

"You are quite welcome."

She opened her desk and withdrew a beautiful fountain pen that looked identical to the one Ivy possessed. With a grand swirl, she signed her name and handed Mazie the proof of her success. "Congratulations, dear." They said goodbye and Kit waved as they left. "See you on the bus!"

CHAPTER THIRTY

"I'm countin' on y'all to tell me the truth. What did you think?"

Tarina's commanding voice seemed to shake Mazie's cell phone. She had the phone on speaker so Addy, Nadine, and Jackie could hear as well. It was late and all of the moviegoers had gone home long ago. The group had just finished previewing Tarina's newest movie, *Love at Last*, and Addy thought the title and the plot were no accident. While the story was about a heterosexual couple, Addy knew Tarina's motivation derived from her own love story with Almondine.

"I liked everything except the ending," Jackie said.

"I liked the ending," Mazie disagreed.

"Why, Jackie? What didn't you like?" Tarina asked.

"It's too pat. And sorry, but it's too corny."

Tarina didn't respond and the group looked around with worried expressions. Maybe Jackie had been too honest. Tarina sighed and said, "I wasn't sure about it myself, but Deenie said people like a Happily Ever After ending."

"We do," Nadine agreed. She looked at Jackie and added, "And just because my wife isn't a romantic softie doesn't mean she knows everything." Nadine blew Jackie a kiss, and Jackie smiled.

"What did you think, Addy?"

Addy grinned stupidly and looked at Mazie. "I loved it. I wish it were two women, but I love the story."

"What about the ending?" Tarina pushed.

"I'm a sap for Happily Ever After." She gazed at Mazie and caressed her cheek. "And since I believe it's possible, I think your ending is perfect."

Jackie snorted and Nadine pulled her into a hug. "Don't listen to my wife, Rina. You'd think I'd be the one who hated sappy endings, given my status as Squeegee, roller derby jammer. Instead it's my wife who hates sap, despite living the Happily Ever After dream, I might add."

"Yeah, that's true," Jackie said, nuzzling Nadine's nose.

"Then I'm gonna leave the ending as is," Tarina said.

"When are you and Almondine coming back to the states?" Addy asked.

"Probably in October. Paris gets chilly then. We'll need us some Oregon weather."

They ended the call and soon afterward Nadine and Jackie went home. Mazie and Addy lingered in Theater One, Mazie's head resting on Addy's shoulder. "Do you believe we're living in a Happily Ever After ending?"

Addy nodded. "I think so. I'm about to be promoted to bus trainer, you're the general manager of the Bijou, and we get all the popcorn for dinner that we want. I'd call that happily ever after." She pulled Mazie toward the exit and the concessions stand. "Let's get a bedtime snack."

They wandered into the vacant lobby, and Mazie squeezed her arm. She stopped in front of the candy display case, pointed and said, "Don't forget your work with Dr. Pfeiffer. You've come a long way with her in the last year."

Addy smiled as she gazed at the case. All of the candy was arranged by price—and only by price. While she doubted she'd ever be able to wear plaid again, Dr. Pfeiffer had helped her work through her color peculiarity, and Addy no longer sorted everything in her life. She could see things for their rich complexity—a kaleidoscope of color.

And it was all because of Mazie.

Mazie grabbed a box of licorice and saw her goofy smile. "Are you on one of your mental vacations? What am I this time? Amazon goddess again?"

"Nope."

"Femme fatale?"

"Nuh-uh."

She abandoned the licorice and draped her arms over Addy's shoulders. "Porn star?"

"No," Addy laughed.

"Sexy mermaid?"

Addy raised an eyebrow and shook her head.

"Then what am I?"

Addy took Mazie in her arms and dipped her for a stunning kiss. When Mazie finally opened her eyes, Addy said, "You're you."

Bella Books, Inc.

Women. Books. Even Better Together.

P.O. Box 10543
Tallahassee, FL 32302

Phone: 800-729-4992
www.bellabooks.com